Libraries

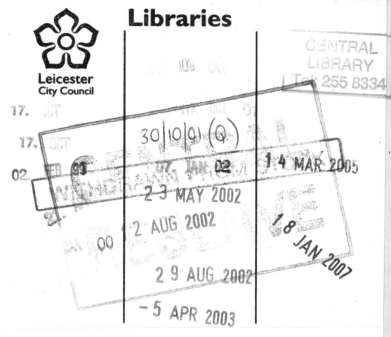

COOPER, C.L.

The syndicate, and, Weed

D1346712

THE SYNDICATE

AND

WEED

Clarence Cooper, Jr.

The Syndicate first published in the USA in 1960 by Newsstand Library Incorporated. *Weed* first published in the USA in 1961 by Regency Books.

This edition first published in Great Britain in 1998 by Payback Press, an imprint of Canongate Books Ltd, 14 High Street, Edinburgh EH1 1TE

The Syndicate copyright © 1960, Clarence Cooper, Jr. *Weed* copyright © 1961, Clarence Cooper, Jr.

British Library Cataloguing in Publication Data

A catalogue record for this book is available on request from the British Library

ISBN 0 86241 718 X

Typeset in Minion and Serif Modular by Palimpsest Book Production Limited, Polmont, Stirlingshire
Printed and bound in Great Britain by Caledonian International Book Manufacturing Ltd, Glasgow

THE SYNDICATE

1

Anyone could tell at first glance that Brace Lilly was a fairy. His smooth skin and neat little lips just didn't sit right on my stomach, and the rest of those goons he had standing around his desk looked just as queer as he did, the only difference being those stiff hunks poking out under the armpits of their dinner jackets.

He waved a delicate hand at me. 'Sit down, darling.'

I sat, but all the rods made me nervous, and I couldn't see the sense in Lou Pulco sending me all the way to the Coast to play hotsy-totsy with a gay boy.

Lilly slid one long forefinger against the side of his cheek and watched me like I was funny, too, and I started to burn just a trifle.

'All right,' I said. 'I know where the hell I am and who the hell I'm supposed to see. Now tell me what the hell is going on!'

'I thought you were briefed in New York,' Lilly said, smiling at the tone of my voice.

'I was told that my services would be worth ten grand, and for ten grand I don't require much information.'

He poked one of his joy boys in the ribs and pointed at me. 'Isn't he darling?'

'And I am also Andy Sorrell,' I said, 'who don't like to play ring-around-the-rosie.'

'I think that would be fun,' Lilly giggled.

'I think it would be fun to come over there and break your head, too.'

All the joy boys clustered around him protectively when I said that.

'I would advise you to keep that joking attitude, Mr Sorrell,' he said icily.

'I'm not joking. If you've heard anything about Andy Sorrell, you know he never jokes.'

'I've never heard of you,' he said casually. 'I was sent a

directive by the syndicate which informed me you would be on the way soon and that I should do all in my power to let you in on a few people concerned in the cross.'

'So let me in, I'm freezing outside.'

Lilly raised his head. 'I *don't* see your hurry.'

'And I don't see yours. There's a tight season on hurries this year.'

'Are you always this sharp?'

'Only when I shave myself.'

He took a long cigarette from a gold holder and got up to walk around where he could face me. 'I must say, Mr Sorrell, that you intrigue me.'

'You should catch me when I'm hot – I'd kill you.'

He turned away abruptly. 'Did Pulco give you a run-down?'

I nodded. 'Harv Cassiday, Al Benedict and Chess Horvat.'

He lit the cigarette and puffed on it reflectively. 'Well, I haven't seen Harv in a couple of months. Benedict used to hang around with the shake dancer outside, Tina Meadows. Horvat – about the same as Cassiday. They all just disappeared a few months ago after that bank job in Jersey City.'

'Thanks for all the help,' I said. 'I'd never ask you to throw me a life preserver.'

'Listen, Sorrell,' Lilly said nervously, 'that's really all I know! What the hell, how am I supposed to know something about five hundred grand?'

'How are you?'

'All I know is that these fellows were mainstays in Hollis-worth up until a couple of months back. All syndicate boys. Cassiday was with the jukebox co-op, Benedict in cigarettes and Horvat in beer. Why they'd ambush a syndicate caper is something I can't understand!'

'It's not so hard when you consider.'

'Consider what?'

'Five hundred and sixty grand,' I said. 'The best understanding in the world.'

I stood up, and all those sissies cringed when they actually saw how far I was up. 'This shake dancer, tell her to shake her ass out front after the next performance.'

Lilly went over to a bar in the rear of the office. 'Care for a drink, Mr Sorrell?'

'When I care for it.' I went over to the door. 'Right now, I want you to take care of business.'

His manner grew cool again, like I'd insulted him. 'Are you actually, really, really, a *torpedo*, Mr Sorrell?'

'In the flesh,' I said, my hands itching to get at him.

Then I went out to the club's lounge, where the air felt a bit cleaner.

2

Talk about a lush joint, Lilly's was the most. That was the name
of it, Lilly's. It was about 300 miles from L. A., in the choicest
part of Gold Coast country.

I used to live on the sea, long ago. My pop used to take me
out on a trawler when I was just a baby; I can still remember
it. That was a long time ago, and it was just Pop, never anyone
else. Like I was something dirty no woman would own.

Lilly's had that sea flavor, that taste of salt air, a sultry place
where the Hollywood jills and juniors could have a few for
the road – the back road, where Lilly had several wall-to-wall
carpeted cabins for those who found the journey home too
long and arduous.

Class, the kind of class I'd been rubbing my hands for all
my life.

The band wasn't big, but it had a big band sound, and when
the shake dancer Tina showed up in a silver mesh leotard, it
seemed as though the roof was caving in.

I've seen shake dancers before, but this gal was something
else. She didn't move – her body did. It scintillated under the
mesh like a thousand angry glow worms, and when she crawled
out of the thing the smooth skin above the wide expanse of
her hips wiggled in two parts, disassociated from her spine, it
seemed.

Her body reminded me of Carolyn, sleek Carolyn, her
twisting thighs and big soft breasts, a thousand years ago,
forever, before she died with my baby.

By the time Tina ended her dance, I was clutching her hard
to me, my breath short, my fists doubled up into two big clubs,
the nails biting into the pits of each hand.

Without concentrating, I could practically feel her body hot
and alive in my hands while she stood thirty feet away.

Then she vanished, and I was left with that crazy, *crazy*
feeling again, getting scared, getting more scared by the day,
and what the hell for?

I came down, like a junkie, snatching up presence enough to notice that even the waiter who brought me a double rye looked and acted like a fairy.

I didn't notice when she came, being wrapped up in a thought wave of nothing.

'Hello,' she said, sitting down, but she wasn't smiling. She still had her make-up on, eyebrows arching cat-like over faint blue eyes, the lips big and red and ripe-looking. She had gotten into a dressing gown.

'Hello,' I said.

'I understand you want to see me.'

'That's right.'

'Well . . . ?'

'I'm seeing you.'

'Look, mister,' she said peevishly, 'I'm in no mood to play games.'

'Neither am I.'

'Then what the hell do you want?'

'I want you to tell me where I can find Al Benedict.'

Her expression never changed. 'And why should I tell you where he is?'

'Because I asked you.'

'And just who the hell are you?'

'A man who wants to find Al Benedict.'

She detected the seriousness in this last statement and looked down at the table to keep from betraying herself. 'I haven't seen Al in months.'

'That's not what I heard.'

'I don't care what you heard!'

'You listen, you big-mouthed broad,' I said softly, seeing the look of fear on her face when I took her hand in mine, 'you're gonna talk yourself right into a nice, deep hole. You know where Benedict is, you tell me, or you're gonna wake up mighty sorry tomorrow.'

That's when the little fella in the pumpernickel pastel came over and tapped me on the shoulder. 'Pardon me, sir, but you're disturbing the other customers.'

I would have crushed the guy but he was so little, and the wild mop of gray hair wasn't there on his head for kicks.

'Why don't you blow?' I said.

'I'd be most happy to, sir,' he said indulgently, 'but it's my job to see that everything goes smoothly here.'

'How would you like to go smoothly, like butter?'

'I beg your pardon?'

'If you don't get the hell away from here I'm going to roll you up like a piece of Kleenex, friend.'

The little guy saw I wasn't kidding and hustled right out of there, and when I turned to Tina again she was looking at me disgustedly.

'I wish all the people like you were dead,' she said earnestly. 'I know what you are and all the rest of them. I tried to tell Al that you were rotten, all of you! And now you want me to lead you to him, so you can kill him. But you're late, muscleman, oh, you're so late!'

She stood and whirled the gown around her, leaving before I could get out another word.

Her so closely resembling Carolyn, that's what got me. She had no right to look just like her, or to say those things like Carolyn might have said! No right!

I got up and followed her back to her dressing room, but when I tried the door it was locked.

I stood there, watching that door, boiling inside and tasting my own bile green and sour in my mouth. I waited a thousand years for that dame, and when she came out, I exploded. I grabbed her, and she was soft and bending, like a willow reed, like Carolyn, and her mouth was saying dirty things to me with its cleanness.

I dragged her to the back door and out into the darkness of the field behind the club. I started to hit her with my open hand, and then the heat got too much and I struck her with my fist, again, again, seeing the blood spurt from her nose and the soft flesh puff up instantly beneath her eyes.

When I stopped, I was sweating and trembling. She lay between my legs, her dress pulled across the thickness of her thighs, her breasts heaving torturedly.

I reached down and dragged her face up to mine.

'Stop . . .' she said, gasping, 'stop . . . no more . . . I'll tell you where Al is, muscleman . . .'

3

Hollisworth is no burg; it's a solid little city, with the exception that it belongs to the syndicate, lock, stock and barrel.

It has a roller rink, city hall and P-TA setup, but it also has gambling, dope from the sea and four efficiently-run whore houses. There was no discord and no hue and cry from the citizens, because those individuals who remained healthy in Hollisworth didn't make it any different.

Lou Pulco told me that I could consider the town mine when I arrived, and he wasn't far from wrong. On arrival, I was met at the airport by the manager of the Hollitop Terraces and given a suite on the twelfth floor.

Everything was lavish and class, nothing like those two-grand bumps, where I had to give up maybe fifteen hundred to keep the cops off my back after the rub was over. This was my big chance.

Lou had given me a down payment of twenty-five hundred, with seventy-five on delivery, and, brother, I had a lot of things mapped out for that ten grand.

The money, that's what was so important now! After leaving Tina at Lilly's, I went back to the Hollitop to pick up my equipment, a .32 automatic, thinking of Benedict, the first of three parts.

From upstairs I had the desk clerk call up one of those auto rental services, and by the time I got downstairs some little jerk was just pulling up front in a black Impala.

'How far's Blue Haven from here?' I asked him.

'The sanitarium?'

'Yeah.'

'Let's see. Go north about ten miles and turn right on 43, the intersection. Can't miss it. It's the first forest you get to, right in the middle. Just keep going until you see a bunch of trees, that's Blue Haven.'

'Thanks.'

'Hey, mister, you're not going there to visit someone, are you?'

'What business is it of yours, punk?'

'None, mister. I just meant that it's almost twelve-thirty. Visiting hours are over at Blue Haven at nine p.m.'

'Thanks.'

I drove off in the direction he indicated. It didn't make much difference whether visiting hours were over or not. I wanted to know if Benedict *was* there, if he actually had the nerve to come back, to be so close, to Hollisworth.

I also wanted to know whether Tina Meadows was lying. It didn't make too much difference, but I wanted to see about her, her closeness to Carolyn. It was crazy, crazy, but I just wanted to see. I felt sorry about hurting her, but I wanted to see if I was right.

I drove for about fifteen minutes, the countryside and the edge of the sea luminously dark, sparkling around the borders like currents of electricity.

When I made the right on 43, I could see the cluster of trees the boy had told me about in the distance. When I pulled up, I had to get out and open the gates of the joint myself. A whitewashed drive twisted through a valley of willows to a large white centerpiece, with a flying white marble cherub, and sitting smack in back of it was the main building, with a garish neon sign as big as any I've seen in Vegas.

I pulled the Chevvy around in front and got out. The doors were revolving, even, and the reception chamber was as big as the lunch room in Grand Central. Subdued fluorescents peeked over the ceiling's ledge, and the lights bounced off the face of the cute little blonde behind the switchboard just right.

'Good morning, sir.'

'Good morning.'

'May I help you?' She smiled, and I had that feeling again. Why the hell did every woman look like Carolyn to me now?

'I'm looking for a Mr Al Benedict.'

She got up and switched her wide ass around to the register. 'I'm sorry, sir, but I see no Al Benedict listed. Could it be another name?'

'Could be.'

'Did you want to leave something? We have no visitors after nine p.m., you know.'

'A friend told me he was here,' I said. 'He's the kind of guy who doesn't like to leave his real name when something's wrong with him. I'm sure he's here under another name.'

'I'm sorry, sir, but I can't find a Benedict anywhere in our records.' She flickered her big eyes at me. 'Are you sure that's who you want?'

'Positive,' I said, almost convinced that Tina had given me a bum lead. Then I had an idea. 'What about a Meadows? Do you have a Meadows listed?'

She flipped through the files again. 'Yes sir. In 309. Mr Charles Meadows, entered by a Mrs Tenna Meadows.'

'Tina?'

'No sir. Tenna. T-e-n-n-a. Would that be the person you're looking for?'

'Possibly. You say he's in room 309?'

'Yes sir. But you wouldn't be able to visit him until later today. One o'clock is our first visiting hour.'

'Thanks very much. I'll come back.'

I started out, but there was something about her, her body and eyes, that made me come back.

'You must get pretty lonely here on nights,' I said.

She smiled up at me shyly. 'Sometimes it gets pretty monotonous, I must admit.'

'Nobody here but you?'

'No sir. We have a full staff on nights. An intern is usually on duty here in front, but it's coffee break time right now.'

That was convenient for me. 'Thanks,' I said and went out. I took the Chevvy down the road toward the gate about two hundred yards, got out and came back.

The sanitarium was a modernized Elizabethan structure, with a broad conical on the fifth and final floor. I went around to the side and found just what I was looking for, the fire escape. I pulled the ladder down and went up quickly to the third floor, where the escape exit was a window leading into the main hall.

I crawled in and went down the hall until I found room 309. I took the .32 out of my breast pocket and tried the lock. The door was open. I slipped in noiselessly. The lights were out and the only illumination was the starlight spray from the night sky.

In one corner was the bed. I went over and found the night lamp.

The light that washed across the bed shocked the occupant to wakefulness. Blood-reddened eyes swept over me frantically, and I could see the fear. I knew this was A1 Benedict.

'Please . . .' he said hoarsely.

'How are you, Al?' I said.

'Don't . . .'

'Lou Pulco told me to come around and look in on you.' I took the .32 and put it on a level with his eyes.

'The money,' he said, clutching at my sleeve. 'I . . . I don't know where . . . I don't know where . . . I'm dying . . .'

'Where's Harv Cassiday?' I said. 'And Chess Horvat?'

'Don't know . . . believe me, I don't know! Never seen a dime of the money!'

'You know why you gotta die, Al?' I said softly. 'You and Cassiday and Horvat did something the big man don't like, plus he don't like people cracking his private safe. He's mighty angry about that. He wants to know how you three guys got those plans. He wants to know where the dough is. And he wants you dead . . .'

'Please,' he croaked, 'I'm dying! Cancer of the lungs . . . gonna die, anyway!'

'Where's Cassiday and Horvat?'

'Don't know, swear I don't know! Cassiday . . . came to me . . . told me about job . . . didn't see Horvat till last day. We all split up . . . payoff in Hollisworth two months ago. It was a cross . . . never seen a dime of money . . .'

'That's too bad,' I said.

'Please . . .'

'That's really too bad, Al.'

I went over and flicked out the lamp. When I came back I could hear his frightened breathing. I put the .32 in my pocket and made my hands go toward the sound of his breathing until they touched his clammy flesh, his throat, then I began to squeeze, harder and harder, ending the first of three parts . . .

4

I went down to the sea after that. I don't know why, I just did. I felt good all over after what I did to him. I felt especially good because Benedict reminded me of a guy I used to know a long time ago, a brain doctor on Ellis Island.

I was hooked for some caper then, I don't know what, but I wasn't much more than a kid.

'Have you ever had nasty thoughts about your mother?' this brain doctor asked me, and I got so goddamn mad I didn't stop until I had my thumbs hooked up in his nostrils and he was screaming murder.

Those saps! They really thought I was nuts after that. But it wasn't that. It was the money, wasn't it? Money was all there was to depend on; it was like going to bed with a woman. You never got tired of it. The money, the money . . .

'I don't know why I love you, Andy,' Carolyn's voice said from the sea, and it was almost like she was sitting right there in the car with me. 'You're horrid and brutal and a murderer. You're killing more than one person when you kill, don't you realize that? You're trying to kill that thing within you!'

'And you died,' I said, clenching my fists and screaming at the sea. 'You dirty bitch, you went and died on me!'

I got out of the car and ran down to the edge of the water. I shook my fists at the sea. 'You don't come back! You come back and I'll kill you again! I'll kill you again!'

It was morning when I got back to Hollisworth. The only thing moving was an old intercity bus. My watch said 3:30, but it had stopped somewhere along the line.

It was funny, but I wasn't tired when I pulled up at the Hollitop's parking area. All day on the plane from New York the day before, then all night last night. I just felt empty, that's all, without any thoughts of today or tomorrow.

I got out and went in. The elevator operator must have been

asleep on nine because I rang the buzzer for a full ten minutes before he arrived, a little freckled-faced kid.

'Oh!' he said, as though surprised. 'I didn't keep you waiting, did I, sir? The signal button is out of order.'

'Put me on twelve,' I said, stepping in.

He shut the doors. 'Twelve seems to be a busy floor this morning.'

'Yeah?'

'Yeah. Must be something going on. A couple coppers just went up a few minutes ago.'

'Cops?'

'Captain Markle and that Hendricks guy. They went up to twelve not ten minutes ago. If you ask me, I bet they got the key to somebody's room.'

'These guys come in here much?' I asked cautiously.

'Only when there's some money to be made, like a crap game or yard party, where they can get the goods on some good-body who shouldn't be doing what he's doing.'

The elevator whirred to a stop. 'Your floor, mister.'

'Thanks.'

I got out and went down to my room. I had an idea that the two fellows in question had come up to have a chat with me, and even if this was a syndicate town I didn't like cops.

I took the .32 out and punched the button at my door.

It was a short, straw-haired guy who answered, and he must have thought I was Western Union or something because he dropped a jaw screw loose when he saw the heater.

'Hello,' I said. 'May I come in?'

'By all means,' the guy said, throwing the door back.

I shoved the .32 under his heart and gave him a pat on the head. 'Where's your buddy?'

'In the kitchen,' he said, tight-lipped.

'Call him.'

'Vin,' he said. 'Vin, come out here a minute.'

The swinging door to the kitchen swung open and a guy came out, a tall, black-haired guy with a drink of the hostelry's rye in his fist. He was swarthy, with a touch of Italian in him somewhere, and more handsome than I could imagine any cop.

'You must be Sorrell,' he said.

'The same.'

'Why don't you get out of Hendrick's ass pocket and put that thing away. I'm sure you're aware that we're playing ball for the same people.'

'I don't know how sure I am.'

Markle went over and sat down on the sectional. 'There's need for you to think otherwise. I got a telegram from Lou Pulco yesterday.'

'How is he?'

'Fine. He told me to look after you. He said that you're inclined to be a little hot-headed at times.'

'That's Lou, always underestimating me.'

Hendricks pecked at my sleeve. 'May I sit down, too? If you're as touchy as all that I don't like to be in this hot seat.'

'Put your gun away, Sorrell,' Markle said. 'We just came up for a friendly talk.'

'How friendly?'

'That's up to you.'

So I put my gun away, just like that, not thinking at all. I saw Markle raise his finger briefly, and in that second Hendricks moved around and sapped me at the base of the neck. I went down, face forward, and all that cushy fur on the floor did little to keep my head from cracking wide open.

Boy, was I a sucker!

I felt Hendricks' hand shoot up under my coat and snatch out the .32.

'You bastard,' he said, and kicked me in the chest.

'No, Pete,' I could hear Markle's voice say behind me, 'he's a sonofabitch!'

All of a sudden it was both their shoes, from the front and back. I doubled up instinctively, but my back was unprotected and Markle's shoe tip cut out a fancy step all along my spine.

Pretty soon they got tired, and a good slam under the Adam's apple made me quit caring. They lifted me by both arms and dragged me over to the sectional, where I bled all over the print.

'A tough boy,' I could hear Hendricks say somewhere downtown.

The Syndicate | 15

'A tough, tough boy,' Markle amended, blasting me with his fist until my mouth was a gummy cushion of blood.

I coughed up a mouthful and, just as I expected, they moved away to keep from getting splattered.

'You guys are gonna die,' I managed to say.

'Look who's talking!' Hendricks said.

I tried to open my eyes, but the water and mush was too much and I could barely make out their outlines.

'I'm a syndicate boy,' I mumbled. 'You push me too much, you're gonna die.'

A wiry hand fastened itself in my collar. 'You know why you're getting pushed, syndicate boy?' It was Markle's voice. '*You're* getting pushed because you pushed someone you shouldn't have.'

'What the hell are you talking about?'

He punched me again. 'Tina Meadows ... Get the point, syndicate boy?' He punched me again, this time harder. 'You touch her again and I'll kill you! I don't care what happens, but I'll kill you!'

I laughed, laughed. 'Love, thy sting doth fill my heart!'

They knew how to work a guy over. They were specialists. They worked me from head to foot.

I didn't know what time they left.

5

When I came back to this world the afternoon sun had focused from the picture window and was burning the hell out of me where I lay on the floor.

I didn't move for a long time, getting myself together.

Ever thought of how one of those big marlins feels after a hard fight, twisting and straining against the hook in its mouth, finally dragged up exhausted and stupefied with pain to the keel of a boat?

That's how I felt, only twice. I pushed my face into somewhat of its former semblance and staggered to my feet, my eyes straining against the brilliance of the sun.

Those guys didn't know it, but they were dead!

I went to the bathroom and washed some of the mess from my face, then, half-reluctantly, I got into a cold shower and tried to rinse away the bruises that covered my body. It was no use, though. They only got bigger and more painful.

I sunk myself in the Sealy mattress and attempted to sleep, but the network of electronic signals sparking from my belly to chest made me work at it only half-heartedly.

So far, it just seemed like I was going along for the ride. The whole show was beginning to get complex, and for a starter it sure put me in one hell of a shape.

I thought about Benedict. The whole thing had been too easy. Markle and Hendricks must have known he was dead, but they didn't say a thing about it. Of course, they were so busy giving me a workout it probably slipped their minds.

It was stranger than fiction.

When I woke up, it was to the tune of the doorbell in high C. The first movement was nerve-shattering, but after a while it seemed as though pain were something I'd been used to all my life.

I got up and drew on my pants. When I got to the door the bell had stopped ringing. I thought about Markle and

Hendricks and started looking around the apartment for the .32. It occurred to me that they might have taken it with them, but I finally found it thoughtfully tucked into the breast pocket of my suit coat. I checked the clip and went back over to the door.

'Who is it?' I shouted.

'Naida,' a woman's voice said.

'Who?'

'Naida Torneau. Brace Lilly sent me over to see you.'

Lilly? I slung the .32 under my right hip and opened the door with my left hand.

'Hello,' she said. She was spraddled-legged, with a round little belly under her sexy suit and a devilish curl around the corners of her mouth as she smiled at me. 'I'd like to come in, but there's something about a man with his shirt off that makes me cautious.'

'Didn't you notice the gun?' I said.

She giggled. 'What can a gun do to you that a man can't?'

'That's something I never thought about.'

She slipped past me suddenly into the room. 'Well, it's something I've thought about, Mr Sorrell. A gun is useful only when you want to use it.'

'Isn't a man?'

'Men are unpredictable.' She went over and stretched out on the sectional, tossing her purse over on the coffee table.

'Make yourself at home,' I said, closing the door.

She grinned up at me secretly, and her eyes were big and gray-colored, like the agates I used to shoot with Pop on the beach, where the sand was so thick I thought agates were a useless commodity.

I saw now that a woman's skull displayed them perfectly.

'What are you staring at, Andy, dear?' she said. 'Why don't you fix me a drink or something? And why don't you put that gun away? Do I look dangerous?'

'Yeah, you look deadly. And the last time I put my gun away, I got taken around the Maypole, on ball bearings, no less.'

She giggled again. 'You must have met Markle and Hendricks.'

'Does it show, or am I blushing?'

'Now, Andy,' she chided, 'don't be angry. They just want you to know how much they *like* you.'

'And I like them,' I said. 'We'd tell the world we're in love, but who'd understand?'

I went back to my room and put on a clean shirt. I could hear her rummaging around in the kitchen with the liquor bottles.

'Don't you have any gin?' she called.

I came back out and pushed open the door to the kitchen, where she stood in the breakfast nook that served as a bar.

'You like gin,' I said. 'I like rye. But I live here.'

'That's not a very sociable attitude,' she pouted.

'I'm not a very social kind of guy,' I said. 'Listen, just what the hell do you want?'

'I *told* you, Andy! Lilly sent me over.'

'And just why would Lilly send you anywhere?'

'Well, Jesus, I'm his wife, aren't I?'

I was shocked, I don't know why. I just never imagined fairies married women.

'I know what you're thinking,' she accused, shaking a finger at me like I was a naughty boy. 'But you're wrong – it's just like you *don't* think it is.'

'That explains everything,' I said.

She brushed past me with a bottle of rye and one of soda and went into the living room, where she spread herself out again all over the furniture. 'Bring a glass with you from the kitchen, won't you, darling? A large one.'

I went back and picked up a couple of tumblers.

'Thank you, sweet,' she cooed. 'Now, after I finish this drink, I'll tell you why I'm here.'

'You'll tell me now,' I said.

She put her hands up in front of her face in mock protection. 'Please don't strike me, Mr Sorrell!' She patted a spot next to her on the sectional. 'Do sit down, darling, and I'll tell you a story.'

'I just woke up.'

'This is not for bedtime, sweets – it concerns Chess Horvat.'

I came over and sat down next to her. 'This story is one that might interest me.'

'I thought it would,' she said, smiling mischievously. 'You and I know that Cassiday, Benedict and Horvat got hold of the plans for the bank heist several months ago, executed it and got away with over five hundred grand.'

'That's the information I have.'

'So much for that,' she said. 'How they got the plans, no one knows, but it had to be on the inside wire. Benedict is dead—' She chucked me under the chin – 'Someone saw to that. He didn't have any part of the cash, but that 60-dollar-a-day fee at the sanitarium was being taken care of somehow.'

'So what does that explain?'

'Why, it's simple, darling. One or both of the boys were taking care of the expenses.' She poured herself a drink and took a long pull at it before she continued. 'Lilly figures that the fellas came back here to split up the money, but something happened and they had to hang around.'

I thought about what Benedict had told me about the arrangement for the divvy two months ago.

'What else does Lilly figure?'

'He figures that both boys are in, or around, town. He told me to tell you that Horvat used to hang around with a little rich deb named Meg Inglander. She lives out near Fernando, with her old man. The joint would make an excellent hideout.'

I started to get moving, but something made me stop and think.

'Just what is Lilly getting out of this?' I said.

She didn't make a very good try at appearing surprised. 'Why, Andy baby, Lil doesn't want anything! He was told to co-operate, you know that.'

'Were you told to co-operate, too?'

'I don't get you.'

I reached down and unbuttoned her suit coat, ran my fingers up around her firm little breasts, felt the nipples rise in response through the thin cloth of her bra.

'Now do you get me?' I said.

She grinned at me impishly again. 'But, darling, we've only just met.'

'Can you think of a better way to cement a new friendship?'

She put her glass down and raised up until her lips were on a level with my own. 'You're not a bad looking guy, Sorrell, give or take a bruise.'

'And you're not a bad looking dame.' I crushed her mouth under mine, tasted it hot and foamy sweet, her breath short and fragrant, like a baby's. It would have been an innocent kiss, except for the way she made her tongue do things.

In my bedroom, she strung it out, like she was experienced in this form of torture. Mischievously, she raised her skirt until I could see her blue silk panties and garter belt, then she slowly drew her nylons from those long, smooth legs. Next came jacket and skirt, blouse, and she paused to watch the hard way I was looking at her.

'*Darling*!' she said with a gushy, bitchy laugh.

I knew women like her. Even when I started to do the rest of it for her, I knew that was what she wanted, what she had planned from the start. The bra was easy enough to get off, but when I got to the panties she made it purposely hard, twisting her hips on the bed so the silk caught under her weight, pushing the bulk of her thighs against me, hampering me.

She made me use my strength against her, force her, and all the while she was laughing, her voice rising higher with her every subtle resistance.

Finally, I raised her body and snatched the damn things off.

'Oh, Andy,' she said in a gusty voice. 'Come here, darling Andy.'

The rose hue of her nipples pointed outward to me, like her arms, the trim little naked belly nestled at her thighs, beckoning with satisfaction.

'Be brutal, dear,' she said, taking me, and I had a sharp instant of regret. 'Burst me, Andy, make me explode!'

The bed received us. I didn't like the way she devoured me; it was the man who was supposed to consume. She drew it out until I felt my bowels were evacuated, then, when she was tired of it all, she siphoned out the very core of my brain.

We lay breathless together.

'That was very good,' she breathed against my ear.

'It could have been a helluva lot better,' I said, coming out of the spider web grasp of her.

I went back to the bathroom, wondering whether Carolyn had seen any of it from wherever she was.

Right then, I didn't give a damn.

6

When Naida left my apartment that evening it was damn near time for supper. I went down to the hotel's dining room, but only wound up having a couple of ryes. I was hungry, but it was for something other than food.

The fixer and in-between man for the syndicate, Pulco indicated vaguely that there was little chance of me getting a direct line on that half million. My job, mainly, was to find the parties responsible for the job and give them the rub. If I bumped into the dough along the way, good and well enough, but Pulco hadn't given me any orders for such an occasion.

I began to think about that dough. All that dough. I wasn't to blame if I happened to find it, was I? And five hundred grand made my promised one-fiftieth seem mighty small.

I paid my check and went out to the parking lot. I expected the attendant to do a double take when he saw my kisser, but he acted as though rubber stamp lips and purple eyes weren't a particularly uncommon sight. They probably weren't, in Hollisworth.

I goosed the Chevvy out on the main drag and started for Fernando, after I got my bearings at a filling station.

I'm a sucker to an extent, but after that point my IQ starts to pick up a little. Naida and Lilly had applied the grease to me in more ways than one. Gay boy's motive for providing me with information about the Inglander broad had designs with a dollar sign.

It'd be foolish for me to think that I was the only one hoping I'd stumble over all that green.

I couldn't seem to fit Naida into the scheme of things, nor Vin Markle and his flunky Hendricks. It wasn't hard to surmise that Markle had a crush on the Meadows dame and came after me because of the workout I gave her. Otherwise, that seemed to be the only thing he was concerned about. And being a part of the machine in Hollisworth, he'd naturally heard about Cassiday, Benedict and Horvat.

And Naida, right out of nowhere, here she comes, easy, pliable. With a husband like Lilly, though, a woman couldn't help but be loose.

The evening sun was hiding behind a hilly pass when I noticed the car behind me. It kept a discreet distance but not discreet enough. I speeded up, it speeded up. I slowed down, it slowed down.

I took a cutoff and detoured about five miles until I came back to the highway. I lost the tail. Or at least I thought I lost him. A couple of hundred yards down the road I saw the car parked next to the pump of a filling station. The guy must have known where I was going!

When I drew abreast, the driver tried to hide his face, but I got a good look at him. It was the little guy in the pumpernickel pastel at Lilly's. I kept on down the highway as though I hadn't noticed him.

Lilly seemed to be covering every angle! In the rearview mirror I saw the little guy bounce out on the highway after me. I pushed the Chevvy up to eighty for about twenty seconds and slowed down at the next bend.

A private road angled out onto the highway. I twisted in quickly and paused, making sure that my pumpernickel pal got a good glimmer before I set off down the road in a cloud of dust.

A winding border of eucalyptus made the thing perfect! I stopped abruptly, flipped the selector stick into reverse and let the rear wheels dig me around so that I was horizontal on the road. I got out, plucking the .32 from my breast pocket, and loped over to the driver's side of the road.

The little guy didn't see the Chevvy till the last minute, and by the time he had brought his car to a sliding halt, I had the door on his side open and was practically sitting in his lap, the .32 socketed just under his left ear.

'Please! Please!' he screamed. 'Don't kill me!'

I took hold of his tie and dragged him out on the gravel.

'I'll make it painless,' I said grimly, bending over to plant the nuzzle gun dead center on his forehead.

'Don't, *don't*, Sorrell!' he pleaded. 'I'm only doing what I was told!'

'Who told you to do what?'

'Brace Lilly – he told me to follow you. I swear that's all I know! He said just to follow you everywhere you went and then report back to him.'

'Aren't you a little old to be playing tag?' I said. 'What's your name?'

'George Eversen. I'm the head waiter at Lilly's. I swear, Sorrell, I don't know what's going on! I get paid good money at Lilly's. There's not much I can refuse to do for him.'

'Maybe you get paid well enough to die for him.'

The little guy saw I wasn't kidding and started to blubber. 'Please, Sorrell, I know something you don't! It was Lilly! Lilly was the one who arranged to get those bank plans from New York! Lilly set the whole thing up through his associates with the syndicate, that's the truth!'

'A few minutes ago you didn't know a damn thing.'

'I hear things, Sorrell! Lilly trusts me!'

I took the .32 away from his skull. 'Get up, Pops.'

The little guy scrambled to his feet. 'You'll never regret this, Sorrell. I'll tell Lilly anything. I'll tell him I lost you on the road.'

'Where do you think you're going?'

'What?'

I waved him back with the rod. 'You say Lilly arranged to have those plans hijacked in New York, right?'

He wrung his hands nervously. 'That's what I heard around the club, Sorrell, I swear to God it is!'

'Where's the dough?'

'What?'

'The half million bucks, stupid! Where's it at? If Lilly arranged to lift all that cash, he must have it around somewhere.'

'I don't *know*, Sorrell. Right after the bank was robbed a few month back, Cassiday and Horvat came to the club to see Lilly. I didn't hear what they said, but I could see they were pretty mad when they came out of the office.'

'Was that the last time you saw them?'

'No, I saw Horvat a few days later. Lilly sent me over to his beach house to pick up a case of champagne from the cellar.

I came in the back way with a key and I could hear Lilly and Horvat arguing in the dining room. They were saying something about the money, but I didn't get a chance to hear anything definite because they stopped talking when they heard me come in.'

'For a guy who don't know nothing, you know a lot,' I said. 'How does Naida Torneau fit into this thing?'

'It was just a marriage of convenience. They were married about six years ago, when Lilly took over the club. Because he's got a morals record, he couldn't get a license to run the place. Everything is in Naida's name. She was a bum when she married him, Sorrell, nothing but a bum.'

I watched him closely. 'Say that again.'

He didn't understand.

'About her being a bum,' I said. 'Say that again.'

'Well, that's all she is, Sorrell!' he said heatedly. 'A bum, a tramp!'

Love, thy sting, I thought. Vin Markle wasn't the only guy in Hollisworth with a helluva crush.

I went over and got in the Chevvy, pulled around Eversen's car and pointed my nose toward the highway. I got out and went back over to him.

'I'm gonna give you a job, little fella,' I told him. 'You're gonna keep your eyes and ears open and every goddamn time Lilly goes to the john, you're gonna rush right over and tell me. Understand?'

'Sure, Sorrell. I don't want any trouble.'

'You won't get any if you do exactly as I tell you.'

I left him standing there and got back in the Chevvy. When I pulled out on the highway, the sudden pall of night required me to switch on the headlights.

I went down the highway about five hundred yards and waited until I saw the headlights of Eversen's car pull out on the road and swivel around in the opposite direction, then I started off.

Like I said, I'm a sucker, but only just so far. It was hard to believe that Lilly had the money. I didn't think Eversen had lied to me, but it didn't make sense that Lilly should bait me with his wife. You don't bait a hook unless you're trying to catch something, and in this case I thought Lilly was fishing for a prize catch – five hundred grand.

There was another way to think about it, too: It was possible that Lilly wanted to make things as easy as possible for me to collect my ten grand, then he wouldn't have to split all that green with anyone.

If that's the way it was, gay boy had another thought coming.

It was nothing to kill three men for ten grand.

I'd kill fifty men for half a millon dollars.

7

I saw the Inglander retreat while I was still five minutes away. It was shiny and big, on a tall slope with trees, like the calliope I saw one time in a circus my old man took me to, high-reaching Colonial spires that looked like eyes staring off over the black, distant land.

It was like a castle.

'See that?' my old man had said of the big, hooting thing. 'That's rare, boy, real rare.'

I don't know why the goddamn house looked like a calliope, but it did, and as I drove up the long, twisting drive to the gaping black mouth of the front entrance I expected to hear those big pipes scream off over the world and hear my old man say, 'That's rare, boy, real rare.'

One pane of glass in the front, almost fifty feet long, let me look in on the cultured expanse of the front room, where bookcases swung around the wall with a thousand teeth. There was a reading lamp burning over the desk, but no one was around.

I struck the chimes with my thumb and watched a slick-faced guy in a black monkey suit and bow tie, through a panel in the front door, march out of a door near the staircase.

'Yes sir?' he said stiffly when he opened the door.

'Is Miss Meg Inglander in?'

'Are you a member of the party, sir? Miss Inglander is entertaining at the pool.'

'I'm the party,' I said, stepping in. 'Where's the pool?'

The guy looked down his nose at me. 'Please follow me, sir.'

So I followed him through heaven. Wall to wall carpeting? This joint looked as though the walls were even carpeted. When I looked at this rich man's world, my mouth watered.

I thought about that five hundred grand and how much it could do to set me up in this sort of shape.

The guy in the bow tie took me through the kitchen and out

a little door that led down a tiled slope. It seemed as though we were going down to the basement, but after a while I saw that the house had been built that way purposely on the flat side of the hill.

In a few seconds I could hear voices and laughter and the sound of strings weaving luxuriously through it all. We came out on what looked to be a patio, but it was bigger than a tennis court.

At the far end was the pool, and guys and dames in swimming suits were lounging around the edge. Occasionally someone would dive in, but it would only be to swim across to the bar, where a waiter stood on call.

The hi-fi, wherever it was, accompanied several swim-suited dancers, and the lighting was obscure, which made the whole thing very cozy.

My escort left and went over to one of the couples. He spoke to a doll with very long but shapely legs. She broke away from her partner and came over toward me. She had those great big luscious breasts, like Carolyn, and the tiger-striped bikini halter was doing all it could to hold them in. The little piece she had knotted around her ass had given up.

She looked up at me inquiringly, and I wondered how Horvat had ever managed to get anything as beautiful as she was.

'May I help you?' she said in modulated tones. 'If it's my father you want to see, he's out of town at the moment – Richards should have told you that.'

'It's not your father I want to see.'

She gave me the once over keenly. 'I don't believe I know you, Mr—'

'I want to talk to you privately,' I said.

'I'm *very* busy now. Couldn't you tell me what it is you want?'

'I want Chess Horvat.'

Her expression became very distressed for a moment, and it was all she could do to keep from pushing me into a little study off the side of the pool.

The room was equipped with a divan and bar, which seemed to be a common fixture around the joint.

She went over and got a cigarette out of the pearl box on the table and set fire to it nervously with the matching lighter.

'May I ask why you want Chess, Mr—'

'Blow,' I said. 'Joe Blow.'

She took time out to make herself a quick drink. 'All right, Mr Blow, or whoever you are, what do you want with Chess?'

I found a spot on the divan, where I could get a dog's-eye view of her figure. 'I want to let him know he's holding a winning ticket in a popularity contest. First prize is a slug in the head.'

She slammed her drink down on the bar. 'Are you mad?'

'Sometimes I wonder.'

'If you've got something to say, say it and get out of here.'

'Where's Chess Horvat?'

She crushed her cigarette out in a tray. 'Are you from the police?'

'Were you expecting them?'

'Certainly not! It was just your manner—'

'Where's Chess Horvat?' I said again.

She lit another cigarette, took a couple of draws and stubbed it out. 'I haven't seen Chess in several months.'

'You're lying.'

She whirled around angrily. 'And just who, may I ask, do you think you are to talk to me that way?'

I got up. I started to burn. I went over, but I didn't touch her. I came over close and stood looking down the deep cleft of her breasts until I thought they'd pop out of that thing with her frantic breathing.

'You know where Horvat is,' I said, 'and you're going to tell me.'

'Please, I don't know where he is!'

'Miss Inglander, you're gonna make me real mad in a minute ...'

'Please believe me!' she cried, clutching me by both arms. 'I haven't seen Chess in two days! He's in some horrible trouble, I just know he is!'

'Then he'll be back here?'

'I don't know!' She looked up at me pleadingly. 'Please don't hurt him! He said someone was looking for him, someone wanted to kill him. I'll give you anything you want, only don't do anything to Chess, *please!*'

She was telling the truth, I could see that easily enough. The fear had her trembling. The desperation in her excited me. If I hadn't held myself, I would have grabbed her. I felt funny again, and I thought about Carolyn. All I could see was those big, motherly breasts and the stiff eyes of the nipples poking out under the stripes, begging me, begging me.

I wanted to touch her, but I knew I'd go crazy if I did. I just stood there, feeling warm below the belly, and I couldn't even think straight. It was the fear in her that did it, and I wanted to squeeze her against me, I wanted to wrap my hands around her big rump and pull her close, tight and close, all the way inside me, like Carolyn.

I couldn't stop thinking like that! Why was it getting worse all the time?

'Please, please, don't hurt Chess!' she was saying. 'I'll do anything, but don't hurt Chess!'

I tried to get out of there before I exploded, but I couldn't. All I could see was those big mother breasts bursting out of the tiger stripes, and her wide hips seemed to be wiggling in anguish.

Before I knew it, I had reached out. That crazy thing in me had made me reach out. My fingers clutched down in the bra and it disintegrated in my hands. I heard her voice saying 'No! No!' but it was too late then. Her full breasts filled my hands, and her fingernails were digging across my face, trying to find my eyes.

Outside myself, I watched me pick her up and throw her onto the divan; then I saw me snatch that flimsy thing from about her hips. She was all mountains of soft flesh, hairless and virgin-like.

In a trance, wild, crazy, I could hear her sobbing defeatedly as I got out of my clothes. But I wasn't really there, even as I did those things, even as I told myself that I was doing something mad.

I watched her trembling, an arm across her eyes, and I was urged on by her fear. But there was something else, something that made me stand there for a long time and watch her that way, naked, soft, and helpless. Made me stand there building up that perverted lust until it seemed to be coming out of my ears, until it expanded and exploded in me, then finally throw myself on her like a wild animal.

It was quick and sudden and good, and though I knew I received no response from her it felt as though I had swallowed her within myself and my swelling, buoyant tides were her own.

'Even this doesn't matter,' she murmured in a dead, vanquished voice.

I lay on her finally, exhausted and somehow ashamed.

'Even this doesn't matter,' she said again, 'for Chess . . .'

When I got out to the Chevvy my heart was going fast and I was sweating. I let the window down out on the highway and the rush of cool air cleared my head, and my mouth felt fuzzy and warm.

I was going crazy . . . crazy, crazy, *crazy!*

8

When I woke up the next day I didn't remember anything, and it was only after I'd laid there in bed for a long time that I could remember the first little bit of last night's events.

My clothes were tossed all over the room and an empty fifth bottle of rye perched up snugly on the pillow next to my head.

I didn't notice I was naked until I staggered into the bathroom and held my head under the shower. I felt rotten and my hands were shaking like a wino's.

Way back in the rear of my head a little voice was scaring the hell out of me. I started walking around in circles, not knowing what to do first. I went into the living room and pushed open one of the windows, looked down on the little people and the little cars and the whole lousy little world. I felt like getting out on the parapet and taking a nose dive, smashing every goddamn thing there under me.

Pretty soon I was able to pull myself together and call room service for a pot of black coffee. In the meantime, I stood under the cold shower until I felt like a popsicle, then got into some fresh clothes.

When the coffee arrived, I laced it with a double jigger of rye and swallowed it down before my stomach had a chance to say anything about it. I warmed up a little, and all the marbles started clicking on time.

What was going wrong with me? I held my hands out. They kept trembling. It was getting closer and closer to me, ever since two years ago and Carolyn. Was I really going off my nut?

I stopped thinking about it. I started thinking about that half million again and tried to keep it foremost in my mind.

Horvat had been around Hollisworth as close as two days ago, Meg Inglander had assured me of that. And with Horvat so near at hand, could Cassiday be far behind?

It was a stickler, and with things happening to me the way they were I felt like an invalid in a sea of jelly.

Naida Torneau's idea about Horvat and Cassiday having the dough didn't pan out so conveniently now. I couldn't see them hanging around with that much green just to take care of a guy who was going to die, anyway.

This avenue of thought led me back to Brace Lilly. It made sense now. Lilly had the money and was making it as easy as possible for me to pick up the trail to his accomplices.

Yet why would Lilly hang around at all? Five hundred grand could have bought a guy an express ticket to the moon, if he wanted to go that far. And Lilly, even if he decided to stick around and make sure the parties in question were all dead, was taking one helluva chance. You don't dribble out that much money, and someone was sure to notice if he started getting prosperous later on.

There was some other angle to the whole thing, I felt it. Eversen said Lilly had arranged to have the plans swiped by one of his syndicate associates. Did this guy, whoever he was, have the money?

It was a provocative thought but not very progressive. There were very few people in the syndicate who had access to the kind of information that would make such a cross possible.

I went into the bedroom and put on a tie, but the door-bell rang before I had a chance to draw it up. Still mightily impressed with my gentlemen callers of the night before, I got the .32 and went over to the door.

'Who is it?'

'Mr Sorrell?' A woman's voice.

'Who is it?'

'Meg Inglander. Let me in, please let me in!'

I went over and put the gun under the sectional's pillow. When I came back she was ringing the bell again and she didn't stop until I'd opened the door and snatched her hand away from the eyelet.

'What the hell's wrong with you?' I snapped.

It was acute relief that made her dig a hand into my arm. 'Oh, please, please, let me in!'

Behind last night, I had to get acquainted with her face once more. The wide, trembling mouth struck up a vague memory, but it was the fear in those eyes again, that tortured fright, that made me see the same woman under the austere brown ensemble. She couldn't look at me, not after last night.

'Please don't be angry, Mr Sorrell. I had you followed last night, that's how I knew how to find you.'

I stepped aside and let her come in. 'What do you want?'

'It's about Chess,' she said, turning to me, 'but you must promise me you won't do anything to hurt him.'

I shut the door and came over to her. 'Have you seen the boyfriend?' I felt odd, talking to her this way.

'Please, Mr Sorrell—' Her eyes sparkled with hate.

'Stop it! You're pleasing me to death. Just tell me where he is.'

'He says he knows you're here to kill him,' she said haltingly.

'You know where he is, then?'

'Yes, but I can't tell you where until I'm sure you won't hurt him.'

I turned away because that frightened thing about her was getting to me again. It wouldn't cost me anything to tell her I wouldn't do anything to Horvat, and I wouldn't – not right away. I wanted to talk to him first.

'Why should Horvat want me anywhere close to him if he knows I'm around to knock him off?' I said.

'He wants to tell you something – he says it's very important.'

I can tell you I considered everything backwards and forwards before I told her okay. The whole thing could easily be a trap. Knowing I was on his and Cassiday's tails, Horvat could imagine better places for me to be than walking around out in public with my hot little hand wrapped around a rod – a very deep hole, to name one. Still, if he had the money, it would be just as easy to pay me off.

'Where do we meet the boyfriend?' I said, going for my coat.

'*Wait*, Mr Sorrell!'

When I turned, the lady had a big .38 perched in her shaking little fist and it was pointed at me, somewhere around the strike zone. I should have known it was inevitable, but what can I expect of me?

'I could kill you now, Mr Sorrell,' she said softly. 'I should – after what you've done to me.'

'I won't argue the point.'

'You're *not* going to do anything to Chess,' she said firmly, 'do you understand that?'

'I'm no dumbbell, but sometimes I wonder.'

'Before you see Chess, you must believe that he has no part of that horrible money. If anything happens to him, I swear I'll hunt you down and kill you. I love Chess more than anything. I'd see every person on earth dead just to have him.'

She wasn't joking about anything she said, and my stomach began to feel a bit queasy under the line of fire. 'Where do we go from here?' I said.

'There's a small art gallery attached to the rear of my home. It's accessible from a back road. Come up at 10:00 tonight. You'll be seen and admitted. And don't come armed, Mr Sorrell, or Chess'll kill you on the spot.'

'I don't like those terms.'

'Those are the only terms under which you'll see Chess.' She backed toward the door without taking her eyes off me. 'And remember what I said. If you so much as touch Chess, I'll kill you.'

After she was gone, I went into the kitchen and hit the rye bottle again, hard. It didn't help much.

Whatever the fatal attraction Chess Horvat had for Meg Inglander, it was certainly a strong one, and I didn't intend to fall victim to his charms. I *would* go to see him tonight, but I'd have on all my clothes, including the .32.

I looked at my watch. 2:25. I had a lengthy waiting period. I went over to the phone and got the broad on information to give me the number of Lilly's joint.

The delicate bruiser who answered the phone told me Mr Lilly hadn't arrived yet but I could talk to Mr Eversen, if it was important. It was important and I did want to speak to Mr Eversen.

'Hello?' the little guy said in a while.

'Sorrell,' I said. 'You haven't forgotten what I told you yesterday evening.'

'Oh, no, Mr Sorrell! I've been doing exactly as you said, only nothing's happened yet.'

'Where's Lilly?'

'He won't be in till later.'

'How late?'

'I don't know, Mr Sorrell. He called from the beach house an hour or so ago and told me he'd be delayed this evening.'

I hesitated for a moment. 'What do you know about a Meg Inglander?'

'Oh, her. Blue book, active in society circles. She used to go with Chess Horvat, did you know? Horvat was the friend of a friend – you understand. They started going around steady about six months ago and her father, Lemuel Inglander, crusty old millionaire, didn't hide his displeasure. They used to come into Hollisworth all the time. The whole town knew about it.'

'The young lady made one of her social visits by my place a few minutes ago,' I said, 'but what she served for tea was a lot more persuasive.'

Eversen's voice perked up with interest. 'Was it about Horvat?'

'The same. We have a date tonight at her place.'

'What do you want me to do, Mr Sorrell?'

'Nothing right now. I've got a hunch about Lilly. I'll call you back in a little while.'

'All right. Anything else?'

'Yeah – keep your mouth shut.'

I hung up. Suppose this *was* a trap. I was wondering now.

Oddly enough, Lilly couldn't be reached at the moment, and if the information Eversen had given me about gay boy was on the level, Lilly and Horvat could very well be composing a funeral march for my benefit.

Only one thing about those sonatas: I don't like them unless they're being played for someone else.

9

I left the hotel at about 9:00 p.m.

Across the street, at a drugstore counter, a guy was asleep with his face in his hat. He should have kept his hat on. I recognized the straw hair.

I was doing forty coming out of the parking lot, and when I made the main way I was marking time with the stop lights. My tail could never make a professional, because he got chicken too easy.

Out on the highway, I took my time.

It was better this way, just sitting and thinking calmly, and I avoided thoughts of Carolyn just like I avoided the thoughts that brain doctor tried to make me think about my mother a long time ago.

Lou Pulco was probably wondering why I hadn't sent him the okay signal, but he told me the job would unquestionably take a bit a time. What he hadn't figured on was that I'd set my sights on the many monies.

If Lilly and Horvat *had* arranged a string of funnies, they had a surprise coming, what with my sense of humor. They would be counting on me arriving unarmed and free of suspicions, but I wasn't built that way.

Then I thought about Meg Inglander, and started having doubts again.

There was something about her that had me thinking screwy. If she loved Horvat as much as she claimed, and he *really* wanted me out of the way, why didn't he have her take care of it? The chance of there being any complications were small, as big as the Hollitop was. And even if there were, the local gendarmeries and I weren't very fond of each other. They would have been glad to whitewash the whole thing.

Here I was again, goofing up the perfect patterns I'd created.

There was something about the Inglander dame's plea that was too sincere. On the other hand, she didn't have to know what Lilly and Horvat were planning and could have truthfully thought that things were to be exactly as the boyfriend said they would.

I pulled off the road at the next filling station and looked at my watch. Only 9:30. I went inside the joint and leaned over the Coke machine to get at the wall phone.

When the guy at Lilly's answered this time he told me that Eversen had stepped out for a moment and Lilly hadn't come in yet.

My doubts about Lilly grew a little bigger. I checked myself and got back in the car. It was all rounding out to a neat package. Chances were that Lilly was one of the welcoming committee at a party where I was to be guest of honor.

I started to burn some, and felt glad about the whole thing, kind of.

I was a clay pigeon on the approach.

The road was framed in the light of bush-high kliegs and the ascent was steep. The art gallery poked out like a bent finger at the fringe of the mansion, shyly exposing one darkened window from a shelter of fruit trees.

Over all this was a soot-like darkness which created too many illusions.

I stopped the car a couple of hundred feet from the entrance and got out. The .32 fitted snugly in the palm of my hand and I held the gun arm half-crooked in front of me, where the heater blended in with my suit.

I walked slowly until I came to the edge of light, then danced out of the illumination quickly, making a wide bend to the windowless right panel of the doorway. From this protected position, I reached around and rapped three times on the heavy facing of the door. No sound came from the interior. I knocked again. Still no answer.

This was something like I'd expected. I reached around cautiously and found the ring latch of the door. I turned the thing slowly until I felt the catch give and the door move back silently a few inches.

I braced myself, put a foot against the door, then shoved.

The darkened inside blazed up suddenly and exploded. A slug whirred itself to a stop in the door facing just over my head. I squatted and pressed the happy button, felt the little machine in my hand buck to life with two brief spurts of fire.

Somebody scrambled across the room and slammed into the wall at the other side. I pointed the mouth of my heater in the direction of the sound and let it cough off three messages deeply.

There was no return fire. I slipped into the room and crouched near the baseboard on the left side of the doorway. No sound. I stood up carefully and ran the edges of my fingertips around the wall until I found the switch. I waited several minutes before I threw the thing on but still didn't get any response.

When the light flushed over everything, I saw that the door on the other side of the room must have delivered my pal with the pistol to the inside of the house.

My immediate surroundings were a jumble of confusion. Statues were broken and paintings knocked from the wall. It looked as though there'd been one hell of a fight.

In the rear another doorway looked like it might be the entrance to a storage room. I went over and gave it a shove with the tip of my shoe.

The first thing I saw was his feet. In the half-light, the little room looked like an artist's workshop, with one huge, clay-ragged table.

He looked as though he'd been dragged under the table. When I bent down I could detect a slight breath, and when I turned the guy over he started throwing up a sweet-smelling greenness from his nose, making the virile young mustache on his top lip look like a dead piece of shrubbery. There was the slight smell of hand lotion that reminded me of the Jergens product.

His eyes parted stickily and swung up vaguely until they settled on my face.

'Horvat,' I said, dragging him up by the shirt. 'You're Horvat, aren't you?'

He understood that much and shook his head weakly.

'The money,' I said, my voice steady, 'where's that money, Horvat?'

Another gush of that sweet-smelling puke was his only

answer. A frame-jarring shudder passed over him. He stiffened suddenly, then became limp in my hands. The eyes stayed open and blank.

I dropped him on the floor and stood.

The whole goddamn thing was getting mucky. I recognized poisoning when I saw it.

10

I heard something almost like the scratching of mice just as I was about to get out of there. It came from around the other end of the table where a leg shield hid the back wall from me.

I hoisted my rod over the ledge and circled around the far end.

What I saw was far from being a mouse or anything related; it was Meg Inglander, and the back of her pretty head was one big grapefruit sop of blood. Someone had sapped her and they hadn't cared how hard they did it.

It was the sound of her fingernails against the hardwood floor that had gained my attention. Half-conscious, she was trying to dig her way up from the floor.

The glazed look in her eyes told me it was a concussion when I rolled her over, but her lips were moving weakly, trying to speak.

'Chess . . . Chess . . .' she mumbled.

'How'd this happen?' I whispered. 'Who did this to you?'

She strained against me. 'Where's Chess? What . . .'

'Don't worry about anything. Just tell me what happened. Somebody meant business, and they didn't mind letting the world know about it.'

She closed her eyes tightly. 'We were waiting for you . . . Chess and I. Someone rang from the front. Chess went out to see who it was . . . it's the butler's day off. I heard them coming back, so I came into this room.'

'Who was it? Who was it came back with him?'

'Didn't see who it was . . .' She shook her head painfully. 'I called out and asked . . . asked Chess had you arrived. He said no . . . and took whoever it was to the front again. In a while, I heard the door open behind me, thought it was Chess. That's all I remember . . .'

I looked over at Horvat's body crumpled on the floor. Whoever had bumped him had hung around long enough to take a couple of shots at me; they evidently knew I was on the way.

My guess was that the rub-out guy had a lot of his plans goofed this evening. Horvat even threw him for a loss. Both guys knew each other well enough for one of them to toss something into the other's drink. That might have been the reason for the return back up front. Meg Inglander would really have complicated things if she hadn't called out to Horvat.

This had been real luck for the guy. After he fed Horvat the fatal double dosage, all he had to do was come back and bust Meg Inglander in the head.

Up to that point, everything must have gone like clockwork for the guy. He probably had a good spot facing the door, just waiting for me to step through. But, right at the last moment, who should show back on the scene but Horvat! I bet the rub-out guy was so surprised he couldn't get himself together right away. Horvat held his own for a while, but the effects of the poison apparently got him.

The sudden rumble undoubtedly threw the other guy off his bearings. By the time I got there, he was too scrambled to carry off the ambush.

I looked down at Meg Inglander. She had lapsed into a semi-consciousness. A dark half-moon had just risen around the top and back of her head. Her full, curving body was heaped upon itself, the big breasts pointing upward helplessly. There was something about her body, the legs exposed up to the thigh, that made me draw up inside. For a moment, I actually couldn't move, feeling warm and cold together. I was able to turn away before the sweat came, but my heart was double-stepping and it was all I could hear.

Somewhere under the shambles I found a phone and gave the operator a ring.

'Send a doctor over right away — emergency!' I left the receiver hanging down and went back to take another look at the girl.

I stopped before I got halfway, crying inside myself, like a baby or something. That feeling was riding me hard again, piggy-backed, with a pair of cold fingers in my eyes.

Then the voice started talking, speeded up, like Woody Woodpecker, and it was laughing at me because I didn't have what other folks had, because I was tainted, like a leper, with a curse on my head.

It was no use trying to get around the facts: something was wrong with me.

And whatever it was was scary as hell . . .

11

Next morning, it was the rye bottle as a sleeping companion again. My mouth was husky, but I didn't have a hangover. I got right up and ordered breakfast. On the way back, I stopped in the bedroom and put five spares in the .32's clip and gave the firing mechanism a good going over.

Guns. I knew them better than anything, from World War II, and those 90-day wonders and the mud. Like we were no better than mud. All of them could go to hell, that's what I told them. But I knew my guns, and they knew I knew. I knew heaters better than people, better than myself . . .

I'd gotten into a fresh suit when the phone rang.

'Yeah?'

'Mr Sorrell?' It was Eversen.

'What happened to you last night?'

'I was trying to get a line on Lilly,' he said from far away, like he was speaking under his hand. 'After you called last night, I went out to the beach house to have a look around.'

'What'd you find?'

'Nothing of interest, but Lilly surprised me before I could leave.'

'What happened?'

'He wasn't in much of a mood to talk. He and Naida were together. I told them I'd come over to pick up a case of bonded. Lilly looked like he'd been in a fight somewhere.'

'About what time was this?'

'Oh, between 10:30 or 11:00.'

'That would be about right.'

'What?'

'Is Lilly at the club today?'

'Not now, but he'll be around later on this evening.'

'Good. Don't call me, I'll call you.'

I put the receiver down. Everything was just gorgeous. Lilly was definitely in the pan. Luck had seen fit to make him blunder just once too often. All I needed now was about fifteen minutes alone with him and I'd know where that dough was.

It was 1:35 p.m. when I came out of the Hollitop. I hadn't even gotten around to the parking lot before Hendricks sidled up next to me and poked something in my ribs. Whatever the thing was was as round as an all-day sucker, but my luck these days always ran against the odds.

'Markle wants to see you downtown,' he said happily. 'I won't have to insist on you accompanying me, will I?'

'Not one bit.'

'C'mon, I'm parked around front.'

It's a funny thing about Hollisworth – nobody in that town notices a goddamn thing. Or at least they act like they don't notice a thing. A man and woman paused together at the front doors to watch Hendricks hustle me into the big Buick between the driver and himself, and they couldn't help seeing the gun. I'll lay odds they were tourists; nobody else gaped that way.

The uniformed driver had us downtown in a trice. Hendricks didn't talk and I was in no mood to carry on a conversation. I had an idea what it was all about, and Hendricks wasted no time relieving me of the .32 after we got to headquarters.

The building was an ugly brownstone. The hallways were dusty and looked unused, but with the syndicate setup in Hollisworth such a place is better unused. Even the pasty-faced cops looked unused.

We came to a stop on the second floor, where Hendricks gave a polite tap under the gold V in Markle's name on the door facing.

'Who's there?' the boss called out testily, as though we'd interrupted him in the bath.

'It's me,' Hendricks said. 'I've got our friend with us.'

After a pause, Markle said, 'Wait a minute.' Then he opened the door.

When you see police captain Vin Markle in his office, you have seen everything. His official garb is a smoking jacket, red silk, and his staff of justice is a good shot of bourbon.

His office is anything but, excluding the bedroom blue desk, which modestly matched those fat sofas and chairs. He was a reader, that guy, and the place looked more like a den than anything else. The lingering scent of perfume and the half-open door leading off to another room told me the place had other uses, too.

'Sit down, Sorrell,' he said, as though my name had a bad taste.

'Thanks.'

Hendricks went over and posted himself by the door.

Markle perched on an arm of one of the chairs and took a swallow of the drink before going on.

'I see you're surprised at my choice of furnishings,' he said finally.

'I'm in the wrong business.'

'Which conveniently brings us to the point. You don't mind my getting right at it, do you?'

'Not at all.'

'It's very simple, Sorrell. You're getting to be a pain in the ass.'

'I could think of better spots.'

'Fortunately, such is not your prerogative.' He got up to close the door to the other room. 'I can appreciate your ignorance of the way things go around Hollisworth. You were sent here to do a job and you've really done the best you could.'

'You can't kick a guy for trying.'

'The same doesn't very well apply for a fellow who louses things up.'

'C'mon and pull me out of the heather, mother, you're not making any sense.'

Hendricks smacked his palm with a fist. 'Boy, this guy is a real comedian.'

'That's just fine,' Markle said. 'He'll appreciate the humor in my telling him he's got just two hours to get the hell out of Hollisworth.'

I didn't appreciate it. 'Are you serious? It seems to me you're forgetting something.'

'If you mean the boys on the council back in the big city, I'm glad to tell you this was their idea.'

'You don't mind if I double check, of course?'

'If you think it'll do any good. I don't think you'll have time for that, though.' He went over to the liquor cabinet and poured himself another drink. 'You see, Sorrell, it's not your fault that you're stupid. I guess you were just born that way. Before you came, we knew Cassiday, Horvat and Benedict were slated to be eliminated and were told not to interfere. The job you did on Benedict was sloppy but adequate. Your low point was Chess Horvat.'

'What are you talking about?'

'Last night, at the Inglander place. You made three very bad mistakes. You knocked the guy off beyond our jurisdiction, beat up one of the richest women in the state and were foolish enough to stick around long enough for her to plate you with an ID.'

'It may not do any good to say this,' I told him, 'but Horvat was on his way out when I got up there. The guy who did it hung around to take a few shots at me. I found the Inglander dame with her head caved in while I was looking the joint over.'

'You're right,' Hendricks laughed, 'it won't do any good!'

'Why don't you shut your fat mouth?' I snapped. 'Maybe if I'd let you come along for the ride, you could verify the whole thing.'

Markle regarded his flunky thoughtfully for a moment. 'He's right, Hendricks. If you'd been on your toes, you probably could have caught Sorrell in the act, if you know what I mean. Think of the heat we'd have saved.' He turned back to me. 'I can't say I regret the whole thing, however, since we're off the hook either way around. Mr Sorrell's penchant for assaulting young ladies has worked out just fine for us.'

'Yeah, everything's just dandy for you,' I said, standing. 'But I'm not going anywhere until I'm told directly.'

Markle picked up a slip of paper from his desk. 'Perhaps you'd like to see the telegram I got from Lou Pulco this morning.'

'I wouldn't believe it, anyway. Now if you'll just tell your lap dog to give me my heat, I'll get the hell out of here.'

Markle gave me a wide, satisfied grin. 'I'm sorry, Sorrell, but we're confiscating your weapon – for your own protection. You see, if you're not out of town at the specified hour you're going to be shot on sight.'

'Sure, I understand. You're gonna make it as easy as possible.'

'Precisely.' He motioned for Hendricks to open the door. 'Oh, yes, that spare you had in your rooms at the Hollitop isn't there anymore, a couple of my men saw to that last night.'

'I expected as much.'

He raised his glass in farewell. 'Bon voyage, Sorrell. It *has* been so nice knowing you.' He looked at his watch. 'Remember, if you're still in town after three o'clock, we're going to kill you.'

12

I was one step ahead of those guys.

I had an idea they weren't going to stick with the two-hour deadline.

After I'd gotten into a taxi out front, I had good reason to believe my doubts were at least half-right. Hendricks and a blue coat got into the Buick and came after me, and they didn't care if I knew it, either.

The cabby shot me right over to the Hollitop, with a fin for encouragement. I got out and went directly to my rooms. I tried to get Pulco at his office in New York, but his secretary told me he wouldn't be in for the rest of the day.

Lou'd given me an emergency address and phone number, but he told me never to call unless it was absolutely necessary. It couldn't get anymore necessary than it was right now, but I didn't get an answer when I rang the number up.

I called Western Union and had them send out a wire asking Lou to get in touch with me as soon as possible by phone, then I slammed the phone down and stalked helplessly around the apartment.

Boy, was I the prize patsy!

As of the past few days, I seemed to be born for putting my foot in it. The frame was a bit awkward but so was my head. I went into the bedroom and started throwing some of my things into a suitcase. If things were the way I expected, I'd really have to be traveling light.

In the back of my head, that little voice started whispering again, but I was already scared. If Lilly was my man, he couldn't have set the thing up better than if he'd planned it. But why would he do that, with my part of the job less than half-done?

It occurred to me then that I didn't know where the hell Cassiday was — for all I knew, he could be dead. The loose ends in this puzzle just didn't fit anywhere!

Where was the dough?

Where was Harv Cassiday?

And why was Chess Horvat dead?

The dough wasn't so hard. Lilly probably had it. I could even figure Horvat in on this. He was pressuring Lilly for his share, Lilly wouldn't come through, Horvat threatened to make a deal with me, Lilly killed him. Okay. Where was Cassiday? He had to be around somewhere, dead or alive. Maybe that's why Horvat had to be removed. Lilly had gotten rid of Cassiday and Horvat figured himself next.

It all sounded nice, but from where I sat – in the middle – it just wasn't convincing enough.

I finished packing and had the desk clerk send a bellboy up for my bag. I sat around for forty-five minutes, knocking off a quarter fifth of rye, then when I thought Hendricks and his buddy were just about ready to come up and see what the hell was going on, I slipped out of the apartment and went down to the service exit.

I was hoping Hendricks would take the precautions I thought he would, and he had. Down past the basement landing I could hear some guy with asthma breathing heavily. The guy was standing in the shadows, and from the outline he cast through the teeth of steps I could tell he wasn't expecting anyone to come through.

'Hey, mister,' I called, exposing myself only partially at the head of the stairs.

'Huh, who is it?'

'The bellboy. Mr Hendricks says for you to come around to the front.'

'Oh . . .' I heard him stumbling up the steps.

I braced myself. When he puffed to the top I hauled back and rammed my fist into his soft gut, feeling his hot breath woosh out over my right shoulder. His gun was unholstered, and as he started falling down the stairs the thing went off twice.

He finally settled in a groaning heap at the bottom and I came all the way down. The poor sucker was damn near dead.

I took the long nosed .38 and a couple of slugs from his belt and vaulted across the basement to the express entrance. Luck smiled on me. The doors opened out on the parking lot, where the Impala stood waiting only about a hundred feet away.

I dashed over, got under the wheel and took off, with several important stops to make before I left town.

I was on my way – or so I thought. Two blocks away from the Hilltop I none too gently smacked into the side of a cruising cruiser.

I have a talent for such things . . .

'You,' said Vin Markle, 'are a damn fool, Sorrell.'

I grinned appropriately. 'What can I say after I say I'm sorry?'

I was back in Markle's boudoir-office, this time with my hands cuffed behind my back. Hendricks, along with four menacing blue coats, including the cop I'd walloped, hovered over me hungrily.

Markle, attired now in a gray business suit, leisurely observed me from behind his desk. 'I've just made a call to the state police, you know. They'll be here momentarily . . . Oh, don't look so relieved, Sorrell. You're going to make an escape bid before they arrive.'

'That's gonna make you look silly, isn't it?'

'Not as silly as it'll make you look, I'm afraid.' He turned to Hendricks. 'Have you got everything set up?'

'We're just waiting on your signal,' Hendricks said, eyeing me with complete ecstasy. 'We'll take him downstairs, he slugs me—'

'You didn't know I was double-jointed,' I cut in.

'—he breaks through the side door, we blast him as he runs for the street.'

'Perfect,' Markle said, then to me: 'Don't feel at all bad about it, Sorrell – we were going to kill you, anyway.'

'I was afraid you didn't care.'

Hendricks came over and gave me a bust in the nose. My head exploded with the pain.

'You should have been a comedian,' he said.

Through the pain, I grasped for straws. These guys weren't kidding, and unless I was able to come up with a stall I'd never be in a position to return the fine favors they'd given me.

'Listen, Markle,' I said, 'you wipe me and you'll be wiping the chance of a lifetime.'

He looked at his watch casually. 'About ten more minutes, boys.'

'The money, Markle – the half million Cassiday and his boys lifted! I know where it is!'

I struck a tender spot. Markle's eyes narrowed and he didn't say anything for a long time, then he got up and came over to sit across from me on the couch.

'You're joking, aren't you, Sorrell?'

'Oh, sure! I'm in a fine position to joke at the moment.'

'If you know where the money is, why hadn't you got it and left Hollisworth before now?'

'Why do you think I was hanging around?' I said. 'I had to be sure I was right.'

The promise of death makes all voices sound sincere. Markle looked up at the blue coats and Hendricks. 'Leave us alone for a moment.'

The blue coats filed out, but Hendricks hung around.

'I said alone,' Markle said.

'But, Vin—'

'Do as I say, you fool! You're not going to be left out on anything.'

Hendricks followed the others out reluctantly, but I could see he wasn't at all convinced.

'All right, Sorrell, let's have it.'

'What do I get out of this?' I said.

He smiled. 'Why, your freedom, naturally. Suppose we let your escape attempt be a successful one?'

'What about my share of the dough?'

He shook his head sadly and clicked his tongue at me. 'Please don't be a hog about this, Sorrell.'

'What's going to keep me from going back and telling the boys in the big city that you've got the cash – that you had the cash all along?'

This point was very effective. 'There's not much choice, is there, my friend? All right, we split—'

'Fifty-fifty,' I said.

'Let's hear what you've got to say.'

'All right,' I said. 'I've got it first hand that Brace Lilly was head man in the operation. He conspired with the three dodos to lift the plans and take off the bank caper. Benedict told me before I gave him the rub that he and the others were supposed to get the payoff here in Hollisworth a couple of months ago. Something went wrong, Lilly stalled them. It's my idea that Lilly never intended to split with them.'

Markle began to laugh. 'You expect me to believe that pansy was the brains in a half million dollar caper! Come, come, Sorrell, you'll have to do better than that!'

'It all figures. When I came on the scene, it made things perfect for Lilly. He sent his wife Naida over to my apartment to give me a lead on Chess Horvat. When I pressed, Horvat wanted to cop out. Meg Inglander came to see me and we arranged a meeting with Horvat. That's when I was fitted with the frame.' I stopped for a second. 'Does it make sense to you that Horvat would let me get close enough to him to feed him some poison?'

I could see the interest peeking out of Markle's dark eyes. 'You say Lilly did it . . .'

'Who else? Remember how the joint was torn up when you guys got there, as though a fight had gone on? Lilly got back to his home later on that evening with his face chewed up.'

Markle was rolling those things over in his head. 'Interesting, Sorrell, but how can you boil all these things down to Brace Lilly?'

It was the same question I'd been asking myself all along, and I still didn't have a reasonable answer. All my evidence against Lilly was circumstantial.

'It makes sense to me,' I bluffed. 'Lilly was central enough in the syndicate's operation and too obvious an individual to take such a chance. It wouldn't have been difficult to con those three saps in on the deal. When everything went against the plans I'd received in New York, Lilly tried to hustle things up and get me out of the way. I've an idea that Cassiday's already dead.'

Markle watched me thoughtfully. 'You portray Lilly as quite an ulterior force, Sorrell.'

'Give me a few hours alone with him tonight,' I said. 'I'll get the money.'

Markle didn't take as long trying to make up his mind as he would have had me believe.

'The money,' he said. 'You say you know where it is?'

'Lilly's got it. Let me go for a few hours and I'll get it for us.' I was sure to add the plural.

He looked at his watch again. 'You may have something, Sorrell. I'm taking a chance. We're going to let you escape — with provisions, of course. You won't be able to get out of Hollisworth, and if it becomes necessary for us to eliminate you, we will.'

He went to the door and called in the blue coats and Hendricks.

'We're going on with the plans,' he told them, 'with a few variations.' Then he outlined it to them, explaining that all slugs fired at me should be aimed a little bit high.

'But, Vin,' Hendricks said discouragedly, 'suppose it's just a trick?'

Markle winked an eye. 'I don't think it would do Mr Sorrell much good, do you?'

The coppers took me downstairs, where Hendricks snapped the cuffs off and I was able to get the blood circulating in my wrists again.

'There's the side door,' he said disgustedly. 'Take out past the garage and around the side drive. A plain black city car is parked at the curb with the keys in it, a Ford.'

I patted him on the head and looked into the glowering face of the copper I'd clobbered earlier. 'I hope your aim's good, fellas.'

So I took off, and those guys really turned it on for the benefit of their fellow officers and anyone who might have been watching.

They were supposed to keep their shots up high, but I heard a bullet whistle past my ear by inches. A couple of them chopped and skidded across the pavement just in front of me, singing like maddened crickets.

But I made it, that was the important thing. It was strange, but the thought of dying didn't bother me so much. I just kept thinking that I wouldn't find that dough or be able to get Hendricks and Vin Markle, if I was clumsy enough to get killed.

I made it around to the side drive, where the black Ford was parked exactly as Hendricks said it would be. I got in and twisted the key starter, rammed the stick shift home to first and squealed out into traffic, scaring the hell out of two women wheelers and a truck driver.

Markle's sudden and urgent interest in the half million might have been surprising but for one thing, and I was slowly getting it together in my mind.

I know he didn't intend to split the money with me, if he found it, any more than I intended to come running to him, if I did. I began to smell another influence, and I mean literally.

I remembered the perfume odor when I came into Markle's office earlier that afternoon, and it was only now that my mind and nose made the association.

I'd smelled that perfume before – on Naida Torneau.

I was speeding down the city streets, but it didn't make too goddamn much difference now . . .

13

I hid out on the backroads till darkness gobbled up everything that evening, like a fat, black glutton.

My mind was going funny again, and I was getting real mad at nothing. My patsy personality was rebelling and I knew it was more than a mere warning.

Naida Torneau had been by to see Markle, assuredly. If her old man had the dough, why was she taking chances? When you're latched onto five hundred grand, it doesn't make much difference whether your true love is a sissy or a fish.

No, it had to be something else.

I found a roadside phone booth and gave the Hollitop a ring.

'Hello, Hollitop Terraces,' the desk clerk said.

'This is Andy Sorrell. Have there been any calls for me today?'

I could hear him choke back the surprise. 'Mr Sorrell? Oh, *Mr Sorrell!* Why, now, no, Mr Sorrell, I haven't received anything for you in the past few hours I've been on.'

'Anybody been looking for me?'

'What? Oh, no, no, Mr Sorrell, no one's called!'

'What's the matter? You think this is an audition or something?'

'Oh, no, no, no, Mr Sorrell! It's – I – well, could you possibly tell me where you are at the moment, Mr Sorrell?'

I laughed at him. 'No, I couldn't possibly. How many cops are there standing around the lobby now?'

'What . . . ?'

'You heard me, Hester. You tell me, or I'm gonna come right over and twist your goddamn lying neck off right down to the quick!'

His voice broke. 'Please, Mr Sorrell, I don't want any trouble! The state police have been in asking for you. They left three men here. I don't know anything about what's going on, please believe me!'

I hung up. Vin Markle didn't waste any time getting the weight off his neck. I looked at my watch and saw it tick out twenty past eight. Biting down on a hunch, I called up Lilly's and asked for Eversen.

'Mr Eversen speaking,' the guy said diplomatically.

'Sorrell, honey. Was just thinking of you and wondering if I should come over and blow a hole in your head for giving me a bum steer.'

'But . . . but I don't understand, Sorrell!'

'You know what I'm talking about. You said Lilly had the money. I don't think Lilly has the money.'

'But it's the truth!' he said frantically. 'From all I can gather, Lilly does have the money! What about Cassiday and Horvat and Benedict? And what about last night – when you were shot at? Lilly came in late, didn't he? It could have been him who attacked you and killed Horvat, couldn't it?'

'You ask too many questions, baby.'

'But I'm right, Sorrell, you know I'm right!'

'Is Lilly around the club now?'

'No. He's supposed to have some of his friends in from Santa Monica later on tonight. He won't be in here at all.'

'That makes it solid, friend. Since Lilly's going to have a leisure hour, I think I'll just stop in before it starts.'

'Sorrell—'

I hung up before he started whining again.

I had to be on my tippy-toes, now that the state boys were after me. No doubt they'd have road blocks set up on the main highways and a couple of stakeouts at the busier joints, if they were convinced I hadn't left town yet.

I took the backroads, running into several dead ends, but it didn't take me over an hour to get within the vicinity of Lilly's beach house.

Remembering his playmates with the over-developed shoulders, I felt a bit naked. I left the car about three quarters of a mile down the road and made myself a part of the crags and jagged upshoots on the beach.

The salt chopped into my nostrils and the wash of the sea and spray made my blood race, like I'd taken a good shot of rye.

The lights in Lilly's joint were just as gay as he was. The house, an eccentric construction, sat right on the edge of the water, with a tide water mark. The basement was above water, and you could have dived in from the second floor balcony when the moon was high.

I galloped over to the side of the building and caught the rungs of a wrought-iron water lily lattice, formulating the obvious pun in my mind a little late. The thing took me easily to the second floor, where I was able to reach over and get a grip on the balcony. I hauled myself over and pressed my back against the wall.

Through a pair of single-paned doors I could look in on the colorful softness of a living room, and squaring off in the center like two game cocks were Naida Torneau and Tina Meadows. It looked like what they were saying was real interesting, so I reached over and twisted open the door on my side until it was cracked about ten inches.

'I'm going to tell every goddamn thing I know!' Tina Meadows was saying. 'You said I'd get Al's share after Sorrell killed him, but all I got was the run-around. I'm going to tell Vin everything!'

'You fool!' Naida snapped at her. 'Don't you realize how high the stakes are now? If you say one thing, we'll both be killed!'

'What about the money? You told me if I buttered Al up enough, he'd tell me. He never told me one thing. All I got was two black eyes and a fractured shoulder where that bruiser worked me over.'

Naida grabbed her by the arm. 'Sorrell is out of the way now, stupid! I didn't find out till today how he'd been used. Now keep your mouth shut! By tomorrow night, we'll both be on easy street.'

Tina snatched away from her. 'We'd better, I'm just telling you – *we'd better*!'

She stalked out, with Naida close behind. I slipped into the room and over to the door. I opened it until I could look out.

Tina had just reached the landing from the circular staircase. She was still talking heatedly, but I couldn't make out what she said. Naida went over to the door with her and slammed it with relief after the visitor had made her jet-propelled exit.

She stood rubbing a hand thoughtfully across the bridge of her nose, then raised her head to call out to the closed doors of one of the lower floor rooms, 'Lil, I'm going out for a while. Be back in time for the party.'

There was a muffled response, and she went back to the rear of the house. In a moment, she returned with a braided shawl about her shoulders and went quickly out the front door.

I tipped down the stairs noiselessly and was able to watch her screech out of the attached garage in a black Thunderbird. The quartet of red eyes on its tail disappeared out on the road in a few seconds.

I swung my attention to that door Naida'd been talking to. Something told me not to, but I decided to go for broke.

The first thing I saw when I entered was Brace Lilly, sitting in the midst of what must have been his private sanctuary. The walls of the room were lined with nudes – all men.

The next thing I saw was red flashes, and everything in front of me became a concave-convex illusion.

I knew I'd hit the jackpot again . . .

14

Whoever it was missed out on his Sunday punch.

Whatever he hit me with chopped away a lot of flesh behind my right ear, but it did little more than knock me down and daze me for a moment.

I reached for him going down and was almost deafened by an explosion. He'd fired right in front of my eyes. The powder flash peppered my forehead, but I was able to swing my arm around, half blinded now, and get a grip on his gun arm.

I dug my fingers in and wrenched. I heard the guy gasp and pull back, yanking me off balance, but he was playing hell trying to get away.

Desperation made him think of his knee as a weapon, and he gave it to me, but hard. I heard my teeth clack against each other in the back of my head. The blow was effective. I loosed my grip and heard the patter-patter of little feet as my guy got the hell out of there.

Way over around South Bend, the sound of a car gobble-degooked around in my brain, as my head and the floor matched grains.

For a long time, I didn't know what the hell I was doing there. I was knocked out somewhere, on my hands and knees, feeling like a little kid who'd had a chance to wash out that bastard neighborhood bully and goofed it.

Finally, I was able to bring myself around. The little voice was talking again, frightening me, and I was so full of frustration it felt like I'd exploded.

My mouth was bleeding on the inside. The blood was good-tasting, warm and full of sea salt. Every goddamn thing in the world was against me, just like it'd always been all my frigging life.

When I could see again, I stood up. I had that feeling, and after looking into Lilly's ivory-pallored face I knew he was dead. I got that smell of Jergens lotion again.

It was a quick death, the kind which left the eyes open and a quasi-life expression on the mouth.

He was dressed for the party in a silky green, Mother Hubbard sort of thing with an open collar. He sat in a deep chair, with his arms at rest in his lap. An empty cocktail glass lay overturned on the floor.

I went over to him. I was so goddamn mad, I kicked him. 'You sonofabitch,' I said.

I punched him in his smooth face, making the head jerk, but I couldn't take that expression off. I punched him till my fist hurt, till that dead bastard hurt me.

Then I realized what I was doing, like in a dream where I'd been watching on, full of urgency in the need to have this dead thing living so that his bruised skin and my own would be gratified.

I was in a mental whirlpool. Where to go from here? What to do? That Lilly had died of poison was evident, and it was also indicated that his murderer was the same guy who'd conned Horvat out of his life.

But why?

I couldn't see the sense in the whole thing. Why was it necessary that Lilly had to be killed?

The only obvious answer was that he knew more than he should have known. The idea that he had the money was shot to hell now.

The complete recognition of where I was and under what circumstances came to me suddenly. I backed away from the body and went toward the door.

At the same moment, I heard a car drive up. I burst through the doors and stumbled up the stairs. I was lucky enough to make the top and fall into the room I'd come out of.

I cracked the door about a quarter inch and kept an eye on the ground floor. The doorbell chimed out. Then a pause. I heard a key in the lock and a quick snap as the door came open.

It was the little guy Eversen. He hesitated for a moment after entering, then passed out of sight under the staircase. In a few minutes he was back with a couple of fifths of something under his arm.

I came out and ran down the steps, cutting him off at the door.

'Sorrell!'

I grabbed him not too gently by the lapels. 'You sure make a lotta goddamn trips for that bonded, Pops. Why don't you hook up a conveyor from here to the club?'

He fidgeted around nervously in my hands. 'It's Cutty Sark. We're all out at the club. Lilly doesn't keep any there – somebody's been stealing it, he said.'

'Why'd you ring the bell?' I said. 'You had a key – why didn't you just come right in?'

He tried to shrug away from me. 'I don't know, Sorrell! It's – it's just something I do, that's all. I've been doing it all along.'

'When was the last time you saw Lilly?'

'Earlier this afternoon, maybe this morning. That's when he told me about the party tonight.'

I grabbed him by the neck and shoved him ahead of me into the room where I'd left Lilly.

He didn't react fast. When he saw that Lilly didn't move, he asked me if he were asleep.

'Go over and wake him up,' I said.

He started over but turned before he got halfway. 'Sorrell . . . Sorrell . . . what's the matter with him? Is he sick?'

'In the worst way.'

'He's *dead*?'

'You catch on fast.'

Eversen gave me a great big horror face and broke for the door, dropping both bottles of liquor. I caught him before he made it, hoisted him up on my forearms and slammed him against the wall.

'Don't! Please, don't, Sorrell, don't kill me, too! I won't tell!'

'Yeah, I'm made to order, right?'

He blubbered all over my sleeves. 'Just let me go! Please, let me go! I don't want to have anything to do with this!'

'That's not gonna work out, my little friend,' I said, applying a little pressure up where his collar plunged. '*You* put the finger on Lilly. *You* told me he was the one with the cash. *You* told me he was the one who'd engineered the heist. Now who else did you tell?'

'Nobody!' he choked out. 'Nobody, Sorrell! Nobody but you!'

'Then that doesn't look so good for you, Pops. If I'm picked up by the police, I'm going to tell them it was you helped me knock Lilly off – and Horvat. I'm not gonna fry-ass by myself, you can bet on that!'

'Wait, *wait*, Sorrell, listen to me! Harv Cassiday slipped in the back way of the club this evening and pulled me off the floor. He said he was fed up with Lilly short-changing him and trying to have him killed—'

'Cassiday?'

'He's been up in Palo Alto. He said he got a telegram from Lilly this morning telling him to meet up this afternoon at the club for the split.'

'Did he see Lilly?'

'No. Lilly'd been in for a few minutes and left. Cassiday said he was tired of the run-around and was going to settle things once and for all.'

I eased up on the little guy's collar. 'What you say would make sense except for one thing – you want me to believe Cassiday knocked off Horvat?'

'But why not, Sorrell? Wouldn't that make the split more promising? Benedict was already dead. With Horvat out of the way, Lilly and Cassiday would only have to split two ways. Now with Lilly out of the way—'

'Just hold on a minute, little fella,' I said. 'Where's the dough? The guy who knocked Lilly off didn't have time to leave with anything, I can swear to that.'

'How do I know? Maybe Lilly stashed it. Maybe Cassiday found the hiding place, forced Lilly into telling him before he killed him.'

In my mind I started thinking. *That might be it*, but I heard something in the distance that made the hair crawl up at the back of my neck.

'Police sirens!' I grabbed Eversen again and shoved him out in the hall. 'I've gotta have somewhere to stay – quick! Where's your car?'

'Outside. The blue Pontiac. Here're the keys. I've got a cottage on this same road, about fifteen miles. You'll find the keys to it on the ring.'

'Okay, but before you try anything funny I want you to give it a lot of thought. When the police get here, tell them you just arrived and found Lilly. Understand?'

Eversen looked scared to death. 'I won't say anything wrong, believe me!'

I could see the headlights about a mile and a half down the highway when I came out front. I sprinted over to Eversen's late model Pontiac and got the thing started right up, keeping the headlights off until I'd gotten to the highway.

Then I turned all the horses loose, mashing down on the accelerator until the road behind me was nothing more than a hazy, gray-black blur.

15

I found Eversen's place easily enough.

It was on the shaded side of a string of wind-blown trees, next to the sea. Perfect. The place was damn near impossible to find in the dark, so I knew it'd be hell to locate in the daytime.

The interior was modest but tastily equipped, with two bedrooms. A canted four panes allowed you to look out on the sea and the highway, simply by turning your head.

A ripple of distant bells came to me, and, looking at my watch with both its hands clasped together over the twelve, I realized with a shock that it was Sunday.

Sunday. All I could see about Sunday was a big wide church with a lot of bent heads and a guy in a white collar saying things he knew the people listening didn't give a damn about anyway.

Sunday.

I had been in Hollisworth nearly a week. It didn't take that long to put my life on the line. I'd come as the hunter, and now I was the hunted, that was for sure.

I fumbled around in the dark and found some cigarettes, lighted one. I let the coal sputter up and peter off with each draw, trying to think the way the guy who was putting me through these changes was thinking.

Three people were dead in less than a week, and I might as well have been responsible for all of them. Perhaps in a way I was.

Then being pulled off the job by Lou Pulco. Lou wouldn't have done that on his own, and I hadn't screwed things up so bad that I couldn't repair my missteps.

Granted, it did look bad for me, being on the scene when Horvat got his, and that Inglander broad put the clincher on. But she must have told them she'd seen me *after* she'd been slugged.

However, the syndicate's gripe was altogether legit – I had

no business being seen at all. My job was to get in and out as fast as possible. Here I was, caught up in an assignment which shouldn't have taken over two days under normal circumstances.

But I was greedy, just like everybody else.

Naida Torneau was after that half million, and so was Tina Meadows, not counting Vin Markle, Harv Cassiday and the syndicate. My friend Eversen had some hidden motive, too, and it was not to play Tom Champion, boy hero.

I let my mind wander, like a magnet in a pin factory.

There was something I wasn't hitting! It was right there for me to see, but I kept putting my own thumbs in my eyes.

I'd get something out of this, or I'd be glad to die!

The conversation between Tina and Naida was provocative, and it certainly proved that my idea about me being a patsy was for real. Naida had an in. She knew a good deal more about the whole thing than anyone else, I was sure of it!

I heard the sirens again.

I crouched down and crawled over to the window. *That bastard Eversen*, I thought, but the car kept right on down the road in the direction of Lilly's.

I got up and stumbled around the place until I found some liquor in a recessed shelf of the kitchen sink. It wasn't rye, but I drink bourbon along with the rest.

I came out and sat down in the dark. My mind started picking those things up again, and I didn't try to stop it.

Where was the money? Cassiday wouldn't knock Lilly off unless he knew exactly where the money was, and Lilly wouldn't be fool enough to tell him unless he'd been unduly pressured. And from the looks of Lilly, he hadn't been forced to give up anything but his life.

Had Cassiday made a mistake? Maybe Lilly'd fooled him into thinking the money was somewhere it wasn't.

Who else could get close enough to Horvat and Lilly to feed them the poison? It had to be Cassiday, certainly. He'd been working with them. They trusted him.

But somehow, I just couldn't feature Cassiday poisoning anyone, that was the rub. Poison was more of a woman's weapon. And why not? Naida Torneau had seemed more than informed about what was going on.

She could have gone up to the Inglander place and fed Horvat the poison.

I bumped my head here. Naida needed more than a round shoulder to send Meg Inglander to dream land, and I knew for a fact that Naida had round shoulders.

By the same token, Lilly wouldn't have been such an easy victim. She'd even called to him before she left – and for whose benefit?

No, it hadn't been Naida. This brought me back around to Cassiday again. But where did that leave me? If Cassiday had the dough, he certainly wasn't wasting time in Hollisworth. In that case, I was left in the cold in my birthday suit.

I couldn't hide out forever, not with the state cops sniffing after me and Vin Markle prepared to sacrifice me at any moment.

For some reason, I had a hunch Cassiday was still around Hollisworth somewhere, which meant he didn't have the cash.

And another thing: Why didn't Cassiday kill me when he had the chance, if it was Cassiday who slugged me? He'd fired once with no effect, but after I'd wrestled with him and got that solid knee jolt it wouldn't have been difficult for him to play duck shoot while I drooled all over the floor.

I stopped thinking. The back of my head was burning now. I went back and found the liquor bottle again and brought it back with me into the living room. I stood for a long time watching the sea.

A squall was coming up close to shore and the first speckles of fine rain drops blew across the canted windows. The night was reasonably clear, though, and in the distance I could see a small white sail. I wondered to myself what goddamn fool was out on a night like this, then I had an idea . . .

Today was Sunday, the last day, and I was going to make it a good day for myself.

I remembered vaguely that Carolyn liked Sunday mornings, two shades of pink beneath the covers early Sunday morning, her breasts rising up under the softness of silk as she stretched her goddess body and breathed that smell of herself on me.

I began to tremble, looking out on the water.

I stood there and drank the whole goddamn bottle ...

16

Somehow I slept.

What woke me was Eversen shaking the hell out of my arm the next morning. I sat up but the roof caved right in, like it always does when I drink bourbon.

'Get me something for this,' I said, holding my head tilted so it wouldn't fall off.

The little guy scooted out and returned in a few minutes with a couple of Bromos and a glass of water. I didn't waste any time getting it down, and I was tempted to put my head in a stocking so none of the pieces would fall out.

'What time is it?' I croaked.

'Almost twelve,' Eversen said. He was dressed for leisure in a gaudy sport shirt and slacks, and I could see now that the little guy wasn't as little as I'd first thought he was. The wide shoulders and thick forearms made his small hands seem almost deformed. Seeing him like that, the gray hair didn't make him look so old, either.

I struggled up. 'You got anything to eat around here?'

He nodded quickly. 'I thought you'd be wanting something. I've got some bacon and eggs going, and a grapefruit for that hangover.'

'You can junk the grapefruit. Where's the bathroom?'

'The door behind you. Oh, yes, you'll find some things I picked up in town for you. I knew you didn't have anything to change into.'

I got up and wobbled back to the bathroom, holding my head with both hands.

After I'd slipped down in the shower twice, I got out and found the 'things' Eversen'd picked up in town for me. It was a beige Bermuda ensemble with white bucks and matching knee length socks. Being a conservative dresser, I really considered this extreme, but under the circumstances the outfit might work out nicely.

I was feeling a little better after I'd got into them, but my stomach went deaf, dumb and blind when I sat down across from Eversen at the kitchen table.

'Just bring me a bowl and the coffee pot, Pops,' I said miserably.

I heard Eversen laugh for the first time, like a little chipmunk. 'I don't see anything so goddamn funny,' I said.

'No, Sorrell, please forgive me,' he chittered. 'I was just thinking, here you are with practically the whole State of California looking for you – and you're nursing a hangover!'

He brought the coffee pot over from the stove and waited until I'd poured a cup and had my first sip.

'Vin Markle was over to the club last night,' he said. 'And this morning, all the employees had to return for questioning.'

'That's not surprising,' I said.

'Markle thinks you killed Lilly,' he went on.

'That's not surprising, either. I was made for the role. And just where am I supposed to keep my stock of poison, in a hollow leg or something?'

'Poison?'

'Didn't Markle tell you? Lilly was poisoned, and so was Horvat. I've seen some poisons work, and this looks like one of the cyanides to me, probably prussic acid. There's a hell of a sweetish smell to the stuff, but the killer probably covered it up in a mixed drink.'

Eversen looked confused. 'I don't understand. It *couldn't* have been you, Sorrell.'

'And why couldn't it?'

'Why – because you're not the type to use a poison. You'd use a gun or knife, wouldn't you? Or maybe your hands, like in Benedict's case.'

'You'll make a fine character witness,' I said. 'Anyway, poison is the woman's choice.'

'You mean Naida?'

'Possibly, or maybe Tina Meadows.'

'I don't think it was Naida,' he said thoughtfully.

'Truthfully, I don't either. Neither do I think it was Tina.' I finished the cup and poured another, my brain beginning to oil up a bit. 'When I got over to Lilly's last night, Naida and Tina were together. I don't think either one of them knew Lilly was dead. Naida left directly after Tina, and she called out to Lilly before she left. She wouldn't call out to anyone she already knew was dead, naturally. I think it was the murderer who answered her – the voice was muffled.'

'Who could it have been?'

'I don't have much of a choice. I think Markle can safely be excluded. That leaves only three other people: Hendricks, Cassiday . . . and you.'

Eversen's reaction was violent. 'But you know I didn't have anything to do with it! What reason would I have for killing Lilly, just give me one!'

'I can give you five hundred thousand reasons.'

'But I didn't know what was going on! I came in and got the liquor, you know that! The next minute you were dragging me into the room! How could I have killed Lilly? I'd just got there!'

'Relax, Pops,' I said, smiling. 'I can't fit you in anywhere as the killer, but I've got an idea you know more than you're telling. Why all the help? Whyn't you just call the cops and get me off your back?'

He was flustered, trying to find a reason. 'Why – why, you *made* me, Sorrell! You're making me do this!'

'Yeah, I'm scaring the hell out of you.'

'But, Sorrell—'

'You just keep right on doing what you're doing, Pops, and no mistake!' I said menacingly. 'Maybe you'll get exactly what you're looking for out of this.'

This pacified him a bit. 'I think Cassiday did it, that's what I think.' His eyes brightened suddenly. 'Why couldn't it have been Lilly himself? He could have poisoned himself, couldn't he? And Horvat – he was even up at the Inglander place the night Horvat was poisoned, wasn't he?'

'There you go, asking those damn questions again. For one thing, Lilly didn't poison himself and then call the cops. Whoever called the cops thought I'd still be cooled there in the house, which would have wrapped things up perfectly. Unless I've taken a hell of a wrong road, I take Cassiday for the kind of guy who plays for keeps. He would have made sure the job was finished himself.'

Eversen looked at his watch. 'I'm going over to the club to supervise the clean-up work. Is there anything you want me to do?'

'Yeah, go over to the Hollitop and nose around. See if you can bribe one of the juniors to release my bags. Get the hell right out of there if you see any cops. Just act like you've got nose trouble. Give me a ring back here when you've taken care of that.' I thought of the idea I'd had last night. 'Is there any place around here where I can rent a boat, a small one?'

He scratched his head for a minute. 'There's a public dock about five miles down the beach, but you'd probably be recognized there. I've got a skiff out in the garage. It may leak a bit, but it's seaworthy. What have you got in mind?'

'I think I'll take a little jaunt over the bounding main,' I said. 'I'll let you know how it turns out.'

'Well, I'll be on my way,' he said, getting up. 'I'll ring you back at the first opportunity.'

'I'll wait until you do.'

After Eversen had left, I went over to the phone and dialed up New York again, the private number Lou had given me. I had trouble with the connection, but finally got it.

A woman answered and told me she was Pulco's private secretary.

'I'm Andy Sorrell. I'd like to talk with Mr Pulco.'

She didn't answer for a long time. 'Mr Pulco is not in at present,' she said finally, 'but he left a message in the event you should call, Mr Sorrell.'

'Let's have it.'

'Mr Pulco says you are to continue as directed until otherwise notified,' she said in brisk, business-like tones. 'Mr Pulco would like to see you personally in his office by the middle of next week. Mr Pulco says he would advise you to finish your assignment with all necessary speed.'

'Does Mr Pulco advise that I sprout wings and fly home?' I said caustically. 'Or maybe I could sail through the Gulf and up the New England coastline.'

'I beg your pardon, Mr Sorrell?'

'Forget it. Just tell Mr Pulco that I got the message.'

I hung up. Mr Pulco sure wasn't clearing this goddamn mess up any for me.

Markle said he'd gotten a telegram from Lou telling me to get home. He could have been lying, of course, but I didn't think so.

Why should Lou take me off the job, then put me right back on?

I could attribute this to my good buddy Markle without too much trouble, at least the part about me being taken off the assignment. Lou'd probably had a change of mind after thinking it over. Anyway, I still had Cassiday to go. I'd dealt with Pulco before, and this was the only time I'd ever goofed. Lou knew it; maybe that's why he was giving me a chance to clean up.

I went back to the kitchen, found another bottle and had a good shot of the dog's hair.

Lou's show of confidence made me feel a lot better.

Now all I needed was a gun, and I'd be in business.

17

Eversen's sporting skiff wasn't in the best of shape.

The stationary sprite had been broken off at the top and the leg-of-mutton sail looked like a piece of somebody's tattered underwear.

It was equipped with oars, though, and I flexed my muscles, remembering the days I could pull a fifteen foot sharpie around the world, and then I was only a twelve-year-old kid.

Getting behind the dolly, I was able to wheel the thing out in the sunlight and check for leaks. I went into the house and got a bucket of water. I sloshed it over the bottom and got down on my hands and knees to take a look.

There were three leaks, one at the bow and two next to the centerboard.

I went back to the garage and was lucky enough to find a can of aluminum caulking. It had hardened some, but was still pliable enough to rake out with the end of a cold chisel.

I went back out to the boat and started giving it a good going over.

I pulled my shirt off under the sun. The sweat started popping out all over my body, and I began to feel goddamn good. It was like my boyhood, on the sea with my old man, him saying, 'Watch your work, boy. You love her right, fix her right, and she'll never let you down. Take some sand and rub her nose . . .'

It was real good. I took the skiff off the dolly and turned her belly up. I got me some sand in the bucket and a piece of the canvas rigging, and I began to rub. I rubbed until her goddamn belly was slick and wood new, and all the time I was listening for my old man's approval, his nod.

All of a sudden, I was looking out to the sea, and my old man was dead, and I was wondering. *Why, why, you sonofabitch up there, why'd you have to take my old man?*

It was no good without paint. I didn't have the paint. My

old man would never have allowed me to rub a boat without paint. My mother, my old man . . . and then Carolyn . . .

I began to feel funny. I wanted to crush something. I got down in the sand and grabbed two handfuls. I squeezed them until the sand was nothing in my hands, like all three of those people. I looked out on that big sonofabitch of a sea and I could hear things, voices, and they got louder and louder, and I stood up and hollered at them, like I'd hollered at that guy who came to get me after my old man had died.

'Don't catch me, you bastard!' I hollered, tears in my eyes. 'I won't let you catch me! None of you can catch me!'

And I ran and I ran and I ran.

Away . . .

I was almost plastered when Eversen called that evening.

I'd forgotten where the phone was, but I finally found it under the sofa where it must have fallen. Luckily, the receiver hadn't come off. The room was a shambles. I'd been throwing things around, and I didn't have any shirt on.

Eversen sounded excited when I picked the phone up.

'Sorrell, I was able to get in with the desk clerk. You got a telegram from some fellow named Lou Pulco this morning. He says for you to carry on your assignment, whatever that means. Markle picked the message up.'

'Okay. Anything else?'

'Markle also confiscated your luggage. The police commissioner has arranged with the state people to handle your case strictly for Hollisworth. They're claiming you for the Benedict murder. A receptionist at Blue Haven gave your identification.'

'I'm glad the state is off my ass,' I said. 'Now I'll only have to put up with Markle and his boys.'

'That may not be so good. I hear Markle's out for blood.'

'So am I. How're things over at the club?'

'Business as usual,' he said. 'Lilly's demise didn't affect Naida gravely. She says it'll be good for the trade.'

'That's one way to look at it. Where is the bereaved widow?'

'Over at the beach house, celebrating, I think.'

'Good.'

'Are you going over?'

'I'm thinking about it. Don't call back if anything turns up. I most likely won't be here.'

'All right. You can reach me at the club, if you need to call.'

I rang off and sat with my head in my hands a long time. I was trembling again.

It was so hard to figure out! Sometimes I would be all right, then *zip!* I'd go off my rocker again.

I went outside and found my shirt where I'd taken it off that afternoon. It was getting dark fast. It was 8:30 by my watch.

I wrestled the skiff back on the dolly and pulled it down to the edge of the water. It didn't take long to drag it out, and in a few minutes I was rowing through the gentle swells.

The sea was unusually calm, and although it was dark you could look around for miles. The sun had left a somber residue of illumination.

The oarhooks protested like squeaky old men under the rhythmic pull of my shoulders. It wasn't long before I saw Lilly's beach house in the distance. I took my shirt off again and dropped it in the bottom of the boat. If anyone spotted me, I wanted them to think I was some college kid out for a night of exercise.

It took me fifteen minutes to pull abreast of the place. I kept on down the shoreline, making sure nobody was hanging around. When I was about a mile away, I stopped and let the boat drift, like I was taking a breather.

I stayed like that for a half hour, waiting for the darkness to thicken, then I swung around and headed back.

I could see the lights burning from the same room I'd gone up to the night before, only this time the doors to the balcony were open.

I made good and damn sure I wasn't sticking my neck out before I came up on the beach. The exposed basement provided an excellent shelter from the front, so I pulled the skiff up on the beach as far as possible, catching hell a couple of times when the centerboard bogged down in the sand.

Since I had such luck the last time with the lily lattice, I tried it again. This time nobody was around when I got to the top.

As I came in, I could hear a hi-fi sounding off somewhere on the floor I was on. When I opened the door to the hallway, the music seemed to be jumping through the open doors of what looked like the master bedroom.

This time I wasn't taking any chances. A nude in ebony stood with her arms over her head under a lampshade near the door. I took the shade and light bulb out and snatched the cord out of the socket, wrapping it around the length of the figurine. The thing had a satisfying heft in my hand.

I came out and went down the hall. I exposed my head, but just enough for me to glance in with one eye. What I saw really jolted me.

Naida Torneau was lounging on the couch in what must have been her private bedroom, eyes closed. She, unlike her husband Lilly, was very much alive, and she was dressed in nothing, from tip to toe.

I saw her mouth part, and the eyes opened and caught me before I could duck out of the way.

'Don't be bashful, Sorrell,' she murmured, smiling at me. 'Come on in . . .'

She covered herself ineffectually with a gown or something. I came in, closing the door behind me.

'Are you sure I won't be a bother?' I said, watching her swing her long legs around and prop herself up in a sitting position.

'I'm just in the mood to be bothered,' she said seductively. 'I seem to remember you didn't have a shirt on the last time we met. I think that black young thing fits you a lot more attractively than that muggy old pistol, though.'

I came over to her, but my mind wasn't clicking anymore.

A long time ago I remember hearing some guy talk of an experiment which had to do with rats, in which a male and female were placed in respective cages. The male rat was starved for several days, then put into the cage with the female, where there was plenty of food.

'It's the damnedest thing!' this guy said. 'That crazy rat'll go after the tail before he eats!'

What that test proved then, I don't know, but it sure let me see that rats and men have a lot in common. Here I was, about to have my ass scissored, staring down at something that had *C'mon, sucker* written all over it.

'I've been expecting you, Sorrell,' she said, extending a hand to pull me down next to her.

'So I see.'

'Don't be frightened,' she cooed, like I was a little kid afraid of the bogey man. 'No one's going to be back tonight . . .' She leaned over and put her lips against mine, backed away when she didn't get any response.

'What's the matter, Sorrell?'

'Don't you feel a little funny screwing around with the guy who knocked off your old man?'

She pooh-poohed. 'You know I don't believe that damn old crap! And even if I did, how will I ever repay you for the favor?'

'In hundred dollar bills.'

'What?'

I wasn't getting through to her, so I pointed to the center of my palm and told her to take a good look. When she had her eyes fastened to the spot, I let her have it right on the kisser.

Her head snapped back with the force of the blow and she grabbed her mouth to see if any teeth were missing.

'You bastard!' she yelled. 'You sonofabitching bastard!'

She made a hook of her fingers and tried to tear out my right eye, but I ducked and let her have it again, this time harder.

She wasn't used to this kind of treatment, or at least she hadn't received a dose in a long time. I took her around the merry-go-round two more times, until I thought the cobwebs were closing in.

'Okay,' I said. 'Do we begin again, or do we act sensible about the whole thing?'

'You goddamn crapping bastard!' she hollered, raking my chest with her fingernails. 'You dirty, crapping sonofabitch!'

I got away from her and cuffed both her ears. While she was trying to dig the bees out of her skull with her fingertips, I found the black statuette and pulled the stiff plastic cord off.

The gown had fallen away and all those pink spots were like

fuzzy peaches. I doubled the cord up and laid it briskly against her thigh.

'I'll kill you!' she cried, coming at me, but I stepped aside and snapped the cord against her rump twice. She tripped and fell. She landed on her side, and I was there to welcome her home.

I beat her ass until her whole body was criss-crossed with welts and her spasmodic jerking accompanied the thunder of the hi-fi. She was making small animal sounds on the floor, and she wasn't trying to get up.

I didn't know what was happening until she dug her fingernails into my leg and began kissing it!

'Darling!' she screamed joyfully. 'My darling baby, my sweet! Please don't stop! Please don't ever stop!'

Her body, criss-crossed with livid welts, wiggled and shook on the floor. Her breasts pressed hot and firm against my knees. I felt myself rising as her hand came to my waist, clawed at my loins. Her buttocks, round, cherubic, seemed somehow profaned with the red stripes, twisted against the floor with wild passion.

It was like a nightmare. I was unable to stop her hands from doing things to me. I pulled away from her, and she sat back on her haunches, a hand under each breast, raising their pink mouths high and questing toward me.

'Oh, you bastard!' she screamed. 'Take me – take me before I go crazy!'

18

There's a little bit of the queer bug in all of us.

Naida's ecstasy was infectious. I got her up and dragged her over to the massive bed. She was wiggling in my hands like a boa, full of strength.

'Quick, Sorrell! Hurry, darling, *hurry!*'

I'd forgotten everything, but absently I was aware of a victory. As I knelt over Naida, watching her firm breasts and their nipples touched with the scarlet of passion, the flesh pulsating along her belly and thighs, I felt the utter conqueror.

I made myself ready, but hesitated purposely, wondering at the thing unleashed within her.

'Please, Sorrell! Please don't torture me!'

With a great sense of objectivity, I sunk myself into her hotness and fire . . .

I saw her come out of a dream.

We were entangled on the bed, and she was breathing heavily under me, her lips shiny with a smear of blood from some small wound.

She began kissing my mouth, my throat. 'Oh, I love you, Sorrell! Honey, I love you more than anything!'

I was suddenly repulsed. It wasn't like the first time I'd had her, before I knew. Now I saw the affinity between her and Lilly, and it was as though I'd become a part of it.

I'd never felt like I'd betrayed Carolyn before by having another woman, but now I felt it as keenly as the pains a woman feels in labor.

The taste of her was in my mouth. Her arms seemed to have me glued to her breasts. I snatched away from her and went into the bathroom attached to her room. I had to wash up, I had to get clean again for Carolyn.

When I came out she had the gown on. She was still on the bed, sitting up against its padded headboard, but she'd gotten up somewhere along the line and made a couple of drinks.

'Come on over here, darling,' she purred.

'I don't need the big build-up again,' I said, but I went over and got the drink, horsing it down.

'Don't be cruel, Sorrell,' she said pitifully. 'Be gentle with me, lover.'

'The next time I'll just use my fists. I think you and I would both like that better.'

She reached out and grabbed me about the waist, put her head against my stomach. 'Sorrell, I can't help it if I'm that way. Don't condemn me!'

'I don't give a damn what way you are,' I said, pushing her away. 'I wanna know where that goddamn money is, and baby, I'm almost sure you know the hiding place!'

'But I *don't!* I swear to you I've no idea where it is.'

'You listen,' I said, sitting down next to her. 'I was here last night. I heard you and Tina Meadows talking in the next room. You told Tina that tonight both of you would be in the chips, after she raised hell about what you'd promised her for being nice to Al Benedict.'

'But I didn't promise her anything,' she said. 'Benedict himself promised it to her. Just before they stuck up the bank, Benedict used to come around to the club all the time to watch her dance. To get on her good side, he told her he had a big deal coming off and he'd treat her right. After he came back to Hollisworth and went into the sanitarium, he told Tina he'd see that I got the money for safe-keeping, that I'd be given her share.'

'You didn't have any private deal with her, then?'

'Of course not, Sorrell! How could I?'

'Tina said you'd promised her a share if she found out where the dough was.'

She knew now that I'd heard a good deal of what she and Tina had been talking about. 'All right, darling, so there *was* a deal. But so what? Can you blame me for trying to get the lion's share?'

'No, but I can damn well blame you for trying to front me off. When you came to my apartment, you told me just the place to find Horvat. How did you know where he was?'

'From Tina, of course. She was seeing Benedict regularly. He told her practically everything, except where the money was.'

'What are you and Vin Markle holding hands about, as if I didn't know?'

Her face blanched. 'Markle . . . ? Why, I don't know what you mean. I *know* him, if that's what you're getting at.'

'You know damn well that's not what I'm getting at,' I said. 'You wear a perfume that's a distinction in itself. I smelled it yesterday when the bulls strong-armed me up to Markle's office. You hadn't been gone more than a few minutes.'

She looked away from me, gathering herself. 'It shouldn't be hard for you to understand, Sorrell . . .'

'Shouldn't it?'

'Well, my goodness, no! Markle isn't an *ugly* man, you know. In fact, he's very handsome.'

'Isn't that playing it a little too close to home? Markle made it plain when he gave me that going-over that it was because I'd jacked up Tina Meadows.' I watched her face. 'Don't tell me you didn't *know*. Tina even mentioned Markle last night – by his given name. I don't think you're in the dark about the romance.'

'What difference does it make?' she said, obviously piqued. 'Who I want to go to bed with is *my* business!'

'Especially if your business concerns half a million dollars.'

She swung off the bed and pranced over hotly to find a cigarette on the coffee table.

'You're not making any sense, Sorrell!' she said.

I began to laugh.

She pivoted around, and I could see I was getting under her skin.

'What's so goddamn amusing?' she said.

'The thought that I'm not the only patsy in this thing,' I said. 'I'd like to see Markle's face when he wakes up and finds himself wearing the blue ribbon!'

She came over to the bed, her manner changed quicker than a chameleon's colors. She sat down beside me and gave me the Lizabeth Scott routine. 'Let's take and get the hell out of here,

Sorrell. Markle doesn't mean anything to me – he never has. I can get the money for us; it'll just take a little time.'

'From what I understand, it shouldn't take you over fifteen minutes. I hear Lilly arranged to lift that poke, along with the Three Stooges.'

'Who told you that? George Eversen?'

'How'd you know?'

'He's always sticking his nose in,' she said. 'The old bastard's got a crush on me. He's always hated Lilly. Don't believe anything he tells you.'

'Lilly wasn't involved?'

'Lil never had a passion for anything but men – real men. I married him six years ago just to get away from Frisco. His old man left him some dough, and one of the provisions of his will was that his son got married in order to collect.' She sighed disgustedly. 'I guess the old guy thought that would make a man of him.'

'Then where is the money?' I said. 'If Lilly didn't have it, who did?'

'Why, the guys who stuck up the bank, naturally. They stashed the dough here in Hollisworth after the robbery, then split up. Benedict went to the sanitarium, Horvat up to his girlfriend's place and Cassiday out of town.'

'Everything is falling into position too easy,' I said. 'Cassiday is the only one left. If he knows where the money is, why doesn't he just come in and pick it up and get the hell out of town?'

She tapped my nose with a forefinger and winked. 'All that would be fine, if things could work that smoothly. But the fact is, the money isn't where Cassiday thinks it is.'

'I'm not gonna play games all night long,' I told her. 'Where is that goddamn money?'

'Be *patient*, Sorrell! Maybe you'd like to know where Cassiday is, instead.'

'I wouldn't give a damn if Cassiday was hung up in that closet. I'm scheduled for the gas chamber, and if I go there's gonna be a hell of a price tag on the chair they strap me in.'

'But don't you see?' she said, almost pleadingly. 'We can't do anything with Cassiday hanging around. He knows I've got a lead on the money and he's going to keep me spotted until

I pick it up. He's got to be put out of the way! You even got a telegram today telling you to finish him off.'

'Did Markle read it to you?'

She smiled secretly. 'How else would I know?'

I smiled back at her, but it was at the thought of how big a sucker *she* thought I was. 'Okay. I knock off Cassiday. When do we get the dough?'

'I thought it'd be tonight, but I've run into some difficulties. It'll be tomorrow night. I'll be here waiting after you finish up.'

'There's something I'd like to know,' I said, getting up. 'Who killed Lilly?'

She took on a modest mien. 'Why, *I* did, baby. He was becoming too much of a bother.'

I grinned down on her as though impressed. 'Oh, yeah, one other little thing. Where is Cassiday now?'

'It's a rooming house on Deacon Street, an old folks' home. You won't have any trouble finding it.'

'How'll I know him?'

'Why, hon, just ask for the youngest guy in the house! I think he's staying there under the name of Anderson.'

'There'll be no slip-ups? No double-cross?' I said.

She got up and put herself against me, her arms around my neck. 'Sorrell, you're the most upsetting thing I've ever met in my life! Just think of the things we can do together with that money.' She pasted her lips on mine. 'It wasn't all together true when I said I loved you – but I could . . . very easily.'

'Don't let me down, Naida,' I said with some authenticity. 'I couldn't stand for everything to blow up right now.'

'It won't, darling,' she said, kissing me again. 'Take my word for it – everything'll be just peaches.'

I wanted to choke the tongue out of that lying bitch.

19

I didn't sleep much that night.

I sat up most of the time with one of my bottled Nemesis, trying to get everything synchronized.

That Naida was trying to make me the goat again, there was no doubt. I didn't believe she had the money, but I did believe her when she said she knew where to put her hands on it. I also began to understand her relationship with Vin Markle: she needed help to get that money. And she needed me as a foil.

I had to play my cards right, or things would turn out just as she had them planned. Her insistence on having Cassiday removed struck me as highly significant. Cassiday *was* hanging around, but it was my bet that he'd been told to.

I could fit Tina and Vin Markle into the scheme of things readily, but I still couldn't explain Horvat or Lilly.

Had Lilly poisoned Horvat, and then himself? For what reason?

I'd had things nicely figured out with Lilly clipped as the head man, but his sudden expiration really screwed up my former ideas. I was positive that Naida hadn't done it, or Tina Meadows. Anyway, that smell of Jergens on Horvat and Lilly told me both boys had been done in by the same person, and I couldn't see either one of the female principles in this act waltzing around that art gallery with Horvat.

I hadn't given up on Vin Markle or Harv Cassiday, and I hadn't failed to notice the interest of Markle's straw-haired sidekick when the subject of that half million came up.

But which one of the three?

I knew the question was going to be answered for me in some way – and soon.

I woke up in bed for a change the next morning.

I showered and shaved, expecting to smell the coffee perking in the kitchen, but when I got out there the stove was bare. I looked in Eversen's room, but he wasn't anywhere around.

I saw by the kitchen clock that it was after twelve. Eversen must have gone over to the club.

There was some bacon and eggs in the refrigerator and it wasn't long before I had a pair of skins and two sunny-sides on a plate. It was the first food I'd had in a good while, and my stomach seemed surprised that I'd cared to think of it.

I was left with hunger pains after I'd finished, but I didn't feel like going through the motions again.

When I came back to my room again I saw that Eversen had dug up a suit and accessories for me somewhere. This beat the hell out of the Bermuda get-up, as far as I was concerned. However, I wouldn't need them till later, since it'd be plain suicide to get out during the daytime.

I lounged around for about an hour, trying to think out a workable method of operation. Then I got down to my jock strap after my food had settled some and went down to the sea.

It's been years since I swam against the sea's strength, let its big rough hands swamp me over with their many tons of water. I forgot all about myself. I swam until the sea and I were one and my waning power was fused in the great veins of that big bastard.

When I couldn't swing my arms any longer, I flopped over on my back and let the swells pillow me in their breasts and carry me slowly back to the shoreline.

I lost track of the time, swimming around out there. It was almost 4:00 p.m. when I got back to the house. Eversen still hadn't returned.

In the bathroom, I found a big terrycloth towel to dry off on. I went into the bedroom with the idea to put on those clothes, but I remembered Eversen had the car and I'd have to wait until he got back, so I slipped into the shorts and shirt again and found another bottle in the kitchen. All that was left was Scotch. It wasn't hard to figure out who'd been lifting Lilly's bonded.

I came back into the living room, and that's when I felt the guy. I didn't see him, you understand. It was just one of those things where you feel somebody staring at you.

He was on the kitchen side of the canted windows, and as I sat down on the couch I fumbled around with the bottle in order to get a good look at him from the side of my eye. I breathed a sigh of relief when I caught a glimpse of the sweatshirt.

I suddenly acted as though I'd forgotten something in the kitchen and went back quickly. Easing through the back door, I tipped around the side of the house, where my guy was still looking over the inside intently.

The soft-soled bucks and sand were made for each other. I came up behind him noiselessly until I was just a few feet away.

'Hey, Rube!' I yelled.

The guy almost jumped out of his britches. I blasted that look of shock off his face when he turned, a thumping left hook that smashed in just under the jawline.

The blow might have been effective if the guy hadn't been so scared. He stumbled back against the house and came at me with a right cross that could have been wicked, but I got out of the way. Then I gave it to him again as he came past, a short, smashing right to the kidney. He did a double take and crumpled in slow motion, a sucked-in expression on his face as he tried to draw wind back in.

He flopped squarely on his ass and stayed that way, both hands clasped to his side.

I had a good look at him while he was like that. He wasn't a little guy, but you couldn't call him big, either. He had that rusty red look the sun gives you, and the bell-bottomed jeans he wore gave me the real clue.

I reached down and pulled him up to my level. 'All right, my friend, just what the hell are you doing around here?'

'I'm looking for a fella,' he gasped shortly. 'You didn't have to go and beat up on me like that, I wasn't doing anything.'

'What ship are you on?'

'The S.S. Maribou. I've got a three weeks' leave. I'm down here vacationing, that's all. You didn't have to go and do that.' His face was still tightened up with the pain. 'I think you broke a rib.'

'You're lucky I didn't break your goddamn head,' I said. 'Who is the fella you're sneaking around here looking for?'

'A little guy. Enderson, I think . . .'

'Eversen?'

'That's it. I saw him down the coast last week. He told me to come over and take a look at his skiff, to see if I could fix it up. I said I'd stop by sometime and see what I could do.'

'If that's all you wanted, why didn't you come to the front door?'

'I was going to, I was *going* to!' he said. 'I just came down the beach, is all. I looked in and saw you. I was just taking a closer look to make sure you weren't the guy.'

'I think you're telling a goddam lie,' I said. 'You must be nearsighted. You stood outside that window a helluva lot longer than it took for you to see I wasn't your man.'

'It's the truth, I'm telling ya! I didn't know who you were. I thought I had the wrong house. I was just making sure, that's all.'

I let him go. 'The more you talk, the fishier it sounds. You get the hell on away from here. If I catch you hanging around again, I'm going to break your goddamn neck.'

I watched the guy take off down the beach, limping on the side where I'd caved him in.

I began to feel uneasy with all this action.

Back in the house, I put through a call to New York, to Lou Pulco's office. He wasn't in, but I was able to get his secretary at that private number.

'I'm sorry, Mr Sorrell, but Mr Pulco left late Saturday night for a four-day cruise on his private yacht.'

'Hell, when I called yesterday you gave me some directives from Pulco,' I said.

'I beg your pardon, Mr Sorrell,' she chirped up in offended tones, 'but it is not strange for Mr Pulco to leave directives in my hands which apply to situations many days in the future. Furthermore—'

'Then it must have been you and not Pulco who sent the telegram.'

'What telegram?'

'The one that contained the information you gave me over the phone yesterday,' I said. 'It was delivered to the Hollitop yesterday.'

'I sent no telegram, Mr Sorrell. It's possible that Mr Pulco may have sent it to you himself.'

'Yeah,' I said, confused for a moment. 'Yeah, I guess it is.'

I put the receiver back.

Something wasn't smelling right. Yeah, sure, it all seemed right, but somebody was crossing the wires somewhere along the line. How could Pulco have sent the telegram if he was out on a cruise?

He probably had a wireless aboard his yacht and I imagine he could have wired the message in. Still . . .

My thoughts were interrupted by the loud jangling of the doorbell. I looked out and saw an express truck parked in the drive. A middle-aged, pot-bellied guy in a green monkey suit had a finger stuck in the bell slot.

I went over and let him in.

'Parcel post package for Mr George Eversen,' he said, picking a good-sized, plain-wrapped package up from the stoop.

'Eversen's not in,' I said. 'I'll take it.'

'Can't,' the guy told me. 'He's supposed to sign for it.'

'What the hell is it?'

'Mister, how do I know? I only drive the truck and dump the bundles.'

'Look,' I said, 'if you wanna come back later, all right. Eversen's not in right now.'

'*Come back?*' he squeaked. 'Look, mister, I come all the way from Alpena – *forty-five miles*, get me? It's the farthest I've been away from home in my whole life!'

'That's a shame,' I said. 'You'll just have to bring it back, unless you want me to sign for it.'

He raised the package for me to read a small white sticker. 'See that? It says "Deliver to addressee". It's insured, even. I can't hand the thing over to anybody but this George Eversen joker.'

I started to close the door. 'That's your tough luck, junior.'

'Hey, wait a minute,' he said, sticking a foot in. 'Are you any kin to this George Eversen?'

'Yeah, I'm Phil, his brother.'

His face brightened. 'Well, that solves everything! All you have to do is sign for him . . .'

'Okay, give it here.'

'Ahn, ahn,' he said, shaking his head shrewdly. 'This will have to be handled with tact. Now you and I know that the trip from Alpena out here is one helluva trip, and we also know that I came out here with the express purpose – *express*, get it? – of delivering a package to your brother George, who is, beyond a question of a doubt, expecting this very important package, right?'

'Ditto.'

'So, solid. Now what I know that you don't know is that the checker is going to check the signatures to make sure they're signed for what they're supposed to be signed for. In other words—'

'You want me to forge my brother George's signature on the receipt slip,' I said.

He coughed discreetly. 'After a fashion, yes – with the knowledge, of course, that you are doing your brother George and myself one great big favor.'

'I'm game,' I said. 'Give me your pencil.'

I set the package next to the door after the fat guy had gone, but after a while I started getting curious. I went over and took a look at the thing.

It was kind of heavy and firmly packed in thick brown wrapping paper.

It was addressed to Eversen in what looked like black crayon. There were two datelines, one at Culver City two days previously and one stamped Alpena, at 10:30 the night before. The return address was a P. O. box in the same town.

I started clicking suddenly like a geiger counter. Could it be possible . . . ?

I didn't waste any time. I went back to the kitchen and found a sharp paring knife. I made short work of the strands binding the thing and it wasn't long before I had the wrapping off.

Inside were five boxes, four the size of corsage containers and the other big enough to set two larged-sized portable radios in. All were plain brown, sturdy boxes.

My hands were trembling when I grabbed the first one, and I was thinking about the way the package was delivered, the Culver City and Alpena datelines, and Naida telling me everything would be bells by tonight.

I was stunned when I opened the first one. All it contained was a filmy black negligee, with matching panties and bra. The second box contained nothing but panties, all sizes and shapes, and seven which represented the days of the week.

I was working on the third box when Eversen came in.

He did something when he saw me with that stuff that I'd never have imagined he'd have the nerve to do – he tried to tear my head off! He was yelling and screaming like a madman, clawing at my face with both hands.

'Leave it alone!' he bellowed over me. 'You have no right to touch it!'

I came out from under him laughing, but the little guy was stronger than I thought and almost broke my shoulder with an arm lock. I wiggled away from him and fell forward on top, his head between my hands, slamming the back of his skull against the floor.

That took all the fight out of him.

'All right, Sorrell,' he said defeatedly. 'Now you know. I should have known you'd find out.'

I got up, but it wasn't much of a joke anymore, not the way he'd tried to yank my shoulder out by the socket.

'I should kick the hell out of you!' I said. 'If there weren't enough queers to put up with in this goddamn mess, I have to have one almost tear my arm off!'

He looked at me strangely for a long time before he got up off the floor. Then he finally got to his knees and started packing the stuff away, his face blank.

I went over and poured myself another drink. 'Don't think you're by yourself, Pops. You've got a psychosis that's a lot less taxing than the one Naida Torneau's got.'

'Sorrell,' he said behind me in a small voice, 'I . . . I can't help it . . . It's something I'm obsessed with – women's underclothes.'

'Well, hurry up and put that junk away. I wanna have a talk with you.'

He left quickly for his bedroom. When he returned, his face seemed to have regained its color and he was even a bit jovial.

'I'm glad that's over,' he said. 'I feel assured that you'll keep this – this trouble of mine confidential.'

'Forget it. I want the car tonight, probably for the last time. I've got a couple of dates.'

He gave me the keys. 'Keep it as long as you want. I'm not going anywhere.'

'I caught some guy peeking in the window earlier this evening,' I said. 'He told me he'd come over to see you. He's a sailor on the S. S. Maribou. Know anything about him?'

'Why, yes, I . . . I told him to bring me some West Indian coral the next time his ship made the trip. You know, for decorations and things.'

I thought about what the guy had told me. 'That's funny. He told me he'd come over to do some work on your skiff. He said you'd asked him over for that purpose.'

'Oh, yes, I do remember mentioning it to him a week or so ago. It slipped my mind. Did he happen to leave the coral here?'

'He wasn't carrying anything, and I don't think he liked the reception I gave him. He may not come back any time soon.'

'Oh, what a pity,' Eversen said. 'I did so want that coral.'

'About that telegram you told me about yesterday – you said Markle picked it up?'

'Yes, that's the information five dollars bought from the desk clerk. Why? Is anything wrong?'

'No, I was just trying to confirm a suspicion. Naida Torneau knew about the telegram. She told me Markle had let me in on it. I think she and Markle are getting set to make off with that dough tonight, and I plan to be on hand.'

'Make off?' Eversen said, surprised. 'You mean they have the money?'

'I don't think so, but I believe they've got things set up to put the wheels in motion. Naida told me last night she expected to put her hands on that money tonight. She also told me where to find Harv Cassiday. It's my guess that she and Markle have things arranged for a fast cross, with me in the middle.'

'What are you going to do, Sorrell?'

I shrugged. 'I don't have anything definite planned yet. I'm going to see Cassiday, but not, as the lady thinks, to rub him out. Mr Cassiday and I are just going to have a nice little talk.' I looked at my watch. 'It's just a little after seven. When I come back tonight, it may be in a rush. Be prepared for anything.'

Eversen put a hand on my arm. 'Sorrell, couldn't I – well, couldn't I go with you?'

'Don't worry, Pops,' I said. 'I'm not going to forget you, if I'm lucky enough to pick up that cash.'

'But I . . . I feel so useless just sitting around doing nothing.'

'You can do something right now. Do you have a gun?'

'Why, yes, but it's a big gun, a Magnum. Haven't fired it in years.'

'Go rustle it up,' I said. 'It just might see some action tonight.'

20

It was good and dark when I left Eversen's place, no stars at all. My timepiece said it was a little past 8:30.

I had the Magnum packed up under my belt. It was bulky and the big round cylinder cut into my waist, but I was satisfied with it. A test firing on the beach let me see what it could do, and I especially liked the quick pin action of the hammer. It was a cannon, but I just might need a cannon tonight.

Monday night is a lazy one in Hollisworth. The most important thing was that I didn't spot any coppers. I wasn't too worried about them, what with Pulco's telegram, but I still didn't want to take any chances with some trigger-happy punk.

Deacon Street is three blocks past the Civic Center. It's drab and broken down, but still fairly neat.

I circled the block twice before I saw the old folks' home Naida'd told me about. It was a converted four family flat, with transoms and fire escapes on both sides.

The sign outside allowed that it was primarily for old people, but visitors were welcome.

I parked the car two blocks away and came back on the opposite side of the street. When the traffic thinned out and I was sure nobody was watching, I crossed over and went directly to the entrance. From the front I could see six or seven old people sitting around in what was supposed to be the lobby. A reception desk sat in the center, where a gray-haired little mama was hunched next to the register, reading a confession magazine.

She seemed surprised when I interrupted her and her false choppers made a condescending clack.

'Good evening, sir,' she said, bowing toward me. 'May I help you? We have some *very fine* accommodations. Are you a stranger to Hollisworth?'

'Yes, I am. I'm looking for a friend of mine. A Mr Anderson.'

'Oh, yes,' she said amiably. 'You mean that fine young gentleman on the second floor.'

'Is he in now?'

She shook her head sadly. 'You know, it's a shame that such a clean-cut, good-looking young man should confine himself the way Mr Anderson does. He's *always* in. Has been ever since he checked in with us last week.'

'What room is he in?'

'Room 211. I'll call right up and let him know you're coming.'

'I wish you wouldn't,' I said. 'I'd like to surprise him.'

'I don't know if I should,' she said hesitantly. 'Mr Anderson left strict orders not to let anyone come up unless I first notified him.'

'That's all right,' I said assuringly. 'Mr Anderson'll be very glad you made this exception.'

'Well . . . if you think it's all right . . .'

'I'm sure it is,' I said.

'I guess it's all right, then. His is the third door from the end of the hall.'

'Thanks.'

I went up the padded stairway. All those old gaffers seemed to be watching me, their lives suddenly titillated by the arrival of a stranger.

The hallway on the second floor was dimly lighted, and I wondered how the grandpas and grandmas managed not to break their goddamn necks coming down the staircase.

When I got to Cassiday's room, I unloosened the Magnum and gave it a quick check.

There was no answer when I first knocked on the door. My second knock brought a rustle from the inside. I moved over to the side and knocked again.

'The door's opened,' a voice said. 'Come on in.'

I put a hand on the knob and released the latch. The door swung open slowly. The inside of the room was pitch dark, except for a slight illumination from the slightly raised window facing the fire escape. It was too damn dark for me to make an ass and a target out of myself.

'Cassiday,' I called. 'Cassiday, this is Andy Sorrell. Put the rod away, I just want to talk with you.'

'I haven't got a rod, Sorrell,' the voice came. 'Anyway, I don't have to kill you – you're as dead as I am.'

There was something about the helpless remorse in his voice that made me believe him. I went all the way, shoving the Magnum back under my belt. It may have been a mistake, but I wanted to play it on the line, sensing that this guy had the answers to everything I wanted to know.

I silhouetted myself in the doorway, but only for a fraction of a second. I saw Cassiday outlined on the bed as I came in, propped up on a pillow with both hands behind his head.

'Hello, sucker,' he said. 'Shake hands with your brother.'

I came over to the bed and got a close look at him. There was light enough to let me make out his gaunt features, the premature baldness of a small head. The body was long and angling, suggestive of death in its easy repose.

I could hear him laugh deeply. 'Get yourself a chair, brother. Sit down while I tell you about the biggest double-cross in history.'

I went over and shut the door. Next to the window, I found a lopsided easy chair.

'That's right,' he chuckled from the bed. 'Make yourself at home, Sorrell. What I'm going to tell you will take some time.'

'Why don't you get right to the point and tell me where the money is?' I said.

'The money?' He laughed again. 'Brother, I don't know where that money is and I don't give a damn. That money's cost too much. That's the dirtiest money in the world!'

'Dirt is something that's never bothered me too much,' I said. 'For a half million bucks I'd gladly be the dirtiest guy in the world.'

'And the deadest,' Cassiday added. 'Let me tell you how all this stuff got started, sucker, and maybe you'll understand.'

'I'm listening.'

'Where do I begin?' he said ruminatively. 'At the heist? No, before that, when Benedict, Horvat and I were contacted by this wheel, this connection. That's how it got started. You see, we didn't even know each other before the heist. But the connect knew us – he knew us well. We'd been spotted months before. When he came to us with the prop, he knew just how we'd react. Fifty grand each, that's what he told us. No complications, no nothing. Just like clockwork, he said.'

'What the connect didn't tell you was that the heist was private property,' I said.

'Oh, sure, he was careful not to say anything about that. But it didn't make too much difference even after we found out. That fifty grand dangling in front of our noses knocked the hell out of all that.'

'So you took off the bank,' I said.

'Just like clockwork,' Cassiday assented. 'One fine Wednesday a few months ago, three smooth operating suckers took off that Jersey bank for five hundred thousand dollars. Our plan was followed right down to the letter. We crossed over to New York in a panel truck, where we met the connect and turned the cash over to him. Two months ago we were all supposed to meet up here in Hollisworth for the split, but our connect said we had to wait a little longer. He said he had to wait until things got cooler.' He began laughing again. 'We didn't know he was arranging to have us bumped.'

'Have you bumped?'

'Sure, sucker! Didn't you know that you were a part of the plan? You were supposed to wipe out a hundred and fifty grand debt. Our man dropped the necessary information to the right people, and all he had to do was sit back and let you take care of us. But something went wrong along the way, Sorrell. You weren't taking care of the job fast enough. After you knocked off Benedict, Horvat and I saw what our pal was trying to do. Horvat wanted to spill, and he thought the best person to spill to was you, since you were out to get us. He rang our friend up and told him what he was doing to do if he didn't come across, and fast.'

'Then it was your connect who fed Horvat the poison,' I said. 'But what was it with Lilly? Why did Lilly have to be eliminated?'

'Lilly got greedy and ambitious,' he went on. 'He's been fronting for this guy for years, you know, and he always got the short end. He found out about the caper and threatened to let the syndicate in if Big Boy didn't come through with the grease. He was a hazard that had to be erased.'

I turned the things over in my mind, slotting them all in their proper positions. 'Why did this guy try to kill Meg Inglander? What danger was she to him?'

'Meg was an afterthought,' he said musingly. 'He thought Horvat might have told her about the job. When you're playing around with half a million bucks, you don't take a chance on anything.'

'What I can't understand,' I said, 'is why the guy didn't bump me off when he had the chance. He certainly tried to up at the Inglander place. Yet, when I found Lilly, he was content to bust my head open and call the cops. He could have wiped me if he'd wanted to.'

'Use your head, Sorrell. It'd look a little strange if the coppers found you laid out with a slug in you and Lilly dead of poisoning, wouldn't it? Uhn, uhn, Big Boy took a chance leaving you. When you got away, he saw he could still use you as a diversion. And since he knew I was in town, he needed you to get rid of me when the time came. Oh, don't fail to keep your guard up, Sorrell – he plans to get rid of you at the right time, too.'

'This guy doesn't know he's about to be double-crossed himself, does he? Naida Torneau talks about the dough as though it's already part of the family.'

Cassiday grunted with interest. 'That ought to be one for the books, sucker, but don't plan on being around to see anything like it go off.'

'I'll only need to know one thing to make that possible,' I said.

'Yeah.' He chuckled to himself. 'The name of the connect.'

'That's it.'

'Well, Jesus,' he laughed at me, 'don't you have any idea who he is? He's the syndicate's terminal here in Hollisworth, the guy with the most to say about everything. He was one of the two guys who double-crossed the syndicate.'

'Two guys?'

'Oh, yeah, that's the surprise! See, I figured it out all by myself. My connect didn't just happen to think of that caper in Jersey. He had inside help, and lots of it. It's just not something you can think up in Hollisworth and engineer a couple of thousand miles away . . .'

That's when the crash came. The window sprayed over everything where I sat, slashing the interior with a wide sheath of glass. A heater bellowed twice and flame-hot next to my shoulder. I heeled around quickly out of the chair, going for the floor. I clawed the Magnum out and held it in a working position next to my side. The big hollow mouth cursed twice with a deep-throated hoarseness, making the whole room tremble with the passage of sound waves. Pieces of the wooden window frame disappeared easily. When I got over to the window, I could see my guy making the alley way on the street side of the building.

I leveled the Magnum at the vanishing shadow and let it ram out two lead-nosed cousins. A scream sounded when my hearing came back, but I couldn't swear it was anything other than a mortally wounded cat.

Out on the street a car screamed past the mouth of the alley. It was a black Thunderbird.

When I got over to Cassiday and took a good look, I could see two round spots, one to the left of his forehead and the other under the right cheek. It looked like somebody had taken a big red thumb and stuck it in.

By this time, the hallway outside had begun to mutter and I could hear some old dame screaming. I buckled the gun again and got out on the fire escape fast. The alley looked clear when I got to the ground, but I could see people gathering out front.

I kicked off down the alley, trying to remember the exact spot I'd left the car in. There was a diagonal passageway that led out to the next street at the end of the alley. It was the only way to go, the quickest way to the car.

I trotted down to the end of it as fast as I could, unmindful of the dark patches. Just as I got to the end, a guy stood around in front of me and I could see he held a great big gun in his hand. I stopped abruptly and the guy held the gun shoulder high.

'You know, I'd just love to kill you,' he said sweetly.

It was Hendricks.

21

'Not as much as I'd like to kill you,' I said.

He weaseled a hand underneath my coat and pulled out the Magnum. 'It sure was nice of that lady to call up and let us know you'd be here tonight, wasn't it? Come on, let's go, big boy.'

He shoved me over to the Buick parked at the curb. The same copper I'd blown in was behind the wheel.

'Your time's run out, Sorrell,' Hendricks said. 'You know what we've gotta do?'

'Don't keep me guessing.'

He pushed me into the back seat and got in, giving the driver a signal to move on. 'You're gonna die, comedian, that's what you're gonna do,' he said, goosing me in the side with his rod. 'All we have to do is *make* you.'

'I don't wanna dance without you, daughter. Why don't we start head-up? All I need you to do is get the hell out of the way.'

'That's the trouble right now, Sorrell – you're the one who's in the way.'

'Sure, I've been the spur in somebody's ass. Why don't we start again,' I said, 'take a rounder route home. If it hadn't been for me you guys might never have believed there was any chance to slip your fingers around that half million.'

He sneered. 'Who needs you, comedian?'

'You do, strawboy. I know where that dough is and you don't.'

The bluff was weak but it struck home. 'If you know so much, where is it?'

'I'd be the most brilliant guy in the world if I told you, wouldn't I, stupid.'

'Maybe you'd be smart,' he said meaningfully.

'That's what I'm being. If I let my insurance lapse in the face of a .45 I'd be a goddamn fool.'

'You haven't been keeping up the premiums, Sorrell. Vin

is picking up that money tonight. He's probably back at the office with it now. We don't need you for anything.'

'Vin *thinks* he's going to pick that dough up,' I bulled on. 'The only payoff he's going to get will come from the business end of a rod in motion.'

'You talk real good, Sorrell. The only trouble is, it's not going to get you anywhere. Vin says it's time for us to make a gift, because the Inglander family is raising a lot of hell.'

'And I'm it . . .'

'With ribbons on,' he said. 'I wouldn't guess at it, but I'd say Harv Cassiday is laying up there in that room with a couple of slugs in him.'

'What difference does it make? I was sent out here for just that reason – only it wasn't me who gave him the shove. Somebody fired through the window up there, and I came back with a few of my own.'

'You understand that I don't really wanna do this,' he said consolingly. 'You've just gotta *go*, that's all there is to it.'

'You'd rather eat dynamite than touch me,' I said. 'Didn't you read that telegram from Pulco? He gave me the go-ahead signal; nobody's gonna interfere with his okay.'

'What telegram?'

'The one Markle picked up over at the hotel. Pulco left orders for me to carry on the assignment.'

Hendricks began laughing. 'If this is a trick, it's sure working the wrong way!'

'What the hell are you talking about, copper? Markle picked that telegram up yesterday. I called New York myself and found out about the orders even before the telegram got here.'

'Somebody's pulling your leg,' he said. 'Vin didn't pick up any telegram for you.'

'You're crazy! Markle even told Naida Torneau what the damn thing said.'

'Listen, Sorrell, I'm not in the mood to argue with you. What the hell difference does a telegram mean to you now? You won't ever have to worry about anything like that again.'

It might not bother me again, but it was bothering the hell out of me right then. Eversen and Naida had both told me about the contents of the telegram. New York had given me the same message. My first thought was that the hotel message could have been a phony, but I couldn't see how it could jibe all the way around.

I noticed we had come a good way out of town. The driver took a beach road. Deserted beach cabins strung themselves out next to the sea.

A mile or so further, we stopped in front of one of the joints. Hendricks made me get out while the driver stayed in the car.

'This is it, Sorrell,' he said, grinning. 'This is where we shot you down tonight. You were hiding out in this place.'

'I don't like the goddamn place,' I said. 'I wouldn't feel right dying out here.'

'Now isn't that just too bad?' Hendricks said.

I didn't rush the thing up any. I tried to take it as slow as I could. Hendricks prodded me up on the porch and through the front door. It was almost black inside, stinking with disuse.

I was grabbing at anything. This scene was sudden death and I had to goof up the script, or else.

Directly ahead of us was a table. Hendricks shoved me over toward the center of the room. When I got over to the table, I stretched my arms out behind me, coiling myself for one last try at that bastard.

My hands touched something long and heavy. It felt like a rod for hanging drapes. My fingers even felt the catch in the thing.

Hendricks was just raising the gun when I shot that rod around. It hit him right above the wrist, snapping the gun over in a corner. He bent over in pain, sucking in wind for that scream I knew had to come.

I raised the rod and brought it down as hard as I could right in the center of his head. His hat sprang off and I could hear the bone popping loose in his skull. He looked up at me with a wild-eyed silly expression and said, 'Ow!' as though he'd just found out what was going on. He didn't even fall, he just froze there.

Then I went crazy. I raised the rod again and slapped it down just over his right eye. His neck jerked back with the force of the blow and I could feel the bone and cartilage pulling away from itself inside his head.

He melted all of a sudden, and I stood over him. I gave him two more good ones, then the blood started to get all over everything.

There was no way for him to live after I got through.

I got down and went through him till I found my gun, then I moved over to the door.

The guy outside couldn't see me, but I could see he was getting nervous wondering why he didn't hear a shot. He got out of the car pretty soon and unholstered his gun.

I didn't even bother with him. I pointed the Magnum at him and let it work out a single. The guy stopped in his tracks, suddenly lifted into the air by the invisible momentum. He crashed over against the Buick and got watery all the way down to his bones.

I ran over and got his heater, since the Magnum only had one more shell, then I got up under the wheel and started moving like hell out of there. When the police ever got to nosing around that place, I'd better be as rare as platinum.

In a burst of genius, I pointed the Buick around toward the police station. Yeah, sure, I know it sounds crazy, but I had to get my hands on Markle and that money before things blew up in my face. The black Thunderbird and the helpful little lady who got in touch with Hendricks told me that my time was measured in minutes.

I remembered the way I'd been brought into the station on my visits. It wouldn't be too hard if I kept right on upstairs, and I didn't expect any of those coppers would be looking for me to turn up right under their noses. If I was recognized, I'd have the advantage of surprise. I probably could scare my way out of there.

Right now I didn't think any plan was too dangerous. With Cassiday dead, the individuals who had taken the fatal trip down that five hundred thousand dollar primrose path had risen to four, not including my last two credits.

What seemed strange was that I'd only been accountable for fifty per cent of them.

22

A few cops were playing ping pong, while several others stood gassing off at the desk in the back.

I came in the side door and went up the stairs to the second floor unnoticed. I didn't hesitate at Markle's door. I went right in – right into the barrel of a gun.

'Come on in, muscleman,' said Tina Meadows.

I'd had a hand on my heater, but the electric fire burning in her eyes warned me against any damn stupid trick.

'Close the door,' she ordered shortly.

I came in and did as I was told.

She moved away from me, got out of reach. 'I didn't expect to see you again, muscleman. I was hoping they'd bump you off quick.' Her face knotted painfully, remembering.

'I've got a charmed life,' I said. 'I'm a man with a goal.'

She went over to Markle's desk and picked up a couple of papers. 'So's Vin. He'll be glad I kept you around when he gets here.'

I grinned at her. 'We're both contending for the crown of this year's biggest sucker, I see. I don't think Markle's going to be coming back anytime soon tonight – or ever.'

'What are you talking about?'

'A good friend of yours,' I suggested. 'The one who was supposed to put you on Money Street. She and Markle have plans which don't include you.'

She jerked the gun up at me. 'You're lying! Vin's got all he needs to get the money. Naida never knew how to get it.'

'I just met Hendricks a few minutes ago,' I said. 'He let me in on the whole story. Naida's been coming up here to talk with Markle.'

'What does that prove?' she said sharply.

'It proves by that look on your face that you didn't know a damn thing about it. Naida and Vin never intended to give you a fair shake on that money. You're stranded, sweetheart. You'll be waiting here forever on Vin Markle.'

'You're lying!' she hissed, coming around the desk. 'Look at these papers! Vin picked them up in the room where you killed Brace Lilly.'

I took the things. 'What are they? They look official, all right, but not green enough to be the government issue I'm looking for.'

'They're a bill of sale and a land deed for Lilly's,' she said.

I read the papers. 'Lilly didn't own the club?'

'That's what those papers say. They say Lilly was only a front for the club, he only worked there . . .'

I could feel myself getting hot all over. My square block of a brain popped out of the formaldehyde for a minute and took a deep breath.

Why I didn't see it before, I don't know. Everything fitted right in, that's why Cassiday had laughed at me when he asked me if I didn't already know who the connect was.

It was funny, so goddamn funny I wanted to cry.

'So Vin found out?' I said.

'Everybody thought Lilly was the syndicate's head here in Hollisworth,' she said. 'The real head is the one who has the money, and that's where Vin's gone. When he gets that money, he'll be right back, I just know he will.'

'Don't hold your breath,' I said, and at the same time I struck her gun with the one I held the papers in. It was like Hendricks all over again. The gun bounced over in a corner, and before she could make a go for it I put a choker on her pretty throat and threw her on one of the oversized sectionals, where she bounced a couple of times with a fine display of well-packed under drawers. I started for her again, but she cowered back, nylon thighs exposed temptingly.

'Sorrell . . .'

'Shut up,' I said. 'If you don't wanna die, keep your mouth shut until I get out of here.'

I ran down the steps and around to the side door at the end of the staircase. Tina began yelling upstairs, but I wasn't worried about it. I was like a boulder rolling madly downhill.

Nothing could stop me now until I struck bottom.

23

There was a light in the study when I got over to Lilly's beach house.

The front door was standing wide open. I came in with the Magnum out, my finger tightened up on the trigger.

He was standing over the bodies when I got to the open doorway of the room off the hallway. There was a gun on the floor between them and the rug was littered sparsely with hundred dollars bills.

Eversen looked up at me sadly. 'They were fighting when I got here, Sorrell. I heard the shots when I came through the front door. I guess it was about the money.'

'I'm *sure* it was about the money,' I said. 'You make pretty good time on foot, or did you use the Thunderbird?'

He purposely ignored the question. 'All this has been terrible! So many people have died because of that money.'

I kept the Magnum pointed at his belly. 'I don't think it's quite over, Pops.'

He turned away from me. 'I've got to have a drink. All this is a horrible shock!' He began to mix it at the liquor cabinet. 'How about you, Sorrell?'

'Rye,' I said. I didn't lower the gun.

He finished and brought a tall tumbler over to me. He'd put something in it to kill the smell of hand lotion, but I got a good whiff of it, anyway.

'Shouldn't we get out of here, Sorrell? The police – they'll probably be here soon.'

'I don't think so.' I handed the drink back to him. 'I want to conduct a little experiment first. I want you to drink this.'

He paled. 'Drink . . . ? But, Sorrell, I don't like rye.'

'I don't give a damn if you don't. I want you to drink this and I don't want you to stop until every last drop of it is gone.'

He didn't take it.

'What's the matter?' I said. 'Can't take your own medicine? I should have known about this crap when I caught the sailor hanging around your place, as much as I know about ships. What you do, buy it from him? Hydrocyanic acid is used to kill rats on ships. It also kills the hell out of people.'

He watched me calmly and I could see the facade dropping off.

I looked down at Vin Markle and Naida. 'Were they dead or alive when you killed Cassiday?'

He went over and placed the hot drink on the liquor cabinet casually. 'I found them here together after I came back – yes, I'd borrowed the car from Naida. Evidently, she forgot that I had my own key. I heard them talking. I couldn't very well let them go through with their plans, could I?'

'At first she was only going to use Markle to strongarm the money out of you,' I said, 'but he had to be taken in as a partner when he found that bill of sale listing you as the bona fide owner of Lilly's. Markle put two and two together. You were the big man in Hollisworth, a secret well kept by Lilly and Naida.'

'I have you to thank for letting me in on Naida's little scheme,' he said easily. 'She and I were going away together, or so I thought. I was to pay Markle off gratis . . .'

'And you found out they wanted all the dough.'

'Precisely. However, I didn't see things quite their way.'

'You have me to thank for letting you in on a lot of things,' I said. 'The night I went up to the Inglander place, I had a talk with you. You beat it up there and did Horvat in with your potion, since you'd already talked with him and he told you he was going to squeal to me. I should have known when you told me in a later conversation about what went on while I was on the premises. You described the shooting and mentioned that Horvat'd been poisoned. Nobody but the killer could have known so much.'

He smiled. 'Strangely enough, you didn't see the relation. I'm not exactly what you'd call a professional, like yourself. Horvat was going to shoot his mouth off, not only to you . . .'

'You slipped up again when you tried to incriminate Lilly. You told me Lilly'd had his face chewed up that night. The last time I saw Lilly, his face was as smooth as a baby's butt. I didn't get the drift then, either. Neither did I pick up when I had a talk with Naida. She *had* been expecting me to come up, because you had called and told her to expect me. You two have been working together ever since she came to me with that tip about Horvat. You also told her to give me that lead on Cassiday, but I told you I wanted only to talk to him, so you followed me over to his place and put the gag on him before he had a chance to tell me who the hell you were. You were taking your biggest chance then, because you had Naida call up the coppers. It had to be split-second timing: Kill Cassiday, get the hell away and leave me sitting on the scene.'

Eversen was unperturbed. He went to his breast pocket, pulled out a cigarette and lighted it. 'You make a better detective than an exterminator, Sorrell. There's only one thing – you don't know where that money is. How much do you want to get out of my hair?'

'Not much,' I said. 'Just all of it.'

He laughed. 'You'll never put your hands on that money without me.'

'I think I can. I've been putting two and two together myself, Pops. Remember that package you got today? Unless I'm mistaken as hell, I'd say the cash was in it somewhere. That's the only part I can't figure out, but I know I'm right.'

His bottom lip trembled nervously. 'Don't be a fool! You saw what was in that package—'

'And I even gave you an alibi for it. Now I know why you gave me so goddamn much trouble about the package. Why, you even told me in so many words that the jig was up – you thought I'd found the money! When I labeled you a pantie freak, that was right up your alley. But I've been doing a lot of thinking about that package,' I went on. 'It went through too many changes to come from Culver City out here, too many precautions. Why so many flip-flops for a gross of panties? No, I think we'll just go over to your place and have a good look at what's inside.'

He dropped his cigarette on the floor and crushed it out with the heel of his shoe. 'Let's not be children about this, Sorrell! We could both be rich. I'm willing to give you a reasonable share of the money.'

'You don't have any choice,' I said. 'You're going to give me all of it. It's worth it for the knocks I've taken.'

'I should have killed you when I had the chance!'

'Yeah, it might have made things a lot simpler. Right now, we're going to get over for that dough. If I have any trouble out of you, I'm going to enjoy kicking your ass off.'

I made him drive Naida's car.

It didn't take us long to get over to his place, and my mouth was drooling by the time we got there. It seemed almost unbelievable that I was going to put my hands on that money at last.

Eversen lagged around when we got there, but I booted him a couple of times and he got to moving.

I marched him right back to his bedroom.

'All right, get it,' I said.

He didn't move.

I laid the Magnum across his cheek smartly, rocking loose a few teeth.

'Don't, don't, Sorrell! Don't hit me again!'

'Get that goddamn money, then!'

He got down on his knees and crawled under the bed. He had a suitcase when he came out.

'Open it,' I said, snapping on the bedroom light.

He freed the catches and raised the lid. That money was the greenest thing I ever saw, all laid out neatly in crisp, new packages.

I looked at it until my stomach started bubbling. 'Now I can see why you tackled me when you found me opening that package. The panties were just a front in case something like that happened.'

'Sorrell . . .'

'Shut up. Lock that thing up and take it out to the front.'

Eversen was just a little ahead of me when we came in.

The voice said, 'All right, gentlemen, if you don't mind, I'll relieve you of that little item.'

Three things I felt at once: the gun in my ribs, both the Magnum and the one under my belt being snatched away and the immediate recognition of who was doing all this.

'Hello, boss,' I said, without turning around.

Who else could it be but Lou Pulco?

'Good evening, Sorrell,' he answered in that smooth voice of his. 'Shame you had to put yourself in such a strained situation.'

'I'll never get over it,' I said.

Lou went over and snapped on the light. He reminds you of John L. Lewis, but he's a helluva lot fatter and better dressed. The gun in his hand looked out of place, but I knew he wouldn't hesitate to use it.

'Now I understand about the telegram,' I said. 'Eversen lied when he told me I'd received a telegram from you. It makes sense that he had to find out the same way I did, directly from your office. Your order fitted in perfectly with his plans.'

Lou's big belly bubbled with a grim laugh. 'My friend Eversen turned out to be a bigger fool than I thought. How he ever expected to double-cross me, I don't know.'

Eversen raised his hands helplessly. 'Lou . . .'

'No lies,' Pulco said, waving him back with the barrel of his gun. 'I knew something was going wrong when Vin Markle notified me that Horvat got tumbled with poison. Sorrell is not so subtle, you know. Then I contacted our man in Culver City and found that you had rushed delivery of the package by four days. I underestimated your nerve, Eversen. You, however, underestimated my perception.'

Can you get any more stupid than me? Lou Pulco was the inside man with the syndicate, the fixer and chief of communiques. He was one of the few people who could get a lead on the organization's plans.

'I know what you're thinking, Sorrell,' he said, 'and there're several people in New York thinking the same thing. I think things would be a good deal more healthier if I left the country indefinitely, the coast of South America, perhaps. That's why I brought the yacht, you see. Unfortunately, I'll be unable to take either of you with me. A regrettable circumstance, I must admit, but the only feasible one.'

'But, Lou, I did what you wanted,' Eversen whined. 'The money – you've even got the money!'

'Please, spare me!' Pulco ordered. 'Our scheme would have gone off smoothly, had you not interfered with Sorrell. Your eye was on the sparrow, was it not my friend? Five hundred thousand of them.'

'But I *had* to, Lou! Sorrell was getting too close. Vin Markle and Naida Torneau – even Lilly – wanted to get in. I couldn't help it!'

'Let's not hash this thing out,' Pulco said reprovingly. 'It's a pity you had to start thinking for yourself.'

He raised the gun deliberately and it cracked twice, three times. Eversen fell over on his face. The blood spread out quickly under him.

Pulco looked over at me. 'Sorrell, I've always liked you, though you seemed a bit vacillating at times. Up till now, you've been able to handle all assignments I gave you. I imagine that your attention was distracted through no fault of your own this time, plus an irresponsible temptation. However, I can't permit you to tell anyone about what you've learned tonight. I also carelessly mentioned my destination.' He raised the gun again. 'Too bad, my friend . . .'

His shot was half good. I felt the bullet dig around my waist line, just over the kidney, the force of the bullet rocketing me against the wall. The pain blossomed and things got hazy red in front of my eyes. I did see him raise the gun again, but this time there was another explosion and I heard the lead plop into him.

He made a little squeak and dropped the gun, waddling as fast as he could for the doorway. When I looked toward the canted windows I could see Tina Meadows standing in front of a broken portion, screaming, her voice a jumble of wild words.

'You've killed Vin!' She screamed. 'You bastards killed Vin!'

By this time, Pulco was hotfooting it out on the beach. I pulled up against the hot spot in my side and tried to ignore the rapid flow of blood. I started after that sonofabitch. It hurt like hell, but I wasn't going to let that fat bastard get

112 | Clarence Cooper, Jr.

away with anything, not as long as I had another ounce of strength.

I could barely make him out on the darkness of the beach, but he wasn't far ahead of me. He was snorting with the sudden exertion.

Down at the edge of the water, I saw a small motor boat with its nose in the sand. About two miles off shore Pulco's yacht bared its white side to the mainland.

He was pushing the boat out into the water when he saw me behind him. By the way he held his right arm, I knew Tina's bullet had got him there.

I'd forgotten he still had the Magnum and the police service pistol. He saw me balling down on him and raised the big gun and fired. I hit the sand just an instant before. He was cursing and snapping the trigger.

I got to him before he thought about the .38. I took him in my own time. I ducked as he tried to nail me with the butt of the gun and latched my fingers around his goddamn throat. He'd dropped the suitcase in the water, where it kicked around in the surf restlessly.

Pulco was infused with the strength of fear, but he couldn't get away from me. I felt monstrous with strength. I was killing him for everything that'd ever happened to me, all the way back to my old man, and it had almost a sexual goodness about it.

We struggled out in the water, him trying to get my fingers out of his gizzard. I didn't let him go. I held him until we were out where the water was about four feet or more, then I dragged him under, I dragged that sonofabitch under. His legs kicked up out of the water and he lost one of his shoes.

I was down in the water up to my neck, kneeling on the frantic whiplash of his good arm. The bubbles didn't come up long. I still held him after they stopped. I held him till I couldn't hold him any longer and the top of his head came to the surface.

Then I thought about the money, but the loss of blood didn't leave me anything to get myself moving with. I managed to wade up on the beach, but when I got there I saw the suitcase had broken open and the money was drifting out to sea, all of it! I scrambled after it, but I couldn't get any, not any of it! It seemed as though I could hear five hundred thousand voices laughing at me.

Then I began to laugh. I was crazy and I began to laugh. I wallowed around there in the water, laughing just like all those goddamn voices were laughing at me, like that goddamn voice in my head had been laughing at me for days.

I just sat there in the water and watched that money floating away, listening to the cry of police sirens, knowing they were only minutes away. I watched my money drift away from me, *my* money!

And I could see my old man coming across the sea to get me, walking on the water, just like Jesus . . .

WEED

For Ada

1

Kick!

The damned door shut, everytime she came in off the street that way. And to Cannonball Adderley, the alto sax whiz – after Charlie Yard Parker, that is. He strained to hear over her entrance, but he should have known the needle would jump. It was Cannonball and Barry Harris, he thought, that Detroit boy, and Tommy Flanagan, who was from Detroit, too – he remembered, or seemed to – that Tommy had gone to Northern High with him, Ned Land. Or should have, since they were about the same age now.

Detroit. That's what her kicking the door shut was like. A long time ago, he liked to think. From Detroit to this broad here kicking, slamming shut, the door to his record shop in Westphalia.

'Hi, honey,' she said.

'Coral,' he said, moving from his place by the machine jack, lowering the outside volume at the same time, so he could hear what the hell she had to say this time, as if he didn't know.

'Ned, my figures-man was by, and – well, you know. I'm a little short.'

He did force himself to notice again, a thousandth look, that she was a well-stacked broad, that she was soft as hell and all juicy-like with a man when she loosed up, and none of her was in any way a bit concerned with the complication of a man: her husband Burris.

And that wasn't all – only he couldn't think what else there was at the moment, unless you counted the sexuality, the musky-love smell of her.

He thought she actually might have been a mulatto, for there was so much of that ofay thing about her, that better-than-average switch of hips. Not that his being black as a berry had anything to do with it – he was a handsome man at twenty-seven. So what was the point in even bringing that up?

– though there did seem to be some amoral virtue in covering her near-white body with his black one.

So, anyway, what was this feeling? He couldn't explain it: he wasn't one of them psychiatric cats. No, he couldn't begin to tell you. No, man, all he knew was that here she was, begging again, and he could see all these things about her and still not feel a little mad with himself for ever letting it come this far.

She smoked a cigarette, a ring of red around the tip.

Cannonball was teasing him, and he turned up the volume a bit, letting Adderley do those things to that helpless horn, letting that colored man named Flanagan whip down the keyboard like a demented sprite, damning each keynote with a bash of tingled cymbals.

Then he turned it down again. 'What now, Coral?'

'Twenty-eight dollars,' she said, watching him as though she were saying, I'm telling a damned lie; what are you gonna do about it?

But what could he do, other than freezing into a solid body of salt, thereby making his pockets salt, his wallet and all therein, salt?

'You're makin me hurt my pocket, baby.'

'But so'm I hurtin, Ned,' she said, still watching him.

He knew her kind: there had been Roslyn, and Joyce, the unemployment clerk, when he was getting it, there in Detroit. And it always seemed to be *despite* them that you got ahead, or cleared away some of the bigger hurdles.

He didn't know – maybe a guy needed them, when he wasn't anything but average, when he couldn't expect anything unless something was taken from him against his will: his pride, his money, or something – and he just had to go pass the rules of defeat. Something like that.

Now, this bitch knew that he'd just opened the record shop, that it was the last phase of a new attempt at something, he didn't know what – that he needed every crying quarter he could lay his hands on. She knew it, and yet she, with her sonofabitching numbers-playing was here now, sucking him dry, fighting him, choking him, just because he had screwed her a few times.

He remembered somebody saying (was it Ruckson, with his

little mouse face and tough little dreams?) that she, Coral, was the kind of woman to be a whore. That kind who lean. Not quite but almost. Capitalizing on that inner, fleshy, hypnotic thing. All women had it, and she had her nerve, for twenty-eight bucks.

'Here,' he said, and she took the cash, with her screwing eyes.

'I don't know how to thank you, honey.'

'That's okay. Will that be enough?'

'Oh, sure. You're a real help.'

'Is that all I am?'

He turned up Cannonball, in time to hear the climax.

But now it all seemed like a lost cause, especially when he thought about them being Detroit cats and all. It was getting more and more like that with him, these few years, and he was even able to see it more clearly, what with the broad, standing there, staring at him.

Man, oh, man, Ned thought, calling on that basic thing of himself, the thing that kept refusing him, the thing that would have made it possible for him to tell this bitch to go to hell and she wasn't about to get twenty-eight bucks from him.

... when here she was, stuffing the bread down safely between her wide breasts, those firm, luscious breasts, that made his mouth want of her.

He selected another album and clipped it down on the plate.

She's got what she wants, he thought. Why doesn't she pull?

'Thanks a lot, honey.'

'That's all right, baby,' he said, and as he said it, he knew what it was she was waiting on, and he said it, so the whole damned thing would be settled: 'When will I see ya?'

'I'm not doin anything tonight. Burris is workin late at the meat market.'

'Well,' he said, and he remembered the delivery of new albums from the wholesaler, and his one-sided debit, and the Christalmighty work he had to do, and even the insides of her near-white thighs and how they would feel. 'What time?' he asked, when all the while he knew he wouldn't be able to make it.

'What about ten, after you close up?'

'That's all right with me. I'll meet you at the same place – Ernie's Bar.'

'Bye, bye, baby.'

'So long, sweetheart.'

Her hips left the room, and he was reminded of that gray way about her.

The next time, he resolved, it won't be a married broad; I've had my share of 'em.

Yet he knew the fascination of them, the freedom from obligation – his conscious obligation – they gave him.

He started the jam to whirling, and found with the needle's knife Conte Condoli, indecisively somewhere on trumpet: Why did they make it sound so threatening, when really it wasn't? When it was really like a prayer.

. . . yes, that's why he liked married broads; in bed they did things to you that they didn't do to their own husbands. Why? he went on, digressing into a subject he held so little knowledge of. Why was it?

Was everybody an animal, like that, black or white, all the same? And the way they seemed to infect a guy! Like her: the patent way – again – in which she had sold herself for twenty-eight bucks.

He got up, because night was coming and he wanted to see it.

There on the street. It looked like rain, kind of, the dark clouds reflecting themselves on the silver of the big front glass, with the words neatly printed just today: *Ned's Record Shop.* Like that, and it was almost like you could tell. A man didn't need to be God to see those kinds of things.

And, as he stared, and as the night came on, he could see himself reflected in the silver, and the world, a short guy, you could say, in the printed sport shirt and the neat clip-on strides, rust-colored, they were. And the blackness of his face: he couldn't see it, truly, not the straight black lips, or the hunches under the eyes that shone sometimes when he got excited or nervous, or the slow rolling of black broad brow.

Only the eyes were specific. They glistened, small and brown (black in the window-mirror, and white), seeing that black night and coming rain – and he more than ever looked at himself.

He saw the neon sign across the street, in green (green made him mad to look at sometimes, he couldn't tell the reason), and the hump of the whore-building, where you could buy a piece now and then, but he wasn't going to, not this evening.

He had to work! Damn it.

And if he couldn't get to Coral, which was already paid and bought, how the hell could he get over there? To Wanda. Actually, if he went, it would only be to see her.

Man, that girl.

He turned up the volume.

Wanda.

Wonder why a girl like her would be a whore. Wonder. The smoothest skin, the firmest bouncy cans, the rounded resilient ass, the yielding curve of stomach: this, all this – and, when she let you, when she really wasn't trying to end the trick in a hurry and even went for the way you did it a little: the most expressive insides any woman ever had. Expressive of night, expressive of warm, enveloping, liquid night.

Ned Land saw himself dying away in the night, and he turned his eyes from the green light.

The record was ended. Something by Stitt now, that should pep things up, that gingery tenor ax. With Gene Ammons on tenor repartée. That was a duel that really wasn't a duel at all – it was an old man bending to a young one, it was youth and fiber asserting itself, it was the tyranny and ridiculousness of uncalled-for competition. Ned Land, for a moment, was frightened by the viciousness of music, especially that which strives ahead, drunken and terrified explorers.

Stitt and Ammons blasted into 'The Chase', a famous piece.

A man came in and bought a record, Ned didn't know what it was, some juicy boogie, perhaps, by some juicy black vocalist.

He thought it was time to go to the back of the shop, but he still felt a nice buzz from the Boo consumed. Pot, Gangster (because everybody used to think gangsters smoked it, and found out they didn't, all of them), Weed, Reefer – all the same thing: Pot, Boo, Gangster. All of it was the same, and it seemed so silly, with all those names. He felt like he should, but not yet, not yet, not until you need it for real, kid, that's the time – when you just can't stand it any longer.

Beebedippybeebedippy, that was Stitt, riding down the scale behind that scared old man who was probably wishing he'd never arranged for this record date.

Dah-whip, dah-whip, dah weee-dee: 'All God's Chillun'. Sure, everybody knew that one.

He thought of David, his son, when all the time he'd been trying to keep the kid out of his thoughts. Life is like that, man, making you become involved in things you never even thought about before.

But he was doing right by the kid – he *knew* he was. And Doris, whatever she had to say, support and all the other things (because he had never really loved her to start with, not *any* woman yet) – what she had to say, she could shove. The bitch.

Yes, David at seven years old. The way they act when they're that age; they make people hate them, the way they act. And her following him here to Westphalia – that's what it amounted to – bugging him, following him around forever, it seemed.

Hell, Ned Land thought. Damn. Piss. Crap: or really, just plain shit.

Wherever did this stinking world get the right to stick its stinking nose into a man's life?

In Detroit, where Doris had been knocked up, devouring him with that lousy style of lay she always gave you? These damned women nowadays.

Or maybe in Cleveland, with its dirty streets dirtying a man's soul. Or New York, probably, with its phony cosmopolitan sheen and gangrenous inner rot of prejudice and inequality – for *everybody,* as though *nobody* was right: could this have been the place, man, this and the others? One of them, sure enough.

Maybe I'm twenty-seven, man, but don't call me one of them angry-young-man type of guys, Ned thought.

He just wanted to *know*, that's all he wanted. Was that so

much for a guy to ask? A guy who would probably never develop into a worthwhile kind of person, to himself, to his kid, to nobody else? Hey! he thought. We, just as the meat we are, don't we deserve an answer to some of this?

Ned Land didn't know. The music played out. This time he felt like digging Ella.

I shouldn't smoke Reefer; it accentuates these things.

And he knew he was going to do it even before he did. He locked the front door and turned up Ella a little, and went back to the rear of the shop.

He hadn't rolled it, and he should have, because it gets away from you so fast when you keep it loose. A shady green, coarse, like tobacco chips almost, but with that feel, that wet feel, clinging to your fingertips, that you couldn't mistake as anything but Pot. He dumped it out of the penny papersack on a newspaper, on his table of all work. He moved an album of Montovani aside, the kind of music he was getting more call for these days. Some people were rising up.

In a battered desk, album-piled, he took out his Top Papers and brought them over to the table.

Man, this was going to be good.

He rolled the joint for action, nothing huge, no bomber, but just a nice joint, one in which the marijuana packed together firmly snug. He guessed he had been thinking of this all day. He closed the curtains to the outside and sprayed the room with Glade, until it was smelling too sweet in there almost, and then he made himself comfortable and lighted the joint, sitting at the table.

Awareness spoke out: The Taste. That was the first thing. Even if you've only just smoked a joint, you get that taste again, that, unlike tobacco, is phoenix-like, ever returning. What was it, actually? Green, certainly, like winterweeds burning, but with a greenness that is so difficult to imagine. Biting? Yes. Like good tobacco might, like the nose-mouth-taste smell of a dirty burro, so like a brother, at the cracked fountain of a Caliente Province well.

Man and sweat, the burning elements of Ned Land's Boo, Pot, Gangster: animal and sweat. Hot sun on a waving sea of weed, there in that dry climate, being baked like fine dough.

Hands picking, pulling, and a bruise bleeding green, with that smell, that nothing-else-like-it smell, that lingers in your head and makes you awake, aware and alive.

His lips tightened about the joint, and he moved his head to one side, keeping out that burning smoke rising from the tip.

His Reefer bill. Above all else, that dulled his enjoyment as he smoked the joint, looking at what was left there, green, on the newspaper, the remains of a full matchbox of Weed. Very small. Money again.

How it gets into your high, he thought. And his highness leveled off, due to rise again. So temperamental, Boo was, like a bitching woman, changing moods with concomitant mental action.

How could he bitch, though? You couldn't do business with anyone more reasonable than Ruckson. Funny little guy. Big dreams. Broads ontoppabroads. Funny.

Yeah, Ruckson wasn't a bug.

Look at that: he had never noticed the Montovani album really before. Look at that lovely bowl-and-cherries white girl. Delicious. She made him hungry. He felt himself looking at her and wanting to have some action with a woman, Coral, Doris, Wanda. He didn't know what made him think of Doris, rising that way.

The pottish aftertaste lingered in this mouth.

The first thing to do was get those albums straight, if he didn't take all night with it, being as high as he was beginning to be. It was some good Boo. Ruckson and his happy Brazilian.

He picked up a copy of *Jet* he had bought somewhere and thrown here on the table. He turned to the centerpage immediately, let his eyes crawl over the half-naked, half-white colored girl pictured there, all her rounded insouciance, thinking, if I could get your simple, lovely ass in bed I'd show you a few things. You who dream of being a model for Lady Clairol or Coke. Fifty bucks an hour. I'd give you fifty, you devil, you rounded soft woman, and I'd show you for it too.

The way he could sink her, he could almost feel it.

This wasn't getting anything done, this. Just sitting and thinking. Why did Gangster do you like that? And make you so hungry, so ravening, both for food and the food of woman?

How many knew that it was an aphrodisiac? – that was the word. Florence, the civil service girl in Detroit, had told him that, and, 'Oh, the way you *do* it when you're high, Ned!' Or maybe he was fooling himself, and Florence cooling him too, because she smoked such a hell of a lot of Pot herself and was an awful liar, and you just couldn't believe it when women told you things like that.

He knew he was very high from that joint, and he was very surprised. I came back up, he said inside his mind, a little glad to realize it, because he had been getting set to roll another.

Doris, what she said, her face, he seemed to see it all again:

'The kid don't even know what it is to have a father. Seven years old, Ned! The other boys at school kid him about it.'

And he saw himself again sitting in the leather easy chair, the one he had convinced the manager to put in his room when they changed the lobby furniture.

'Why don't you get married, Dorry?' he had said.

'*Married?*' And she looked at him with those eyes, those sometimey eyes, that frightened him at moments. 'I don't think *I* have to go lookin, Ned. I don't think any other man owes me anything but you.'

'What is this?' he said. 'You just wanna be a germ, hangin onto me for the rest of my life? You're makin this one damned mess! Ain't it enough, what I do for ya? I know what it is you want, but you can't *have* it!'

He saw her again in his mind, positively, just as she had been, the light red dress for early summer hugging her slim body – and those tiny breasts with tiny nipples – and the hash-marks of her brow, accusing him behind that yellow-smooth skull and fresh-done blossom of soft red-black hair, and those conniving, trying-to-catch-him, brown eyes.

Yes, he knew what it was she wanted, and the kid probably wanted by now, having listened to her bitch about it all his life.

And he wasn't going to give them the only thing he had left.

'Ned, we wouldn't even have to sleep in the same bed, if you hate me that much.'

'Hate has nothing to do with it,' he said, in a press, uneasy in his easy chair (and he remembered Frank Sinatra had sung that somewhere). 'You know I couldn't marry you now, even if I wanted to. How the hell could I stand the expense?'

'It's *your* kid, Ned,' she droned.

'Damn it! Don't you think I know that?' he shouted. 'Of all the things I know about you, don't you think: I know that best?'

'You *owe* it to him—!'

'Listen, Doris, I owe you what you're gettin – sixty-five bucks a month, from me. And what are you doin? You're spendin that to follow me here from Detroit, just *blowin* it up, tryin to make me do somethin you know I won't do in the first place.'

Her eyes blinked at him, then had a shiny film. 'Do you know what it's like? No, Ned, you don't know what it's like and you don't give a damn. Living with my mother and father, livin offa them. And here I am, twenty-five years old. Eatin offa old folks!'

'Stop it!' he snapped out at her.

'Well, it's true,' she said in a blue, moaning, breaking, last-breath voice. 'I'm sittin right in the middle of nothin. Ned. I don't belong to anything.'

'Goddamn it, Doris,' he said, getting up, 'can't you understand that I *want* my freedom?'

Then she blazed; her face reddened as she stared at him and mouthed the words: 'And I want other kids to stop calling my son a bastard, that's what I want!'

Of course he knew it was useless to go on, and so did she, after a while.

He didn't love her.

A man could never sleep long with a woman he didn't want in the first place, and he had never loved Doris in any place.

Sure, that was the only thing, he kept telling himself – sure, the biggest thing. He couldn't admit to himself that he was afraid – afraid of David. He didn't know, maybe he was like God might have been: made His creation, then left it, afraid to see what the thing He had done would turn out to be.

His son.

His son was conceived in ignorant lust, which didn't seem to serve to make David legitimate enough.

What he held against circumstances – not Doris, he had to admit – was the fact that he had been too young. That was it. He hadn't felt or stroked or kissed enough of the thighs of other women to know this was just another piece, and it not good as most, or this was nature's way of protecting the bearer and the born, of insuring their continued sustenance by mesmerizing some foolish male in furbelows of passion for a thing withheld from experiencing passion itself.

The mother.

The lie and the trickery of motherhood.

Ned Land remembered vaguely the service that begat his son, wincing a little. Like something from an obscene 16mm film. Fresh home and hard-on, he'd found the street and apartment through the address the schoolgirl Doris had given him. Even her mother and father seemed to leer pornographically as he entered – and the broad way they excused themselves for a movie . . . why hadn't he seen the conspiracy?

And the way she came to him after they'd gone, with her hot mouth and hot little breasts under his hands and face. Was there any other way? Because, God! he needed it – he needed his hands up her skirt and on her slim thighs and his fingers pubically submerged – nothing else would have made him feel fully the man.

And in a second it was all over, like passing through a subway turnstile, and he was rumpled in his once-neat khakis and Doris was speaking of a date which (he did not know at the time) he would be forced to keep.

At least, they had *tried* to force him. He had been a little bit quicker than the erotically leering Mom and Dad and compliant little trap of virginity – no. They didn't have to be scared, not like him, they didn't.

What they wouldn't understand was the fact that he was less a father to the son than the son an actuality to him.

His son.

Then this thing: Boo, Reefer, Weed, Pot, Gangster. All of it being the same, all of it affecting him the same, a green escape.

But it was better than the heavy stuff, he reflected, not reasoning that it *was* the heavy stuff, that anything, women, whiskey, Reefer, security, heroin, *became* heavy with use, with need to die artificially, with need to be not.

Then, as he realized, as he saw it clearly through his high, Ned Land said to hell with it all. How could you really ever win? Against things like Doris and David, or Boo even, or Ruckson with his Reefer bill, or a useless black man on a new, useless start, or Coral, with her blackmail eyes and sponge-rubber thighs?

Ella died away in a moody, big-woman, beauty-meshed moan.

Oh, well. No more just now.

He glanced through the *Jet* and found out just how many Negroes had raped white women in the deep South, in the last week; how many white men, in the big cities, had retaliated in kind (and it was easy to see why with things like *that* in the center pages).

He thought, to hell with it, Boo-high, he was. But it didn't do any good at all. It was all intertwined some way, this life, and Ned wouldn't understand why it embroiled you, whether you wanted to be embroiled or not.

He stood and stretched himself; the effects of Pot made his head swim for a second, whip-waving the room, bouncing his eyes around redly in his head, but he found himself in an instant, and stood looking down at the table, at the girl in the centerpage of *Jet*.

His throat felt warm and dry, and he felt like a beer. But the albums . . .

And he retraced his steps to his desk, resigned all of a sudden, out of necessity, to something he could no longer avoid.

A bell rang, but it wasn't his phone, halting him abruptly as it tanged away in his head. He stood waiting. It was like ground shocks from an explosion, like something he remembered from another country, and his kid's eyes looking on it all, a tiny, closed-mouth people, abjectly opened-faced as they watched all they had be destroyed. Korea.

Ned sat down again, thrust down by the chapel chime. And the faces of those people, that was the important thing about it all. You never know what a man is made of until you see his insides, their rare, purpled redness, and sloshed muck left by a fifty caliber. No. Or just a man dying.

And I was a kid, Ned Land thought, seeing it all again, remembering the crying tears a man never loses, always the childish crybaby within from life's inherent anguish.

He remembered:

BLACK BOYS DYIN!

'Hit hard on that left flank, Ned! You got a rod up yo ass? Push that goddamn platoon, ya hear me!'

'*You* don't have to be scared – not like me, you don't!'

'C'mon, boy, I mean it! This is Sarge talkin' to ya! Dig them sonsabitchin Chinks out! You *do* what I tell ya! White folks watchin us! We gone show 'em! Take that *hill!*'

And they took it.

A bell rang.

Ned Land felt his insides churning.

It wasn't really so bad, not when you took a good look at it. Man, you listen to those sounds in yourself and you'll go crazy! No, you can't listen. This goddamn good Weed . . .

Sarge, blacked-faced, shiny like his own hunches under the eyes, but Sarge's was perpetual. Georgia nigger, tough with Georgia-nigger perseverance. A man to be respected, and yet – when Ned stood over him there, trying to crouch at the same time to keep out of the line of fire, and feeling a chilly, world's-end horror of what he saw was left of Sarge, his half-head carried away like that from mortar shrapnel – a man who was to be detested, a thing to be loathed, a loamlike mushy feces.

Oh, Lord!

With white folks watchin, like a battle Royal, ring full niggers killin each other!

And remember the Chink Lieutenant, the one who said he'd been educated at Oxford and acquired his accent while learning English? And when they flushed the bunker, and Brother Red, who took over after Sarge, with freckles and the long grin, from Royal Oak, salted it out with his Tommy, and they found the fat little Looey cowering in a corner near the radio set-up, and the way, when he saw them, he said,

'Oh, I thought *you* chaps'd be somewhere in the backlines, shooting craps!'

And Brother Red started to kill him, then saw the guy was doing it on purpose. And didn't.

Ned Land began to laugh, not on his own: the Boo made him laugh like that, for no reason.

The bell rang once more.

Warm mud warming boots ankle high, as they moved toward the Buddhist church in Kwihan, leaning, broken spire from tank fire, but still intact. The sun was red hot, burning, antithesis of the freezing winter of a few days before. Slowly moving in that warm mud, with Brother Red chewing on a dead rice reed, hefting that dirty blasphemy of steel and explosive lovingly, unleashed passion of the kill like a kiss on his sandy, freckled face.

Oh, God, the *way* they killed!

Easy out. Okay. Hands high. Get 'em up, you punk.

He can't understand you.

High, I said!

He don't dig English, man.

Hold it, Red! Don't shoot him!

Katahkatahkatahkatahkatahkatah.

Hey, look out! Up there, by the bell!

Red raising Tommy; Tommy talking. Two men in six seconds.

Katahkatahkatahtah.

Blood, from up there, splattered down in Ned's looking face.

The body slumped, lifeless, as though it had always been so, falling as only a body without life can fall. Against the bell.

And the bell began to ring.

They ran and dug in, away from the falling grenade, and they covered up, until they realized it had been a dud.

And that had been the last time he had heard that bell, ringing, accusing, cursing, damning all of them, until now, right here in his record shop, in Westphalia, Michigan.

Ned rose, feeling that thing again, that what-the-hell-was-it feeling of loss. A man never got hard, no matter how many tough outer crusts he grew in defense. There always seemed to be a chink somewhere, a little defect, open and suppurating, that drew in the germs which could fester.

He looked at what was left of the joint, the roach, and decided to let it ride, being as low as he was. He could utilize it later.

Again, this thinking that Gangster gave him.

Kill every goddamn one of 'em, Red had said. We'd get court martialed if we shot who we'd like to shoot. Kill 'em; they're the closest thing to white a black man can kill.

And before: 'It's crazy, killin this way,' Sarge said. 'Crazy man kills the only thing he got.'

Ned whirled round his shop, looking frantically for something that did not exist. He closed his eyes, and was high again, thinking about Velma, the white wife of Ruckson's happy Brazilian, and what he could do with her to help himself forget that he couldn't forget.

That integrated Army, like a big joke laughing at itself.

And he remembered, for some reason, that he had hated Brother Red. That Kankill sonofabitch – like *God*, he was! that smell of creosote and pestilence about him. Where was he now? In Ford's, Chrysler's or one of GM's plants in Detroit? Sweating the dollars down through his red skin by the hour, all twisted and hunched in a contortion under the body bridges of a Plymouth, wrenching against the criminal resistance of new nuts and bolts?

And him like God, the red-black bastard!

Oh, Lord, Ned said inside, I *didn't* want to kill that man. Please believe me when I say it: that man, that kid, that little almond-eyed boy, only a few years older than David, and the big silly automatic in his two hands, and him probably high off an opium smoke a few minutes ago, and thinking that this was HIS world, that nobody else counted not when they defied your reason for existence. This, along with the charge of sweet-tasting dope, still there in his hot mouth, cleansing it with terrified compulsion, then . . .

A nigger in a foul U. S. Infantry uniform, standing there with the M2, turning, frightened, and giving way to the squeeze of terror latent in finger . . .

Then a man with a cause killed by a man without one.

The way he looked. Ned Land knew the look of a new baby, all curled and fetal-formed, because he had seen pictures in high school of babies that way, and he knew the close association, that feeling that he was there once and the thin division of man and babe.

Then, this dead boy: he was Ned Land, there, so beautiful in spite of the two slugs in his guts, in spite of the mud, and the stink of a body somewhere, and, off to the side, the picturesque block patterns of rice paddies. Here, dead, gone, with a smear of mud on his right cheek, like a little kid who had played longer than his mother intended. Mother and death, lying there, fetal-formed. The burpgun he carried had flown from the body with the momentum of the M2's slugs, and now stood upright in the mud, like a steel flower, like the stick of surrender, or grave, in some child's game.

And Ned saw through it all that this *was* him. From the day of his birth in a shabby storefront, his first dog, his first hard, scraped-up-by-the-old-man electric train. His first screw in the home of a girl who was fourteen, and older than him by two years, and whose parents were away in some Hastings Street bar, dredging their systems with the arsenic of inconsequential life. This face before him, mud-smeared . . .

And he cried out, even as he saw it happen again, as his soul cried out now in the solitude of his shop, *Leave it alone!* Don't touch it. Keep your hands off. This is MINE!

And there, in the Korean mud, he had done unto a brother exactly that which he would not have had done unto himself.

No, say what you want; he would never forget.

2

Ruckson's eyes were two gleams that never flickered, and so sure in perspective his hand never faltered. He may have been littler than most men, but on a pool table he was huger than God and twice as mighty.

Snock. Cueball in the face of the eightball cross-corner. That was the third successive plunk.

Ruckson stood back on strong bowlegs and faintly smiled around his cigarette at the dark faces hovering torsoless in pooltable light, and his opponent, Black Casey from Grand Rapids, fresh out on a seasonal tour of the Midwest and very unhip to the hands that held his fate. That was the way most pool hustlers got cut down, and Casey hadn't become aware that he'd victimized his own bankroll in a subtle, smalltown cross until Ruckson's stick of genius began to cut it out from under him, a hundred at a time.

The gamekeeper clicked a disc over on the wire line with the tip of a poolstick and said quietly, in Ruckson's favor, 'Three.'

Casey, a tall, dark-skinned man, no longer young, the anxiousness for his fading youth evident in features that were thickly troubled, eyed the smoothness of the last shot-in ball.

'You sure you ain't Willie Hoppe in blackface, man?' he said, in a try at humor as his bankroll inched away. 'It's been two games since I lifted this stick off the floor.'

And Ruckson winked. 'Every man has his day, friend.'

'It looks like you're havin yours,' Casey said, not ungently, as though his loss was a curse Ruckson was relieving him of.

The rumor that a battle was raging in Ross's Poolhall had circulated freely, and now the two wide front doors bent inward regularly, admitting the curious male Negro populace; fellows who, by virtue of and disrepute through, a personal knowledge of Ruckson's amazing gift on the green, came gaw-grinning with the hope of seeing the village pool genius vanquished by an upstate outsider.

But even though the calm little man won, they were not disappointed, for in Ruckson's hands the 22-weight pool-stick became an astounding Excalibur, demonstrating poise and beauty and total devastation.

'Four,' said the gamekeeper, and Ruckson chalked up. Now he surveyed the table. He knew he was in for trouble even before he took a look – this had been heralded in the last shot. In leaving the table at the far end, the sixball had interrupted a crip, it being an easy straight-back or cross-corner; now the twelve and nine ball, which had composed the choice, had strolled over, on brief contact with the cue, to hide their noses in a cluster of tight-knit companions, as though informing their unwise fellows that the sky was falling.

Down the table, where Ruckson was, the cueball stood as though ostracized, at right angles to the threeball on the spot, and the seven right behind it, these two engaged in an act of love so binding as to make a clean shot impossible.

The green field was otherwise clear, and it was a long time before Ruckson made his eyes flicker once. But flicker, they did, at the sight of opportunity. The eleven ball had not completely tucked in her tail, seeking anonymity at the wall of green, thus providing a tip of butt Ruckson felt the cueball could touch. He looked once at Casey, who knew if there was ever a chance to recoup, it must come here.

Ruckson knew, too. And he bent over the table to aim the blue tip of the cue at the white waiting ball, his eye had closed to a tiny definition.

'Two rails and the side,' he said quietly.

The cueball suddenly danced away in a straight line toward the cluster of balls, as though it would smash into the pile, but amazingly it passed a hair-space away and solidly smacked the tail of the eleven ball and glanced innocently away, like a grinning pervert who had squeezed the soft young rear of a girl in a bustling crowd. The frightened, struck ball hit two rails as predicted and vanished quietly in the side pocket.

'Ruckson's five,' said the gamekeeper in an admiring tone.

Now the real work began, for he had misjudged his english and the cueball had come to opposite angles of the pile, not disturbing its solidity as he had intended. He came slowly around the table, lighting a cigarette and wishing he had taken time to get sufficiently high before the game commenced.

This thought added a slight terror to the tenor of his movements, since it had been quite a while when he had been entirely sober; it was an unnatural kind of fear, for Ruckson imagined he would react like a fish out of water if he ever allowed his mind to become completely cognizant.

He hurried over the balls, but not too much – nothing but haste could defeat him now.

Crouched in the pack, the fifteen ball said, Here I am – don't you see me, Ruck? and he examined the situation. Then smiled a trifle as he realized. Bank pool was like a woman saying, I have nothing to offer – when all the while she was saying, Take me, I'm yours – and more, I'm anything you'll make of me.

He placed his cigarette on the cigarette-scarred table ledge, chalked his cue and bent to the table. 'Tenball off the fifteen ball cross corner.'

The cueball discharged the entire cluster in all directions. But, like crazy cars at an intersection in a silent picture, none collided, and the fifteen ball, as though remote-controlled, plunked graciously into the corner pocket.

The rest was easy. With six to his credit, the table quickly and obligingly gave Ruckson the remaining two he needed. It all really happened too fast. When the last ball led to the side pocket, even the gamekeeper was silent.

Only Casey made a move, flipping a hundred dollar bill across the table to Ruckson. 'I don't think I need to play another game to know who's best, brother.' He went over and put his unused cue in a wall slot. 'I'll see you fellas around.' He started out.

'Wait a minute,' Ruckson said. 'I'll walk with ya, if you don't mind.'

And Casey waited while he came.

Outside, it was still early, though heavy in darkening. The cool breeze was slightly damp on Ruckson's black face, and he pulled his hat over his eyes a little as he walked beside the larger man.

'Gonna rain,' he said.

'Lot like it.'

'Been to Westphalia before?'

'Once . . . but not again, if I'd met you that first time.'

'I'm new since last year,' Ruckson told him. 'I lived in Detroit for a while.'

'Then you know where the Canfield Poolroom is.'

'I played a lot of games there, but that was a long time ago, too long for me to try to remember now.' He looked around at the two-story buildings and the faint light in the sky that illuminated their crests. 'I'm gonna stop here in Westphalia for a while. I guess I been everywhere and done everything there is for a man to do. I only got one dream now – that's a pad in Frisco with a bunch of fine Chinese serving-girls.' He heard Casey laugh, and lighted a joint in the quietness of the street.

'Man, man,' Casey said in a long, sad voice. 'It seems like every place you go is somewhat the same, don't it?'

'I guess. Depends on what yer lookin for.' He passed the sweet joint to Casey, who accepted and took big large drags that made the coal glow and flicker like a red warning.

'I used to live in New York,' Casey said after a long, held-in breath. 'And that wasn't too long ago. Told myself I wasn't gonna hustle the poolhalls no more. I ain't young no more, little man,' he said, looking down on Ruckson. 'A man's gotta stop someday, ain't he? Yeah. Well . . . told myself I was gonna stop and try to find somethin that meant more than the way I was livin. I guess I was gonna try to find God.'

'That's what we all try to do,' Ruckson said.

'It's funny as hell, the way a man tries to find God,' Casey said with a searching voice. 'All my life I hadn't give Him much thought. Then I found out I was scared because of how little I knew about Him and what He was tryin to do.'

'I know,' Ruckson said. 'Like you'd be left out, if you didn't know all the rules you had to know, to be one of the club.'

They came by one of many benches in a small park, under a monument with a man riding a horse with a sword uplifted in the air. And they sat in silent agreement.

'When I was tryin to find God,' Casey said, 'I lived on the west side, near the park. It was the damnedest place for tryin to do what I wanted to do, and it was a long time before I found out I was trapped, Mr Ruckson.' He paused for a draw on the joint and passed the remains to Ruckson.

'Tryin to find God in New York is like tryin to grow pot in a rock garden,' the little man observed. 'I've been there before. When a man gets as old as me and you, he should never go to New York to look for anything.'

'Yeah, man. It wasn't too late when I found that out, and when I did I got right out and went back where I came from.' His face became shadows, except for the whites of his eyes as he looked, remembering, to the evening tranquility of the small town street. 'You know one thing? There ain't no dirt in New York. I mean, not dirt like here: somethin you can dig your toe down in and see that it's black or that bugs live in it or that somethin will grow in it. The only dirt New York has is in the center of the tenements and apartments, and you'd never know it was there, passing down the street – unless you lived in one of the rear rooms or apartments. Then all you'd see is bastard trees or somebody's face starin at yours from a window. That's what I had,' Casey said, 'a room on the third floor lookin out at a brick wall and one window where some spic family lived. In the mornin, I woke up to Spanish music on the radio. There was another window I couldn't see that was open and had another Spanish station goin. Down below me, a bunch of faggots lived, always partyin with the radio turned to rock-and-roll. I got up and went to bed with all this stuff. All night long, you could hear the garbage fallin from windows . . . bottles crashin in the catwalks. Voices. Some screamin – all fightin. Here's some nigger callin a broad a mothereff and some broad callin a nigger a mothereff. All night, Mr Ruckson. It got to the place where my room was full of the smell of garbage – till the walls kinda tape recorded the spic music and punk music – and I went to the streets, tryin to find what I couldn't find inside the four walls.'

Ruckson unhappily knew what Casey was speaking of, and he sat back to listen, as though paying some sort of special penance.

'I went to the streets, tryin to find a little dirt to jam my fingers in,' Casey recalled quietly. 'But Central Park was the only place I could find it. And at that time of day, it was gettin dark. I didn't find no dirt, not dirt like I thought about it, not in the way I had come to think about God and dirt together. But I did find green, wild grass growin, right at the top of one of those rock hills in the park. I sat up there, right at the top and pulled it out of the ground. But it didn't make me feel no better, Mr Ruckson.

'Below, I could see the cars with their headlights just goin on, and the old men in white shirts, them pasty-faced fags, roaming the sidewalk, tryin to find youngsters, or other fellas like them. And it come to me, you know what I mean? They were tryin to find God, too, no matter if it happened to be a pecker or pat or squeeze or two. It come to me that everybody had to try to find his God in his own way, no matter if the way was told in spic music or nigger rock-and-roll. Man told me once, a fella who painted: I don't wanna see nothin ugly, 'cause God ain't ugliness; I don't wanna see spit or puke or shit, because it's ugly, and God don't love ugly.' Casey laughed. 'New York made me know how dumb I was. Taught me how to appreciate another kind of livin that didn't need no answers. I looked at all those millions of people – everyone of them just like me – and I come to know that God had millions of faces and was made up of millions of things. Yeah,' Casey said. 'I come to know that God was God only insofar as man desired a chosen dream, and that was Him. This man who thought of God as beauty was the closest thing to shit I ever seen, but that didn't make his dream any less real or his God any less beautiful . . .' He paused for a long time before continuing, and Ruckson could see that the whites of his eyes had lifted again to the sky, then down, to observe the slowly moving cars. And he lighted another joint to pass over to his new friend.

'I'm fifty-five years old, Mr Ruckson . . .'

'I'm fifty-three,' Ruckson said.

'Sometimes, when I have a mind, I can put myself 'tween a woman's thighs, but I hardly get a mind lately.'

'I know what you mean.'

They smoked until marijuana induced a verboseness in Ruckson that he could not resist. 'I like the way you explain how man created God in his own image, my friend,' he said. 'I guess you might say my God is the coastal image of a half-dozen oriental broads, a featherbed and a waterpipe full of Boo. But that don't seem to be all of it, right now – not all of what I'd like to do, and I've done quite a bit so far. But I haven't done anything . . . good. Not really good. You see, what I've done don't balance the sheet the way it should be. I know I'll probably get what I want, because I'm a hustler, and I'm good because Napoleon set the best example for me better than a hundred and fifty years ago. I deal successfully in pot, pool and people, in that order. But I'm like a woman who's never had a child – I don't feel like I've completed my purpose . . .'

'Sometimes we overlook the very thing we're lookin for,' Casey told him.

'Sure,' said Ruckson, 'it was ignorance kept your painter friend from seein that even crap has symmetry. See that shop over there across the street?' he said, pointing. 'If you listen, you can hear music – not spicky stuff or sissy, either, but new young men, a lot of them junkies and social freaks, one kind or another – but a fresh sound of the world goin on despite everything else, is what they have to say. And they say it better than anybody else, so far.'

They listened to a bass that was dominant, even this far, over lighter strings, from the loudspeaker.

'There's a young cat over there who owns that shop,' Ruckson said. 'He's young enough to be my son, and his name's Ned Land. I wish you could know him, because you've seen him before. He's been any face in the poolhall. You know him – he didn't shoot, not because his hand wasn't hip but because he didn't believe there are two ways out of anything. You know him . . .'

'Yeah, man, I know him,' Casey nodded.

'It was simply a matter of me rememberin what you said about people lookin for that one thing, and I thought of Ned Land second to myself. You see,' Ruckson said, pointing to a small pink palm, 'it's my idea that a man don't ever find what he's lookin for, not because it's not around for him to find but because fate knows once he's found it he'll stop lookin, and a man standin in the middle of the road gets in somebody's way, somebody who's got to go on a helluva lot further. Me and you, we've passed a half hundred. We know what we want, but we can't stop. That's what we're afraid of, the stoppin.

'Take Ned Land, there,' he nodded. 'He's close to me not because I mighta been him; he's close because he's everything I could'a been, because he never started lookin – he was smart enough to get scared right at the beginning.'

'One day he'll have to,' Casey said.

'Maybe. But maybe life'll kill him before that happens.'

Casey laughed softly. 'If you try to interrupt her plan, she'll kill you, too. What she does to that Land might make you curse, Mr Ruckson, but there ain't nothin you can do about it. All a man can do is dream his own dream and stay away from other people, no matter how hard they get shook by the neck.'

Near the edge of town a train hooted a distant whistle.

'That's *my* voice callin,' Casey said. 'I've been answerin for a long time now, and I guess I'll be answerin it for a long time to come. One day, I'm sure, it'll leave me standin in the middle of the road. But I gained sense enough, now, to step out of the path of others who still got a little way to travel.' He stuck out his hand. 'I'll be seein you, Mr Ruckson – in case we're both goin the same way.'

In Ruckson's hand, as they shook, were two bills. But Casey acted as though he had not noticed and turned to walk with heavy, moderately long strides down the darkening street.

Ruckson watched until the man turned at a far corner, and stood seeing nothingness for a long time after.

He finally turned to walk slowly in the opposite direction, pulling the mild evening calm down deeply to his lungs. He did not recall Casey's face or the mouth that said them, but the words that belonged only to the big man repetitiously massaged his mind, and it felt good, like a back that badly needed scratching.

In passing, he looked at Ned's shop, but he did not let his urge to cross and enter overcome him, and so proceeded once more to the poolroom. He was, after all, the only reefer man in Westphalia, and there were many ungentle, tired souls that needed the vaccine of its relief.

Strangely (for he had never let his thoughts call attention

before), he heard the all-aboard lowing of the evening train and felt a kind of pain at Casey's journey onward.

He stopped for a moment to look back at Ned Land's shop and saw that Coral was just leaving, and, automatically, his gaze straining the street, he saw her husband, Burris, leaning near the shadow of the monument. He had probably been there all along, but Ruckson hadn't noticed.

He saw Burris follow Coral, unseen, down the street.

Ahead he heard an organ grinder, a fellow he'd seen before who used a monkey as beggar. He traced the tune in his memory, then went on slowly down the street, singing to himself.

But then he stopped to look back once more at the record shop, and he was forced on by the words he'd heard Casey say,

'All a man can do is dream his own dream and stay away from other people . . .'

And he went along to take care of his own business, but with no immediate idea of personal safety.

Only a little anger at how big a bully life was . . .

3

It was evening and time for his shift, and he felt it rising in his throat already, that desire, that something he couldn't beat down for her. And shame.

All alone in the big house his father had built, Detective Cullen could almost imagine a remonstrative voice as he shaved and prepared to leave for work. Sometimes he almost seemed to hear the damn thing coming out of the picture of his old man, The Preacher. Surely, that's whose voice it was if it was anybody's voice at all.

He'd been wanting to move out of the house ever since the old man had died ten years before, but there was an Aunt Maida he'd have to deal with, and a couple of the city fathers, banking brothers, who held the mortgage.

He hated the goddamn place.

He wiped and looked at his face in the inlaid bathroom mirror and listened to the whiskery water gurgle out of the ancient bowl, and it seemed that the grimy bubbly sounds accompanied the fringes and hollows of his face, which, considering the small head, was so completely out of proportion to the rest of the pudgy body.

Eighteen rooms and one man.

He wiped his face thoroughly dry and brushed his teeth and combed his straight brown hair with water. Again, as he thought of her, a voice seemed to chide, but he went right on thinking of her anyway, because what else was there for him to consider in a place like this?

Creepy damn house. He hadn't gotten over it yet, not even this long. He felt a blush come over his face as he thought of how he slept sometimes with his head under the covers . . . as though he expected to look up some night and see him, the old man, standing over the bed like he used to do when he was a kid, and asking him whether he remembered to say his prayers.

Even now he said his prayers, just to make sure that the old bastard wouldn't come around checking up.

He almost hated the memory of his old man, regretting that he knew little of the soft woman that was his mother before she died. But that old man . . .

Detective Cullen came out of the bathroom into his first floor bedroom and began to dress. He wasn't in any special hurry, so he took his time, picking out something to wear. It was all ill-matched, the stuff he chose, but it was neat, and the sport coat was large enough to hide his schmoo belly and the .38 revolver he was forced to wear. He had never liked guns, and sometimes he faked, wearing only the holster and a lighter plastic replica. In a larger city, of course, you couldn't do that, but here in Westphalia eight policemen were all that was needed to take care of any trouble they were bound to have. Chief Belmont was never finicky about anything, and he particularly gave Cullen a lot of elbow room, since he and The Preacher had been close friends.

The Preacher.

Cullen sat on the bed and closed his eyes tight as he pulled on a sock. Actually, he didn't feel like a detective, for he had never stopped feeling like The Preacher's son. And this had complications in a job in which you were supposed to be a tough guy, or impressive enough at least to make people respect you as a stern individual.

Cullen knew he was lucky. In a big city department, he wouldn't have lasted a week. But here in Westphalia it was a different matter altogether. Every once in a while there were a couple of drunks, and sometimes the Chief had him go down with Bill Mullins to the train station and keep an eye out for two or three pictures on a wanted poster. That was just about as far as it went.

Life would have been easy for him if he could just forget about The Preacher. Talk about a real policeman . . .

Cullen pulled himself into his trousers.

It always amazed him how the old man could be so cherries-and-creamy in church, then come home and raise so much hell about things like the lawn being mowed or the dishes washed, or the care of the boarders' rooms, all of which were his appointed duties. He guessed that was when he began to hate the old man, after listening to him preach about tolerance for two hours in church, then coming home to hear him bitch in an entirely opposite abstract.

He was a bastard, Cullen said to himself, but low enough in his mind so that it was barely audible even to him.

And he didn't believe in ghosts.

No.

Not even the way the steps creaked at night sometimes.

Or the way the old man's picture kept falling off the wall.

No, no. Not even the one night on which the phonograph played 'Just A Closer Walk With Thee' all by itself. Of course, he'd been drinking pretty heavy that day (a thing The Preacher abhorred) and might have left the damn thing on himself.

He told himself he would have gotten married if he could have found a woman easier to live with than the old man. But she somehow never seemed to come along.

That's why, when he allowed himself to think about her, he closed his mind to Society's preventives, and even to the fact that he was a policeman, a detective . . . and the son of The Preacher.

He was finished dressing now. He checked his pistol before strapping it on, then lighted a cigarette. Through his raised front windows he could hear an organ grinder passing, and the music made a pleasantness course through him suddenly, and the smoke from the cigarette gave a good brown smart to his tongue.

He passed through the crinoline curtains to the front hall and adjusted his hat in the full-length mirror there before going out. He usually felt ambiguously thrilled at this moment, enjoying and deploring the action, remembering that his father had done it, and he had seen it done, a million times.

Then he passed out, locking the door behind him, pulling in the fresh air of nightside deeply.

He noted with a slight satisfaction that the grass needed cutting and the picket fence could stand a new coat of paint. He could remember when these things had been done regularly, but he could not remember the last time he had done them.

What was nice about Westphalia was, it was small and comfy. At thirty-nine, Cullen had come to a ledge of life that demanded no interference with routine. The only thing that impaired his sensitivity was the house with the red light in the window, and he didn't count this as a difference, or a bother. It was. It must be.

Pleasure.

Peace.

The night was wonderful as he walked.

'Hi, Officer Cullen.'

'Hi, Joe,' Officer Cullen said.

He walked briskly to the police station off Main Street, glad that he was alive – and glad, in a way, that the old man was dead.

The thing that shook his serenity was Bill Mullin's face when he came in, and Bill came over to him, with a look on his pan that made it look cracked in several places.

'Hi, Cull?'

'Whatsa matter, Bill?'

'The Chief wants to see us, boy.'

'Goddamn,' Cullen said. 'Sounds like work to me.' His favor left as he accompanied Mullins over to the Chief's office.

'Evenin, fellas,' Chief Belmont said as they came in.

'H'lo, Chief,' Cullen said half-hopefully.

And Mullins said something, too, but he did not sound hopeful at all.

Belmont, a ruddy-faced fat man in his sixties, was a sort who hurried to the point. 'Boys, we've got reports from Detroit that dope's comin in through Westphalia, that it's bein sold here and checkpointed. I want you to keep your eyes and ears open and investigate any new arrivals. We don't wanna let that kind of stuff get a foothold here, you know. Westphalia has a fine reputation.'

'Dope?' Cullen said.

'We'll check it out, Chief,' Mullins said.

'That's all, boys. I'll be at home if you happen to need me.'

Cullen and Mullins came out.

'Aw, shit,' Mullins said. 'This is more than I'm gettin paid for. I'm not goin up against some combine, believe me.'

'Dope?' Cullen said bewilderedly. 'Maybe we oughta have the state police in on this.'

'A feather in your cap is no substitute for a bullet in the gut,' Mullins told him meaningfully. 'I'm on my way, Cull. If you happen to need me, I'll be at home.'

Cullen followed him outside and watched as Mullins got in his private car and drove off.

'Dope?' he said again, then wondered at the sound of his voice.

He started walking down the street, toward the house with the red light.

Mama Harper, huge, black and eternal, met him as he came in. 'Say there, boy, you early tonight.'

'Yeah, Mama. Listen, is Wanda around?'

'Don't you worry,' Mama said, wobbling into the front room where the red light burned. 'She'll be out in a minute. C'mon in and hava drink.'

Cullen followed her through.

In one corner was a bar, where Mama Harper seated herself. Cullen could never get over the feeling that she stared through him when he came around, but his sense of fear was overshadowed by his sense of authority. It was he who let Mama's whorehouse operate undisturbed, and it was Wanda who prompted his presence here.

In the corner, a stereo phonograph began to play loud, fusion-like jazz, and the various weird sounds cascaded against the sensitivity of his inner ear.

'How's the police business, boy?' Mama grinned whitely at him from behind the bar.

'Still arresting,' Cullen said, but doubted whether she got the point.

'Wanna drink?'

'Not tonight, Mama, I'm just startin on my tour. Maybe I'll stop around later.'

'Lorraine,' Mama hollered, and a svelte brown girl came to stand smiling within the Chinese curtains.

'Tell Wanda to hurry,' the big woman said. 'She know Mr Cullen got his business to tend to.'

The girl left while Cullen sat down.

'What's new?' he said.

'Nothin now,' Mama said. 'But we coulda used you the other

146 | Clarence Cooper, Jr.

night – a trick got bad, and we had to hire a man off the street to get him outta here.'

'Anytime you have trouble,' Cullen told her, 'you just call the station – the desk sergeant and I are pretty good friends, and he'll send somebody around. Don't worry about anything.'

'I sure appreciate that, boy. C'mon, have a drink. This is on me.'

He stood and went over to the bar. 'Make it bourbon, Mama, and a quickie.'

She poured and he drank. The music swelled within the room. He looked within the black woman's face and found her grinning at him.

'Wanda'll be along, boy. Yes, yes. Ain't that right?'

He shifted nervously. 'That's right, Mama.'

The curtains parted and Wanda stepped in, almost tall in a tight red dress but very wide across the hips, a dark brown-skinned woman with big breasts that stood upright and a face as untroubled as ice cream.

'Hello,' she said.

'H'lo,' Cullen said. Then, quickly, 'Wanna see you for a minute.'

'Let's go to my room.'

'Well, I only wanna stay for a minute.'

'As long as you want is all right with me.'

'Remember you owe me a dollar for that drink,' Mama called out behind him.

Wanda's room was a green light that permeated the bed and furnishings and warmly entered him.

'I just thought I'd stop around,' he said, grinning nervously.

She sat on the bed with her beautiful legs apart. 'I wondered why you haven't been around since the last time.'

'They've got me on special duty, Wanda ... You know I would have been around before now.'

'I've missed you,' she said, but he could not see her face distinctly in the green glow, and he felt the rising thrill of himself underneath.

He went to sit on the bed next to her.

'Look,' he said, finding his words hard to capture. 'Wanda ... you know I like you a whole lot.'

'You seem to like it.'

'Well, I do, I do! I want you to know that.'

'Is there something you want to tell me?'

'Yes. Well, yes, there is. There may be a little trouble in town. I want you to keep your ears open.'

'Is that what you wanted to tell me?'

'Well, yes,' he said. 'I want you to help me all you can, you know what I mean? I just don't want any trouble here in Westphalia.'

She leaned her face close to his. 'What else do you want to tell me?'

He could not speak for a long time.

'Do you want to tell me you've missed me?'

'Yes, that, too. You know I like to come and see you.' He began to feel awkward.

'How much do you like to come see me?'

'Jesus, Wanda, you know how much. I've never lied to you, have I?'

'I don't know . . .'

'Listen, you believe it, I've never lied to you. I don't care . . . you know what I don't care about. I think you're swell. Well, hell, you know what I mean. I don't come in here to *take* anything – I have a sense of values, Wanda. I know what you do, and you know what I do, but that doesn't keep us from being good friends.'

'I like you a lot, Cullen.'

'That's the way I feel about you, Wanda.'

They were silent, looking at each other.

After a while, she said, 'Is there something you want me to do for you?'

But he felt a voice, and could not answer immediately.

'I'm supposed to be on tour, honey.'

'Would you like to stay for a while?'

'Hell, you know I would, but—'

'I won't keep you long.'

'Wanda . . .'

'Yes?'

'I want you to know . . .'

'What do you want me to know?'

'I want you to know I think you're a fine person. You know.'

'I know that you mean what you're saying.'

'Well, I don't care what anybody else says, and you don't have to worry about anybody else, you or anybody in this house, not as long as I'm on the force.'

She made her hand come to his chest and pressed it palm-flat there.

'None of us can help who we are,' she said.

He touched her hand, and then her arm, then he seized her and kissed her mouth.

'You can stay with me if you want to,' she said.

'I want to,' he breathed heavily.

She rose, and he watched as she began to undress, exposing the wonders of her smooth body in the green light. Her breasts had nipples like the caps of gushers, and her belly was a wonderful, black, inverted pyramid.

He held his breath, and she took one of his hands and made it come across one smooth hock of her wide behind. He smelled a quiet perfume emanating from the lower part of her as she stood before him.

And then he was breathing hard, grasping her around the hips with both arms and kissing her belly.

'I'm yours,' he said. 'Just tell me what you want me to do.'

As he undressed, he repressed the shrill, sanctimonious voice of his dead father, aware only of the golden brown gift that lay awaiting him on the green covers.

4

Doris saw the curtains go down in the record shop, and she saw the lights go out eventually. And she stood in the shadows. From where she was, Ned couldn't see her, she knew. Her hand went to one of her small breasts.

Oh, a blues was going around through her head, and she couldn't get rid of it, a crying thing, a pleading line, a dazzle of earthy words for a woman.

> You knows you mine, dear,
> Don't care what you say.
> I'm gonna win you, on
> My lucky day.
> Caterpillar Daddy,
> You got yo squeeze on me.

Gee, gee. That was the way, the way she would round it out. Geee, geee, with that deep tone. She had a talent for singing; she even won a couple of amateur contests, just like Ella.

What *she* could do with that song. Maybe that's why it kept going around for her: it wanted to be done. Funny how she kept thinking she should *do* something. Funny with David, and Ned, even. Funny that she should think of being that way, when really, all she wanted was Ned.

Oh, that little black man!

You knows you mine, dear.

And why she needed to have him so, she didn't know. Maybe it was the way some men leave a woman, pulled and stretched, exhausted, worn, *used.* The way they went into you and dug everything out, then twisted it like wet laundry.

After that first time, and even after David, she knew she had to have Ned.

Doris warmed herself in the shadows, waiting.

Over the night-tight city of Westphalia, Northern Lights seemed to be a blinking part of the sky. Slow moving, lazy early summer evening, the turgid moving of summer-struck people on the neoned streets. Doris thought everybody looked like they liked everybody else, this evening. Only, there was a rain in her heart, and she could almost smell it on the air. And she watched it all avidly, knowing how Ned loved to watch the night.

Ned saying what he said yesterday, he shouldn't have said it. There seemed to be no way of explaining it, the way she felt, with the few scanty words of her mind. She was here, and Ned was here, and it was religion-like, like the sanctity of the baptismal, the drowning choke of holy water.

Almost eight years ago, Ned had had her, had made of her, and that was all Doris needed, openly exposed to the moving power of the flesh and the heart, pushed on in her actions by some heathen feminine worship of woman's need to be owned, absorbed, by man.

Oh, how he had wrung her out.

Again her eyes strayed toward the shop. And she saw a movement at the door across the street. Then she hid herself more deeply in the dark.

Her mind was a heroin haze as she remembered, for she felt as though there was no beginning or end in her life. It had been so easy to be seventeen and meet that Army boy, fine and black, in the coffee shop next door to Cass High School. So easy to forget the song of her soul – and maybe not forgetting at all, since Ned had that same rhythm in him from the start – to surrender to the frightened and tentative probings of a man beginning.

They didn't know what it meant; no man would ever know what it meant: to find cleanness and goodness suddenly, to see it begin, with manhood, to see it die, and not be able – them not being women and knowing – to halt that deterioration with the only thing any woman had to give a man.

What she had to give was not sufficient, and it was only after Ned had gone overseas that she knew how insufficient it had been.

Then he, flying on arrival home, to Cleveland, and, after several months, on to New York. He hadn't had time to see his son.

Maybe that's when she resolved it. To be his ghost. He would never understand what he had taken, and given, to her. So when he finally got back to big D, when his mother died, and there was no one else, nowhere to go from there, she began her haunting.

Well, yeah, Ned was nice to her. No man had been as nice, and there *had* been other men after him. He took care of the kid, sending him things on his birthday – the fruit of some sweat-stinking, gelatin-black crap game in one of Harlem's back alleys. But that wasn't it; it was more than that.

Blessed Lord, why couldn't he understand?

He had taken her song from her and wouldn't give it back!

He had taken that surging, moving, womb-warm child from the pit of her and pummeled its undying body with his massive black fists, those things that could be so gentle, those reaching fingers into her.

Geeee, geeee.

It was so easy to see why it had to be this way. Her song for the world was taken from her, and she *could* have been immortal, like Ella or Billie Holiday, or even Bessie Smith; seen Paris, or South America, maybe, like Josephine Baker; or done that real thing for the world – take out the heart and give it – like Marian Anderson: this was the life of her stolen song, peopled with the throng of Love's many-billion children.

This she had given to Ned Land, and because of it she was dead.

She had every right to haunt him. Though there was much more she couldn't explain – so much that was a tone, a resonance, a triumphant sound of grinding finality: so much, so much. So much that was David, Ned, the both of them, and more of herself than she had ever dreamed would be.

And why wouldn't he *see* that? Didn't he see that David was her own indelible failure? In everything?

Oh, Lord, God, she could remember when she used to live on Cameron Street, and that old rickety house there, with the big rats that used to sit at the bottom of the basement steps, their eyes gleaming in the dark, looking up at her, defying her to panic them into flight. Like they were saying, C'mon. C'mon down here, you, I'll eat your ass off.

And right on the corner there was a bar, with a local vocalist, and (Doris remembered she had just graduated from Sherrard Intermediate, still wore the white fluffy thing resplendent about her smooth yellow legs) she used to hear this woman going on with that doing-it, deep, breast-soft voice, late into the night, from her bed by the street window.

And it was then she thought: 'Nothing could make me do anything more than what I should do: like you. Nothing could mean more than what you tell me to do.'

And now she looked over at the shop, wondering at the thing that made her turn from that woman, and her pledge, her eyes hungry with the transference of this great love, and she thought, remembering an unavowed vow about Ned Land:

Geeeee, geeeee.

Come make me sing, my Ned! Let me love you, love you!

For he was what that singing woman had, and she had, that was the thing so vital to her now, even more than David, even more than the memory of her dead, dead mother: his reefer smoking, his loving, the very way he cried out against her, was like menstrual flow, pulling her from within, thick, abundant, warm and cleansing.

Doris pressed her tongue-worried mouth together, moistly, thinking of him as she watched.

Somewhere down the night time streets, an organ grinder came toward her. *Frankie and Johnnie, dah, dah-dah.*

A neat, big yellow man in sports coat and trousers came toward her standing there in the shadows, walking slowly, hatless, hair honed short.

'Hello,' he said, as he came abreast of her, but she kept her mouth shut, thinking that he might be thinking that she was a whore and out there trying to sell herself, which she didn't have to do.

He stopped, and she saw a fine face, ageless in a way; but you could tell it had been around: Detroit, Pontiac, maybe Jackson, 4000 Copper Street there.

'I said hello,' he said, looking at her and drawing in smoke from the cigarette he was smoking.

'Listen, mister, I don't know you,' she told him. 'I'll call a policeman.'

'I wouldn't for sure want you to do that,' he said, grinning. 'Maybe if I introduced myself, you wouldn't have to do nothin like that, now would you?'

'I don't wanna know you.'

'But I know you,' he said, smile fading. 'And you'll like to know who I am, 'cause we're both in the same boat.' He pulled in hard on the cigarette, and for an instant his eyes shifted to the darkened windows of the shop across the street.

'My name is Burris,' he said, grinning again.

5

Ned came out, the door slow in clicking behind him. He checked it with a backward hand and continued on.

Late, and nothing done. Nothing but Pot smoked, burned up in twisting headbands of nothing but disturbance. Still, he carried a joint in his pocket, for later, for the other hours when he would need to be unlike himself.

The ashlike sky reminded him of burning coals of weed. That rain was coming, fast. Despite the parent sky, the city was dark and impenetrable, like the humps and crevices of a deep cavern.

The green light across the street blinked at him as he walked away. The whore shadow on the flecked-coal sky seemed the bent head of a woman.

Ned paused.

What now? His room, with the record album covers plastering the roach homes of the upturned, dirty green wall papers? This much didn't seem to be enough just now.

His separate eyes saw the woman's head nod behind him with his going steps.

Coral?

Was that what he wanted? Yes, that was what he wanted, but not like she would do it, not with her sucking mouth at him on his face, that way in which she did it to him instead of he doing it. That wasn't the way he wanted to explain it to himself. But something like that. And a woman didn't know how much she debased a man, by making him *pay* for it that way.

But however else was it meant for a man like him to be?

Ned went on, then paused again. Music, somewhere, told him for the millionth time of '*Frankie and Johnnie*', that mad ofay ballet.

Two cars whizzed by. In sports coat and sweater, he watched three men in windbreakers. The sharp breeze rose under his chin. Westphalia was a nice place.

Yes, yes.

Almost like New York, in a tide of day at morning, huge with that same huge yet tiny, gentle hugeness, omnipotent, really, like a big kind dragon rising from sated sleep. Across the street, he saw the open windows of lunch-rooms and nice bars and nice beauty shops, and much nicer things in shopwindows.

Ned turned. Across the street the green light faced him squarely. A drop of rain fell on his nose. He stepped into the street, and a brief flurry of wet touched behind his shirt collar and began to dribble down his back. It would rain for a long time sometime tonight.

He eased easily through small-town traffic, some of the farmers' cars, dirty and beginning to catch a few of the borning bugs of summer in dust-scarred lacquers. He passed a little man with a little dancing monkey on a chain, on a box which he wound to tune with a long handle.

Dance to the right, dance to the left. Ned watched for a moment, becoming a little sick. A little slave. The monkey grinned at him, a hateful thing.

He thrust his hands into his pockets and began to walk in the direction of the shop, on the opposite side of the street. He stopped at the house of another century, where a red, good luck candle burned in the front window, in a tall red glass. How many cops knew of this place? Surely Cullen, the one Wanda had told him about.

Ned went up the steep steps, cursing himself, and thinking what was left after the twenty-eight dollars. But it was too late now, and he wondered how long it had been too late for him.

He rang the old cowbells and waited. Lorraine came, and she smiled when she saw who he was.

'Hi, c'mon in.' Her wide, red whore mouth pursed, O-like, as though she were drawing in on him, as though he were a cigarette. 'Well, c'mon in, daddy.'

He came.

'Wanda?' She stopped him in the hall, that way she did sometimes, testing him, letting him bump up against her plump buttocks in that tight black dress, letting his loins and thighs rub against her for a long time. 'Nobody but Wanda, huh? What's Wanda got?'

'Nothing special,' he said.

'I just can't understand it,' she said, watching him side-ways, her eyes flickering a bit wantonly over her commercial mouth, still leaning hard against him. 'What Wanda can do, I can do,' she assured him, sticking her tongue out a little past her lips.

'Better?' said Ned.

'If I have to.'

She tore away from him, and it was almost like the parting of two sticky fingers. 'Wanda's upstairs. She'll be right down.'

Chinese curtains filtered the living-room light, red from the candle in the front window and the red bulb of the overhead ceiling light. Cushions everywhere. Mama Harper was behind the bar, big and black, a nightmare female, illumed in the work of her daughters and something blue and funky from Miles Davis, on the stereo, a long time ago.

'Hi, boy.'

'Hi, Mama.' Ned walked over. 'I think Davis was a young trumpet then; I got the album over at the shop. A man ages in everything, you know, Mama?'

'That's the truth, boy, you take my word for it,' Mama Harper said in a voice that was as big as she was. Her eyes twinkled in the blackness and distortion of her face; her huge breasts were animated under the simple print, bursting about her. 'Wanna drink, boy?'

'I'd like a Scotch, but my money's kinda short.'

'Don't worry 'bout nothin,' Mama said. 'You can pay me some other time. You'll be back, boy. You'll be back.'

Ned noticed again, with fascination, how white her hair was. Mama. And she truly was to Lorraine and Wanda Terry, whom he saw at work rarely. And there was Denise, who was her daughter too, now a big-time whore in New York, in a mixed call chain. Lois, and Carla, the white girl, didn't count, since Mama picked them up off the street, gave them a meal, now fed from them.

And again he marveled at how they, her daughters, all of them, could have come in their beauty from the ghastly wound of Mama Harper. Mama told him once, how they all had different fathers. Trick babies. And yet, so all alike, as though one starving man had waxed magical with his hunger and flushed Mama Harper with his immense vexation, and love. And that four were the daughters of love.

Ned turned from her, as her fat black fingers handed him the glass, and as he could look at her no longer. He sipped, and the whiskey inflamed the marijuana he had smoked a little while before. The room only gradually turned redder, and Ned belched an aftertaste of Pot. His stomach began to swell a little. He went to sit on the couch.

Miles was swinging along in a bluesy groove, talking in that funny voice, like an infant crying in the night, twisting away into unheard-of things.

'Now what do I ask you?' Mama grinned over at him.

'You ask me if that is nice,' Ned said.

'And what do you say, boy?'

'I say I can't explain it, Mama. It's too beautiful. I never was no poet or anything.'

'Man *is* poetry, boy!' She squinted an eye at him across the room, like one light going out, then on again. 'What you talkin 'bout?' in that child-chiding way she had.

Ned smiled, mostly from the Boo again.

Lorraine came in the room, seeing him there with his drink. Her eyes were big and Spanish like, with a color in them, unlike Mama Harper's – but he never liked the weakness of her breasts, although her rear was roundly planted. There was something wanting in a woman without much breast about her.

'Hey, there, man,' she said.

Ned smiled on, seeing her twist across the room toward him that way, and it began to seem as though it would take her a million years to do it, weaving her hips, and they, bouncing from their bigness, making her look all open and deep in front.

'Wanda told me to tell you it won't be long.'

'Thanks, honey.'

'Oh, s'nothin.'

Miles shambled through the room like thunder, and all the while it being a mere trumpet. Lorraine caught the lyric push, the excitement of the trumpeter, and began to wiggle her hips with a grinding drive standing there before him. Ned saw it all in an hypnotic red haze. Her movements were gaseous, all intertwined some way, and he was most conscious of what he thought the back of her must be doing, two man's hands full of her. Like a big fat black snake in that black dress. All rubbery; and all of it misleading, he knew. All it would take to prove it was a bed. That's one place a woman couldn't put one over on you, unless you let her. And Lorraine couldn't.

His eyes shifted to the curtains as she undulated before him, her body becoming an exclamation of both pretense and truth, sucking in on itself like a moss-soft black mouth, breasts disordinate and divided with her movements, butt swinging round, almost touching his outstretched chin with its infuriated closeness.

'Like that, man?' she said in a long gasp, now actually thrusting her rear into his face, touching, softly, till he could smell the deep woman-scent of her big behind.

'Sit down,' Mama yelled across the room. 'Don't you see he wanna listen to that man blowin?'

'Don't wanna listen,' Lorraine said in a petulant, little-girl voice. 'Do you, Ned?' And she sat down beside him, exhausted, no longer able to relent to the cry of what it was she truly was. 'Do you, Ned?' She breathed hot breath into his ear. 'Pretty black man, you – you don't need Wanda. Take Lorraine.'

'I like Wanda,' Ned said, still smiling, and he saw her hate him for a moment.

'Wasn't that nice, boy?' Mama said as the record ended. She leaned her huge head on an upturned fist on the bar. 'It's a funny thing with me. You know what I mean? People say, Mattie, why you lissen to all that old funnytime music what don't make no sense? But I know what he means, boy.'

'You gotta get that feelin,' Ned said.

''Zactly. Now I'm old, boy,' she said, 'older than you think. Lorraine there, she's thirty-eight.'

'Oh, I wish you'd shut up!' Lorraine said, sticking her red mouth out.

'I been around this world – Johannesburg, that's where I got my start,' Mama said. 'Something from a night-black nigger and a moose, that's what I allus said, since I didn't know the cannibals what was my folks. Pickaninny house-maid, right off the block, sold by some black old sonofabitch with a bone in his nose. Then, when I come to Englun, my bosslady, all the time she's playin Bach or Beethoven, makin me lissen, tryin to give me airs. And that's where I *figgered* to lissen. Goin on eighty-year old now, boy, and I still can tell that sound, whether I hear it 'mongst the gruntin of people lovin or Persian rugs and chantilly wine. I know it. Yeah, I know it.' She pointed toward the stereo, a fat-mouthed old man in the corner. 'Lissen.'

This time the executionist was unknown to him. But it was a baritone sax, deep, soft, ruffy sounds that reminded him for a moment of Harry Carney – but then, something else again.

This number was swinging, chuchuchichichichiswinging! Drums were going, fever in 'em, swinging, swinging, bass behind them, clawed Ned's inner realm of reason, tenor, trumpet, baritone. With the tempo rising that way, he could *know* the pulse of man; warmth of Reefer rising with the insane tenor saxaphone.

'Nice!' Mama said, and Lorraine stopped her probing round him.

A parroty trumpet clashed to the middle ground, and like a terrified old man, finding himself on the banks of the River Styx, cried out at Death's new torment; his breath howled over the river of brushed cymbals and collided in fear against the whole hairy chest of the baritone, which took the little thing into its apelike arms, smothering its forlorn protests, then took off, running wildly, a cruel, crushing, invulnerable mad messenger.

'Man, that's NICE!' Mama said.

Wanda came in.

In the red light, he did indeed see the child of her. The drums expressed her breasts and breathing under him. A slash of cymbal and two-beat pause, preceded her passage completely through the curtains. He and she, it seemed, were entirely oblivious to everything else. He saw her come forward, the red light in the contours of her sleek, silverlike dress making her look like uncertain jelly under it.

The climax was Wagnerian, crying to Christ, and when it finished with a rolling roar that bashed his conscious brain, she was there, smiling down on him.

'How's everything, Ned?'

'I'm not cryin, baby.'

Lorraine stood up, hitched her hip-tight dress saucily, shaking it at him, then walked away.

'She been buggin you, Ned?'

'Not so much.'

She stretched out a hand toward him. 'C'mon. Wanna come to my room?'

'The man's enjoyin the music,' Mama Harper cried across the room. Clifford Brown, the late trumpet genius, pre-empted her words with a wicked A-minor intro. It sounded like Sonny Rollins too, on tenor.

Again, Mama opened her mouth, but this time she did not exist for him. He rose to Wanda's hand, and stood there, close to her. The music swelled around him as he looked down in her painted face, green with orange, almost, and her lips so red, so deep and red.

'You must be nuts, Ned.'

'Why?' he said.

'To feel this way.' She shook her head, sad for him. 'I don't know, baby.'

'You've got me in the wrong boat,' he said over her, smelling the whiskey smell of his breath as it glanced against her face. 'When I was a little kid, my old man and my uncle used to fish on Belle Isle. I was suppose to stay in the boat with my old man and the other kids, but all the time I seemed to get out there in my uncle's boat some way. That's like you.'

'I know what kinda guy you are; don't you try to tell me,' she said. Her fingers closed on his. 'You're makin this hard for both of us.'

'Well, get out!' Mama Harper called to them, aggravated. 'Don't make it hard for *me* to lissen!'

'C'mon,' Wanda said softly.

'That's a buck for the drink, boy,' Mama reminded him.

'I won't forget,' Ned answered behind.

In the hall they met Lorraine with a streetside trick, a regular customer, like Ned, who felt about Lorraine, he imagined, the same way he felt about Wanda. They bowed their heads with customer politeness.

'How's the weather out?' Ned said.

'Rainin now,' the man told him.

'You shoulda worn a raincoat or something,' Wanda told Ned. 'You'll get wet when you leave.'

'Maybe it'll be over then,' Ned hoped.

A piano solo, from the inner room, compounded their attention.

'C'mon,' Wanda said.

He followed her into a ground floor room of green light, one-shaded window and nice curtains, and that broad, made-up ironing board flat bed. The covers were unwrinkled. Wanda sat, one round firm thigh over another.

'You know,' she said, looking up at him, 'I been thinkin since you were here last week.'

'About what?'

'About you, mostly. I mean – the nice things you do, Ned.'

'I hoped you were liking it,' he said, misunderstanding her.

'You got a cigarette?'

He gave her one.

'It's not so much what you mean, Ned. You know what *I* mean? A woman has a hundred men, two hundred. It's all the same. Once in a while, some is better than most, but she tries not to think of that. After it's over, two or three weeks later, she takes off to the doc and lets him clean her button. And it's like none of it ever was.' Her eyes sparkled in the green light. 'What I'm talkin about is something else, honey.'

Ned's ear harkened to the sound of her words and the music that was filtering in under the door, through the walls: to him, it seemed like all the places of the earth – her words, the music, his heart beating hard.

'You got a light?' she said.

He lighted the cigarette for her.

'Thanks.' She blew out an abundant cloud of blue-green smoke. 'I hope you know what I mean.'

'I'm tryin to.'

Her eyes looked up at him, and he saw that they were people eyes, with moisture in them, just like his own; and her nose, just above the cleft of her top lip, had film from the warmth of her nostrils.

'You're being a sonofabitch, Ned!' she burst out in a harsh voice, lowering her head.

He dropped to his knees in front of her. 'I'm not, baby, please believe me, I'm not.'

She raised her eyes and looked at him, found the corners of his face in the green light, traced it lovingly, as though she had tissue paper over a map.

'You been smokin reefer, Ned. I can always tell; your eyes get red.'

'Yeah, I sure have.'

'Do you like it that way?'

'It serves,' he said.

'Will you understand what I say?'

'Yes, Wanda, go on. I know everything you're talkin about.'

His hands gripped hers in her soft lap; then her hands came away and went under his coat, around his chest, up his throat to his chin, the hands perfumed, touching on his mouth, a finger feather-brushing the entrance of a nostril; up over his black skin they crawled, to the edges of his eyes, around them, cool palms on the sides of his cheeks, pressing his face inward with sudden intensity, then on to his hair, short and napped, and he felt her nails at his scalp, tearing into it. Then she pulled his head into her breasts, mouth and nose within the crevice, as though he were the child that had just sprung from her, and he felt her trembling under his hands, her belly quivering.

'Ned, understand,' she begged, tearing him from her, colored above him with a queer thing that distorted her face and made it look more beautiful. 'Black man outta nowhere, doin this to me—' She made her mouth go over his, grease of her lipstick swelling his mouth with its sweet taste, and her tongue.

And she caught bits of his short hair as she pulled away from him, and said, her eyes crying, 'You crazy bastard. I *love* you. Do you understand that? Isn't that as silly as hell? I'd *die* for you, Ned . . .'

Outside, in the rain, Doris watched the house of joy.

6

He awoke intertwined with her. As complete consciousness closed in, he began to feel the warmth of her body. Her body almost made him overhot.

Burris pulled away from her in the half shade of their darkened bedroom. She muttered, and he could smell the sharp awakening in her breath which spoke of living flesh and fluids, and too much drinking of beer and smoking of cigarettes. And frustration.

His eyes popped fully open with a slitting sound. Her hair was in his face, smelling two weeks old and ready for a wash. And a hairdo, and another five bucks from him.

His hand spread open beneath the crack of her wide behind. Her voice was like a moan as she felt it through half-sleep.

She's thinkin about him – but Burris felt his heart expand and hurt, as though pepper powder had been suddenly injected into his veins.

His free hand came over his face, feeling it, and he smelled her again on his fingers, going down now, touching the wide jaw. A reminiscent smell of blood, not actual, forced him to shift a little in bed. Another five bucks.

Well, he had to get up. But feeling better this morning. Better than last night, when he thought she would again. It was the second time that fella stood her up. His fingers tightened with a small surge of anger, and her butt approached the tensile strength of jelly in his hand.

'Listen,' she said against his ear, 'it don't pull out like a snap-button.' She twisted against him. 'Quit diggin round me.'

His voice was hoarse. 'Sometimes I think maybe I can *make* it pop off like a snap-button.'

To show how much she thought of him and what he had to say, she went promptly back to sleep.

Burris lay there, getting madder.

If it wasn't one guy, it was another. That's the way she was. A lot of times he thought he would kill her, but right at the last minute he couldn't do it. Even sometimes when he caught her right at it. And wasn't that funny? Because he'd never had any trouble before. In Chicago, nine years ago, it had been two men. And he hadn't had any trouble then. They were men he hated, men who had pushed him too far. And he killed them, and he was still glad he killed them. He'd kill them again. He wished he could kill them every day, after what they did to him.

And he hadn't been scared about what anybody would do to him for it, either.

Not that he loved her so much. That wasn't it. He'd had women before and they had meant more than her. It was something else, something he couldn't describe or begin to reason. That's why he had to destroy all around her instead of just killing her like he should.

He felt his wide chest expand, and when the covers bellowed down with his expiration, he smelled the harsh tones of two lemon bodies intermixed.

She wiggled and nudged his hand from under her behind. His hand lay with nothing to do, between them, and the fingers clutched at nothing for a moment. Then the wrist reached forward and the fingers clamped about her thigh. Her flesh was tickled at the sudden movement, and it vibrated under his fingertips. His hand remained that way, for as long as he could make it, then the knuckles rose and the fingers creeped upward, turning the slopes and ridges of her upper thigh and belly, like the members of a practiced caravan. Then stopped at the jungle edge of pubic hair.

'Why don't you let me get some rest?' she said in a tired voice.

'That's all you get is rest,' he said. 'Whadda you mean leave you get some rest?'

'Oh, Burris.'

'No, I wanna know just what the hell you mean. Rest! What do you need rest for? What do you do around this joint that takes so much outta you that you say you gotta have some rest?'

'Burris, it's five o'clock in the mornin.'

'I know what time it is. Don't you think I know? I gotta get outta here in a few minutes and get to work. I know what it means to want some rest. Twelve hours a day.'

'Are you complainin?' she said in a graty voice.

'I'm not complainin about anything but the fact that you got to have so much goddamned rest.'

'Now, listen,' she said, rising up on an elbow, 'there's a lot of things you don't think about and a lot of things you don't understand. You don't have to *live* here twenty-four hours a day. *You* got your meat to chop up, and every other thing you wanna do with it. *You* got that. Now what have I got? Burris, I'm a young woman. I'm not gonna be used up the way I've seen other women used up.'

Now he rose, half-sitting. 'Oh, as long as you're used up by some other man, is that it?'

'Oh, you're talking crazy as hell . . .'

'Crazy, huh?' he said, his eyes big. 'Crazy, is that what you think I am? You don't think I know, do you? You don't think I know about *him*?'

'Him, who?' she said with big clear eyes.

'*Him!*' he exploded. 'You know who the hell I'm talkin about! You know good and goddamn well who HIM is, and don't you try to tell me you don't!'

'Just another him in your mind,' she said. 'It's been six years of "hims".'

'It looks to hell to me like there's gonna be six more!'

'Now I'm wide awake.'

'Good!'

'Oh, Burris honey, please stop fightin me . . .'

'I guess you know I could make you, if I wanted to.'

'You wouldn't have to make me do anything, honey.'

Almost as a challenge, his hand came around her buttocks, and they yielded inward toward him.

'You don't have to fight me,' she said.

'You know what I'm talkin about is true,' he said.

Her hand came under his shirt. 'You're just makin up things on me, Burris baby.'

'I've seen ya, Coral, I know about it.'

'You know about what?'

'About the guy at the record shop, that's what. I know just what the hell is goin on.'

'All I did,' she said, 'was to go in there and buy a record by

B. B. King, and that's what you think you know? Can't I even go to buy a record by B. B. King?'

'I never said nothing was wrong with buyin a record,' he half-apologized. 'What I'm talkin about is, I know what's goin on with you and him, that Ned Land. What about the bar?' he sprung on her.

'What bar?'

'Ernie's Bar – that's where you always meet him.'

'Meet who?'

'The record shop man . . . goddamn it, Coral, you know what the hell I'm talkin about!'

'But I don't see what's wrong in having a drink at Ernie's. What's wrong with it? Ain't me and you both gone there before? Don't I have the right to go there? If I feel like a beer, is there anything wrong with havin one at Ernie's?'

'Not with another man, it ain't!'

'Oh, Burris, *what* man?'

He felt his arms trembling. 'Coral, do you want me to punch you in your lying mouth?' He felt them trembling with anxiousness. 'You know what man I'm talkin 'bout! The same guy you been havin drinks with in Ernie's Bar, the same guy you been screwin for three or four hours a night at the Flamingo Hotel. You know what man I'm talkin about!'

'Have you been followin me around?' she said in a high voice. 'If you've been followin me around, then you *should* have seen those things!'

His hand lashed around, but she had been expecting it, and she met it with her teeth and sunk them deeply in the flesh. With a gasp of pain, he tore it away from her. He made a fist, and drew it back, knowing it would go with all his power – and when she saw this, Coral sat upright in bed and poised for the hammer, closing her eyes calmly and resignedly, and looking suddenly beautiful in the warmth of the half-shadows and what he could still smell of her.

'Well, go on,' she said, 'bust my brains out. Beat your nigger-woman.'

He lowered the fist, physically stayed by what she said.

'What good would it do?' he said.

'Well, g'wan,' she said. 'Bust my brains out.'

'Shut up.'

'After seein as much as you did, why don't you hurt me?'

'Shut up, Coral.'

'C'mon, hurt me. Hurt me, Burris. Make my nose bleed. Make my eye black, will ya? Come on, Burris, mush my face in. Hurt me. Make me holler and scream. Make me die, Burris.' She shook her angry head at him. 'As though you could *really* hurt me! You don't call what you've done to me for six years hurtin? This being buried without bein dead? This *ain't* hurtin? Burris baby, you don't know just how much you've hurt me already.'

'I *drive* ya to other men, huh?' he said. 'Is that what I do? Don't I try to give you every damn thing you want? Don't I do that? Huh? Ever since we latched up together after I came out of Jacktown, didn't I give you everything I could? Lookie, baby, I didn't just get borned yesterday. I been around this world. I did right and I did wrong, but I never let no man or woman make me stick my head down an outhouse hole!'

'Tell me I never had it as good since the time I said I Do, and got kicked in the ass for it!'

'Well, goddamn it, you never have.'

'I could have had better. When we were there in Jackson,' she said, 'I could have had a whole lot better. But no, not me. Not me. I feel sorry for *you*. You been locked up so much yourself, you don't know *how* to let other people go.'

'Not when the people you talkin about happens to be my wife and out screwin other men!'

She flounced out of bed. For a moment she stood looking down on him, her eyes fired. Her nightgown had a wear slit in it, and he could see where her breast sloped under, round and soft. He licked his lips, wondering what it would actually feel like to kill her, to feel all of her dying under his hands, and him there above her, commanding her for the first time in his life. How it would feel.

'I'm gettin pretty damn tired of you,' she said.

'Oh, is that the way it is!' He crawled suddenly forward on the bed, his head tilted at her, his lips pulling back. 'Is that the way it is? You're *tired*, huh?'

'Man, I can't make it no plainer,' Coral shouted. 'You, you with your jealous ways and your jealous eyes all the time, always watchin me. If I go to the bathroom, if I say, phoot! you ask me who that *man* was! Burris, you're just the kind of man who drives a woman crazy! You don't do *your* screwin around, huh? I just *guess* you don't try to stick some other woman when you get a chance! What about that girl who used to be the cashier at the meat market? What about her, Burris? Don't you think I know what the hell was goin on? Listen, man, I wasn't borned yesterday, either!'

She was trying to confuse him; even through his anger, he knew that.

He shook his finger at her, like a whip. 'You better be goddamned careful what you do from now on, Coral, I MEAN THAT!'

She went out of the room, and the old floor creaked its boards at her barefoot steps.

'You better remember that!' he yelled after her.

He knew where she was going, just right down the hall, and in a little while he heard the hissing sounds when she released her urine.

In their attic rooms above the other sleeping tenants, or those who couldn't sleep because of them, Burris lay spread-eagled in the bed, boiling with a dangerous mad. The clock began to alarm on the bureau, a quarter to six, and he let it ring until it rang down.

'Why didn't you shut it off?' she said as she came back in.

'I just guess you don't know he uses dope,' he said, sitting up on the bed, facing her as she came over to the bureau to take out fresh panties and bra.

She turned her head toward him. '*Who*, Burris? Who uses dope?'

The sides of his jaws began to tremble. 'That record shop fella, that Ned Land, that guy who's been getting into your lyin drawers!'

'You can just go to hell if you have to talk to me that way!'

'Oh, don't be so holy with me,' he said, shaking a fist at her. 'I know things about him you don't even know!'

She slammed a drawer. 'Goddamn it all right back to God!'

'He uses dope,' Burris said again. 'Yeah! Reefer. He smokes reefers!'

'I guess you *seen* him,' she hollered at him.

'Yeah, I seen him!'

'Don't you tell that goddamn lie, Burris, because you know that's all it is!'

'I seen reefer in my time, lady,' he said with mad importance. 'I know what it looks like when I see it. I seen that Ruckson, too, that little poolroom hustler. I know what he does, and because I know what he's doin I know what Ned Land's doin too!'

'Why the hell don't you go right back to Jackson Prison,' she said, 'where you'd know what *everybody* does! Sugarman of mine, why don't you do that? Why don't you leave me alone with your pickin and pullin, and just get the hell on back to Jackson Prison!'

'I wouldn't make you that happy!'

The sun bloomed hotly through the shaded window and made them pause. Below, a toilet flushed. Her eyes made targets of his face.

'Sometimes,' she said, 'I think you're crazy – I think you need to be put away in that crazy house up at Ionia, that's what I think.'

'He's gonna be investigated. You don't believe it, you watch and see.' He got out of bed, stripped off his pajamas, and began to dress. She began to dress. 'You're gonna get yourself in a lot of trouble, Coral.'

'Sure, I will, that's what you always say.'

'You'll be beggin for my help, Coral.'

'You'd better hurry,' she said. 'You'll be late for work.'

He pulled on his shirt. 'I'm *tellin* you – I've had too much, Coral, I'm full up with you and everything you been doin. I been doin right. You never want for nothin. It ain't like it was in Jackson, when I had to take what I could get. Now it's different, Coral, I got some say and I'm making some money. Sure, I did wrong in my life, but now I'm straightened up and flyin right. You're gonna get your asshole tore right out, treatin me like this.'

'You don't realize how *you're* treatin me,' she said, getting into her brassiere, with those wobbly yellow breasts and their deep brown tips that jiggled down, then paused at the lips of her brassiere cup, then sunk under, like the face of two drowning brown men. 'Bring home some beef for a stew tonight, will ya?'

'You're gonna get in trouble with that Ned Land,' he warned her, and watched as she wiggled agitatedly into her panties, then seemed to swell to his own dimensions.

'You know what you can do?' she said, and her hands came to her hips, over the rounded belly, and the shadow, through her pink panties, of someone's head below, while at the same time her knee buckled inward and she rocked on the axis of her hips, daring him with them. 'You can just kiss my ass,' she said. 'That's what you can do.'

'And do you know what you can do?' he shouted. 'You can just fix me bacon and eggs and ham this mornin, and that's what you'd *better* do!'

Just a skirt and sweater, and it was all over for her. But he still had trousers yet, and socks and shoes, and the adjusting of that sonofabitching belt that kept squeezing him to death after three in the afternoon.

She went downstairs to the community room where he could hear pans rattling and grease popping in a while, then the first frazzle of ham as a side was lowered into the sizzling liquid. Pretty soon he could smell that sinus-raking odor of ham cooking, peppery and gentle at the same time; something like a crowd of people who didn't know anything about underarm deodorants on a hot day. So good it smelled, it made his stomach ache.

Well, he could bet he made her do it.

She was just mad about *him*, that's all. Last night, and her waiting at Ernie's Bar. She sat there alone until twelve-forty. Then she came home with a lie. And all the time he was sitting across the street in the 12-cent hamburger joint, watching that place, and every now and then going through the front door of the bar to peer through the other door with the little glass window, to make sure *he* hadn't got in through the chimney, or some other place around there.

Burris got into his socks and shoes. He stood up from the bed. He began to hitch the belt. Getting too fat.

He hitched it to the other side. And it was only ten minutes after six in the morning. He *was* getting too fat.

He finished soon and went into the bathroom, which they had alone, since there was no one in the other attic flat. He relieved himself and brushed his teeth and washed his face and hands, and he pulled out a facial hair that had festered when he shaved two days before, somewhere there among the thick new growth.

He should have shaved again, but he didn't. People didn't look at the butcher's face; they watched his hands instead. As if that kept him from cheating.

Without a word he went downstairs and broke his fast and found his coat and hat. Coral left to do something in the kitchen as he started down the lower stairs. She didn't even say goodbye. He stood there. His lips hurt with his teeth biting into them. He felt his eyes get small. He thought about Ned Land. He remembered belatedly that she hadn't cooked him a lunch, that he would probably have to eat coldcuts from the counter freezer.

He went back to the kitchen, where she stood washing the breakfast dishes, her eyes not seeing him. He stood there, mad as a sonofabitch. His eyes fell to her wide behind, and his hands recalled the feel of the rounded, bottom parts, and that long crack there.

He went over quickly behind her and grabbed her butt in both his hands. It was too wide for his hands, and he was astounded that he'd never really known how big it was, and knowing too with a stab of pain that this firm, round woman was one he could never leave, no matter how much he hated her. Her flesh was stronger than his reason.

'I hope that squeeze brings you luck,' she said, still washing the dishes.

Burris turned and went down the steps.

Another hot day. He hated summer's coming.

The early morning sun blazed down hatefully. He could not even remind himself of the fine breakfast Coral had fixed for him. His steps became more anxious down the morning streets as he thought of Coral and Ned Land.

'Hi, Burr!'

'Hi, Mike,' Burris said.

Mike, big young Italian, bigger than Burris, stood looking

down on him as he opened up the meat market with one of the keys on the ring with the one he had his Cadillac key on. 'How's everything?'

'Everything's goin fine, Mike.'

'Let's rake 'em in, boy,' Mike said, wide white grin.

'That's really what we're gonna do today, Mike.'

Mike became confidential. 'Listen, kid, I've got some things I've got to take care of. You pull in three hundred behind the meat rack today and I'll *give* you twenty-five bucks.'

'You're throwin your money away,' Burris told him. 'We'll make that easy.'

'Don't mind about that, Burr,' Mike said. 'Just make that three hundred for me.'

One of the white butchers came in.

'Hi, Joe!' Mike hollered.

'Hi, Mike!'

'Rake 'em in today, boy!'

'Don't you worry, boss.'

Burris went over behind the wholesale counter, hung up his coat and hat, then went over to the main counter where he found an unbloodied apron. Side meat came in two minutes later, and he had to cut the strip in two, and later carve the carcass crossways. He had begun to work even before opening time at seven-thirty.

'I'll give you a hand,' Joe said, hair in eyes already, and Burris couldn't see why he didn't have it cut.

At seven-thirty-four, Mike at the checkout, where he could take in the money and flirt with the broads at the same time, Burris got his first customer, a bent-old Negro with a black leather bag.

'Two pounds of neck bones,' he said in a rickety old voice.

Burris served, then served two more.

Eight-forty-five. Cullen came in, and Burris saw him immediately. It was like that with him about cops.

Cullen, kind of fat, but kind of handsome in a pudgy way, with a vest that was in style and a sports coat that was completely off and couldn't hide the bulge of small-town thirty-eight, came over casually. Burris tensed.

'How ya doin, Burris?' Cullen said in his high voice.

'All right,' Burris said, wiping the blood from his hands. 'Been keeping your nose clean?'

'Like always.'

'We have to watch you boys on parole, you know.'

'Ask my parole officer, he can tell you.'

'Sure, I already did. I just wondered what.'

'You wondered what about what?'

'What you know about some things,' Cullen said.

'What have you been hearin?'

'About a narcotics ring,' Cullen said. 'I hear Westphalia is a center for Detroit.'

'I never heard anything about it.'

Cullen tilted his head back and leaned on the white freezer counter. His eyes were gray. 'I like Westphalia, Burris, you know what I mean?'

'So do I,' Burris said.

'That's why I like to know if anything criminal is going on.'

'I know you do.'

'And that's why I'd like you to help me, whenever you hear something wrong is going on in Westphalia.' He winked. 'I don't mean like that cathouse that everybody knows is operatin; that's harmless. A man works hard all week, he's gotta have something like that. You know what I mean?'

'Sure, I know what you mean.'

'Well,' Cullen tipped his hat down. 'I'll be seeing ya.'

'I'll be seein you, Detective Cullen.'

He watched the man walk out.

It didn't strike him until after Cullen left. Then he knew what he should have done. He couldn't understand why he didn't think of it.

He still wiped his hands of blood, staring out into the awakening streets. He smiled to himself, remembering Doris, that Ned Land's woman, and what he had done to her thoughts.

And he laughed out loud.

Subsiding, he grinned at Joe, who was watching him.

Then he went into the freezer to steal the pound of stew meat from smiling Mike for his and Coral's dinner that evening.

7

Two kids were dancing outside his shop, brown little moppets, and he knew they should have been home from school for lunch a long time ago, but he didn't have the heart to make them go away, when they were so happy. Grown ups paused to watch them dance.

It was music from the loudspeaker outside they danced to. One of the new albums, something swinging by Count Basie.

He came around in front of the counter to watch through the window. The music was that strong, power-packed kind of jazz, one that tore through the clouds of inhibitions in every listening ear and snatched out the common gift of rhythm.

And these kids exemplified it. The sun was red in worship, and hot, and their movements became a oneness in the air that was almost tangible. And how big and dominant they were becoming! The one of them with short sleeves and bucked teeth slightly in a child's way, swung around with the slim fury of a jubilant black god.

Woodwinds blasted out strongly, paving a broad, bambooed plain in the introduction of a virile young tenor sax. Then at the moment they could go no farther, and you had to know that these were happy men making happy music, there was a pit of brief silence.

The smaller kid fell into this pit, just as though he had stepped from the wing of a winging jet, and when he crumpled downward, Ned could barely repress a cry of horror. But it was all in fun, that's what the band said. After the first four measures, the tenor convinced him, and then he saw the kid break, this little kid, like a glider, and come smoothly, arcingly down, like a little brown bird, resting on the big wind of the mellow tenor swinging.

And then they met each other, this bucked-toothed kid and the little one, feet flashing in tempered time, like little lights in the daytime. This time, Ned did gasp, for it seemed as though they, infra-red in the glow of the sun and the happy, joyous music, had moved inexorably together, face to face, and then had seemed to pass right through each other, as though the music were, for them and everyone who watched them, a fifth dimension, where all things, and man especially, were indeed possible.

The street, the day, the air, was all left charged by their going. It seemed somehow criminal that they had to go, that the music had to end. It was like seeing something supernatural and being blessed by it.

Reality was slow in getting back to him. Still enchanted, he went to the back of the shop and lighted a joint, and turned the fan on his desk to swinging round, blasting away the smell of weed.

It was his first joint of the day, the one that always seems to feel the best. It – the taste of it – made his nose well inwardly around the sinuses. The green glow was lavender-like on his tongue. The inner sides of his jaws began to feel warm and, as the first flush of highness got through to his brain, were victims of a triggered flow of new saliva. And he sucked in on them. The taste of Weed now began to feel thick in his mouth. It burned unevenly as he smoked, and he knew that it was old stuff, stuff picked a year ago maybe, part of a pile the grower and his wholesaler probably had a hard time getting across the border to Texas or California, or maybe up through Louisiana. But age had mellowed it, and he thanked God for the slow operation of the underground.

The fan hummed away on the outer reaches of his consciousness. The smell of weed had exploded in his head. Breathless, and excited, for a moment, he felt the slowing of blood to his brain, and the vacuum that feeling suddenly left, as though he had fell, like the kid, into a pit of something, but that he plummeted instead of gliding, and that he physically crashed and was instantly one with pain, good, glowing pain.

Ned savored the feeling until it was too delicious, and he had to release it or die. He settled his rear on the table, unable to take another drag on the joint, breathless. He looked at the little thing, a quarter of an inch still, in the grip of his forefinger and thumb. It was colored with a brown-yellowish Reefer stain that was a particular kind of nicotine, and above it was that gray, circular ash, that sometimes stuck onto the red coal for a long time, and sometimes disintegrated like dust when least expected. At the blunted smoking tip, he could see two strands of green weed, wet with saliva from his pulling inward, and a little warm with the heat of Pot burning, which burns, sometimes, faster than a cigarette, sometimes much slower. This was the slow kind of marijuana that puts itself out when not in use.

The joint had gone out. But when Ned lit it again, it was like an enemy, not smooth like it should have been, and he was only able to get a few drags from it before he put it out again, mashing the coal down on the table top. A little of the coal squashed outward and got into the print ridges of his thumb; it burned like a fire of purge.

Ned cursed.

He felt good, but the stinging in his thumb reminded him of marijuana's evilness, too. He got up, feeling like some music. He found an album by Yusef Lateef and Donald Byrd, tenor and trumpet, two other Detroit boys.

As he came out with the record to the front, Ruckson came in the front door. He sniffed, eyes widening in his small skull under the short brim of his black flat-top, and he shook his black head at Ned.

'Man, you can almost smell that on the street. You oughta watch out during business hours,' he said.

'I'm careful enough,' Ned said.

Ruckson was sharp today, Ned could see, especially in his dress. Ned guessed he was going out of the city, a dapper little black satchel of connections, and destruction too, when you came right down to it.

Ruckson's two-colored lips of pink and black combined, pursed like a third orbless eye at Ned.

'I'm rememberin the first time I met you, kid, at Ernie's.'

'That wasn't so long ago,' Ned said.

'I dug you to be righteous and a kid who knows a little somethin,' Ruckson now said in a buzzing voice. 'That's why I made myself known to you.'

Ned turned away in growing agitation. 'Awright! What are you gonna do, preach to me?'

'I just don't wanna see you hurt up, kid. It's easy to get hurt. You know how the game is. You been around. A small town like this, you'll get your throat cut by bein careless.' He came over to the counter. 'You know what I mean, Ned.'

'Yeah, I know what you mean.'

He laid the piece by Lateef and Byrd onto the plate, and set the neeedle in the groove. The shop thundered with a hiatus of young music.

He didn't know why, but Ruckson worried him. Looking at him now, Ned felt like a man dissected by the tiny eyes. Only once in a while had he met people like Ruckson, those people who, through what it is they are made of or what it is they think, are able to look into other people, as though they are soul-searchers for God.

Perhaps the feeling was accentuated by Boo, but Ned could swear that this was so. He tried to keep Wanda out of his thoughts and at the same time look Ruckson squarely in the face, but this was useless, for his eyes strayed from Ruckson's eyes and crawled with their gaze along the bony ridges of upper cheekbone, and a little scar under the eye that Ned had never noticed before.

'Listen,' he told Ruckson, 'I don't have no dough today; I can't pay you for the B. You'll have to wait on me.'

'That's okay,' Ruckson said, and his voice approached croaky proportions: somehow this was a part of him, the voice changing with everything he said, whole sentences, and sometimes just words, like an Oriental speaking new-learned English. 'I know you're a right kind of fella, Ned. One of these days you'll be sittin on top of the world, and you'll remember old Ruckson. That's *all* I ask.'

'Sure,' Ned said, 'I'll hang you up just like a suit, in mothballs, and I'll take you out some day and think about you.'

'You really touchy today, kid. What's the beef?'

'I don't have any.'

'C'mon, don't pull my leg. Who else you got to talk to outside of me?'

'I just feel kind of drugged today, don't ask me why. I guess that's all it is.'

'What have you been doin for yourself?'

'Same old thing, tryin to make some dough.'

'Shop doin okay?'

'I'll manage,' Ned told him.

Ruckson rubbed his chin, lighted a cigarette, and looked at Ned. 'I just wondered how things were going with you, since they were goin with me so well. Man, I'm gettin closer and closer to that pad in San Francisco, right downtown, with Chinese broads for serving girls.'

'You'll get it, man, I know you will.'

Ruckson tilted his head at Ned. 'You know one thing, Ned boy, you're the first guy I ever really liked. I mean liked. Because I never had no dubs or buddies, real guys to talk to, and here I am fifty and more – much more.'

Ned laughed and listened to the music.

'Maybe you think this is bull,' Ruckson said, 'but it's the truth, Ned. You're ... man, I don't know how to describe you. You're like me being friends with a nice guy who is dead.'

'Dead?'

'No, no, man, you don't get me. Yeah, you're dead, but not *dead*. Do you get me?'

'Hell no,' Ned said.

Ruckson spread his long fingers. 'Ned, you're like a painting. Like somethin done a long time ago, like in Paris, where I did some time after the first War. Or like in a cave I seen there in France.'

'A cave? Ruck, you're making so much noise I can't hear the music.'

'C'est la vive,' Ruckson said in a high, piquant French voice that made his black stature seem foreign, other-worldly.

'Don't give me that,' Ned said. 'Just give me one good reason why you're here.'

'To see the beauty of you, boy,' Ruckson grinned, 'and to ease your jeans a bit.'

'How?'

'Don't tell me you don't need some money?'

'Sure, I need some money. Where's it comin from? Are you gonna loan me, say twenty, for a couple weeks? Or fifty would be better.' Ned was laughing now.

Ruckson turned around in a quick half circle. 'You don't believe me, I can see. Take it easy, Ned,' he said in parting.

'Hey, wait a minute,' Ned called out. 'Let me hear some more of this.'

'You really interested?'

'If you're not kiddin, you know goddamn well I am. I could use some bread right now.'

'I thought you might be able to.' Ruckson came back over and stood in front of him, and his eyes watched Ned for a long time, looking into him with an X-ray force; made Ned listen for the close of the Lateef-Byrd piece.

'Somethin's worryin ya,' Ruckson said, looking close.

'No,' Ned told him, surprised that Ruckson said what he was thinking, 'nothing's bothering me.'

'Is it Doris?'

Ned almost raised his voice. 'No, it's not Doris. I told you it wasn't anything.'

Ruckson's voice changed to a deep basso. 'It must be Wanda, then.'

The record ended. Ned put on some Stan Kenton.

'I've got a picture of Doris,' Ruckson said.

'You always got pictures of people. They don't mean anything.'

'No, listen, give this a hearing. Doris is an oyster who's growin into a clam and you're a pearl diver. One day you steal that little bit of grit of a marble from her, and there's nothing she can do about it. But she gets another grit, and starts to makin of it, and she starts to grow at the same time, until she's round and big, big as an airplane tire.'

'I don't want to hear it,' Ned told him.

'Of course you don't.'

'What happens then?' Like all of Ruckson's 'pictures', Ned couldn't wait to see the last of it.

'After she gets big as an airplane tire?'

'Yeah, that big.'

Ruckson closed his tiny eyes and pursed his lips again. 'She goes crunch on your leg when you come back to steal that other grit; she's waitin on you, and her big mouth goes crunch on your leg so you can't get away. She holds you there while yer runnin out of breath.'

'I don't know how to swim.'

'That's okay, it doesn't make no difference,' Ruckson grinned. 'I just wanted you to see that picture I had.'

'You were talkin about money,' Ned reminded him.

'I wasn't kiddin. You can pick up three hundred Thursday night, if you feel like you can.'

Ned saw three hundred-dollar bills in his mind. 'That much? What would I have to do?'

Ruckson waited, then said, 'Make my run for me, to Detroit.'

'Why can't you make it?'

'The local fuzz is watchin me, for some reason.'

'How much is goin?'

'Six pounds – fifty bucks for each one, Mexicali Green – and a can for yourself when you get back here.'

Ned waited, thinking, and the loud brass clashed against him from the turntable, making it difficult for him to examine all the angles.

But this much he did know, and that was Wanda, and the things she had said to him, and the violation of his lover's body which had until now seemed of little importance, that he had to end some way.

Why this intense thinking like a square, he didn't know. Wanda had been doing it for most of her life, and it was a certainty that no one could take anything from her now. Yet just thinking of her there beneath some man's body in her green-lit room was enough to make the world turn, or simply stop altogether.

He jerked at the touch of Ruckson's eyes on him, as though the little man were reading his mind. No, he wasn't able to see it. This new thing in Ned Land, this questing pain unsatisfied that he had to sate. No one else but Wanda knew it, and he was *sure* that she knew it.

It was like a dream come suddenly true. All the while he had had Wanda, he had never had her at all: and now he had her in truth. It was too much for any one man, and he wished that he were two, so that he could really feel the joy that needed two of him to express itself.

'What time Thursday?' he said.

'You could catch the 10:20 P.M. to Detroit. I could see you a little while before and give you what you need to have.'

'When would I get the three hundred?'

'When you get back here. I'll take care of tickets and everything.'

'Where would I meet you?'

'At Pancho's place. If me and him ain't there, Velma'll take care of you.'

'Can I have some time to think it over?'

'Sure, but today is Tuesday. You'll have to think fast, kid. I gotta know by Thursday mornin.'

'I'll let you know by then.'

Ruckson turned to go. 'Don't worry; it's all safe. You know *I* know, man: Look how close I am to that spot in Frisco. Chinese girls and a waterpipe full of weed. Think it over, Ned. The only thing, sometimes a man thinks himself out of safety, you know what I mean? He gets a big break, a chance to do somethin for himself, and he thinks himself out of it. This is a chance for you, kid.'

'I'll think it over,' Ned told him.

'How are ya fixed for weed?' Ruckson grinned at him.

'I'm okay till tomorrow.'

The little man took a little packet from his coat pocket, cellophane, and Ned could see the Reefer within. 'Pay me later — or better, take this on account.'

'I still haven't decided yet,' Ned warned him.

'S'okay. I won't lose nothin. Well, I'll see you later, kid. I'm on my way downtown to price one of Caddy's Eldorados.'

'I personally go for Thunderbird this year.'

Ruckson guffawed. 'May the Lord give it to ya! So long, Ned.'

'Bye, Ruck.'

And it was just possible that Ruckson wasn't lying, that he was on his way downtown to buy a Cadillac. You could never tell about a guy like that. Why else was he so sharp?

Ned put the Reefer in his pants pocket, exulting at the feel of it and what might be possible because of it.

Just as he was turning around, Doris came in the shop. Her face was blanched and a little frightful.

'Hello, Ned.'

He waited, half-turning to her.

'Just thought I'd stop by,' she said.

'Well, how are ya?'

'I'm okay.'

'How's the kid?'

She smiled a little. 'He's okay. He's the reason I came over.'

'What is it? Are you goin back to Detroit?'

'No, not yet,' she let him know. 'I planned to stay for a while. Until after Thursday, at least.'

'What happens Thursday?'

'It's the kid's birthday,' she said.

'Eight years old, then! Doris, I didn't realize how long it had been.'

'Yeah, it's been eight years,' she said.

'Eight years,' Ned echoed.

'I was just thinkin, Ned . . .' Her eyes were high brown this morning, and she wore a brown cut mourning suit. 'I thought I'd come over and ask you.'

'Ask me what?'

'If you'd come – to David's birthday party.'

Ned turned away. 'The kid should be at school instead of some goddamned birthday party.'

'Well, we're goin right back this week.'

'He should still be in school; you shouldn't have brought him up here.'

She came around him, where her eyes could see his face, her slim, dim body over the counter, like Ruckson almost, and he almost said, Ruckson, why the hell don't you get away from here?

'Ned, will you come?' she said.

'Thursday?' he said.

'Thursday,' she replied.

He was aware that it was all like a conspiracy: Ruckson with his Gangster and Doris with the kid's birthday, and he remembered Wanda at the same time.

'I don't think I can make it,' he said.

'It'll be the last time for a while.' Her eyes pleaded at him. 'I can't come up here for a while. I won't be able to afford it.'

'That'll be just fine,' Ned said.

'. . . You don't know how happy I would be if you could come, Ned. You don't know.'

'I've made arrangements for Thursday night,' he said. 'You got to understand, Doris. I'd like to come, but can't we put it off for a while?'

'Till when, Ned?' she said. 'His *next* birthday? I'll be gone come Friday.'

'But I want to buy the kid some things.'

'You'll have today, and tomorrow, and the next day,' she told him.

She started away, but he reached over the counter and grasped her arm as she was going.

'You wait just a damn minute,' he said. 'You won't be able to blame this on me.'

'I'm not trying to blame you for anything.'

'Then why won't you understand?' he said. 'This is my son too, I love him. I don't care what you say to yourself, I love him, and you're not going to tear it up.'

'I'm not trying to.'

'Oh, hell yeah, you're trying to, but I won't let you, Doris. I'm telling you that.'

'Then you're coming to David's birthday party?'

The insidiousness of her got to Ned. 'No! No! I'm not coming!'

'That's all I wanted to know.'

'You wait! You listen to what I got to say!' he shouted at her. 'You're *tryin* to make David think I don't give a damn about him.'

'I'm not trying to do anything.'

'Oh, yes, you are, Doris, and I'm hip to you! I *can't* come, can't you understand that?'

Her eyes came upward, and he saw most of the white parts of her eyes. 'I saw Ruckson come out of here a few minutes ago. Ned, I know that reefer smell. Is that what you're givin up for David?'

184 | Clarence Cooper, Jr.

'I'm not givin up *anything* for David!' he said. 'That's what you don't try to understand. All you think about is gettin me, that's what you're tryin to plan. All you care about is *you*, Doris, and I know about you.'

'Thanks, Ned,' she said, going out. 'You know where I'm stayin. If things do turn out where you have a chance to stop in, stop in.'

She went out.

Ned was consumed by the heat of himself.

Three hundred dollars was what it would take, for him and Wanda. This was the chance, this was the bit that could free them both. With three hundred dollars, he and Wanda . . .

He compressed his thoughts.

Three hundred dollars, Ruckson had said. And for three hundred dollars he would give Doris . . . David, really.

Ned slowly shook his head without his knowing of it.

He put on something by Babs Gonzales, not really guessing what to do.

8

She began to die when the lights came on. Not really die, but dying anyway with that perpetual feeling of living death. She opened her mouth, lying there on the bed. The air was breathless and hot, sticking to her.

Lorraine came and knocked on the door, but she didn't answer.

'Wanda?' Lorraine said through the door.

She closed her mouth.

'Wanda?'

Another knock, then walking footsteps away and down the hall, and Wanda knew where she was going now.

The lights were from the outside, and green, like the one she now switched on in her room. Tuesday nights were easy. Usually they were, but it didn't seem to begin so easy this evening.

She came to the window and stared out on the street. As she looked across to Ned's shop, she had an almost overpowering desire for sexual intercourse. She had utterly no idea where it came from, and it wasn't a thing her mind was partial to at the moment. Still, the tingle was there, a little capsulated now by her thoughts, and she tried to defy the odd sensations.

She felt herself in a slip without any panties, and as she shifted before the window the silk of the slip caught in the contours of her bare body and was electrified by the contact. She felt an inner running of tiny feet under the flesh, in the blood, of her body. Her roundness, contacted, warmed, she felt that need again: that crazy need that held no sense and no real, *real* relief.

She turned away and felt herself below, with her fingertips. There were things to do in getting ready. Maybe the first man tonight, she thought – then knew that this would not be true, and she wouldn't be able to feel anything anyway. Ned came to her thoughts.

Oh, *why?* She couldn't understand.

Until him, everything had been centerpieced, like a fine table in a big fine room: she was just an adornment, that's what she was. And she had been content with that, until Ned, the sonofabitch, like he had been sent by someone . . .

She pressed her lips together and felt her breasts. The nipples were lax and tired, and so was the firmer flesh. She inhaled until her breasts spread out youngly over her ribcage. It wasn't bad at all, she thought, looking down. Thirty-four, and still that way about the chest. She wondered what Ned would think of her vanity.

Ned was twenty-seven.

She wouldn't let herself think of it. She wouldn't let it get any more involved. She wouldn't let it. She wouldn't think of this thing she had for him. She wouldn't recall the last thirty-four years, no, God, don't let her.

In the coming light of night, the furrows in her face were plainly seen in green. Mama started something playing on the stereo out front, blue and swinging, and Wanda knew the night had begun.

She tried not to think longer of Ned, but it did no good. He was everywhere about her, like a crime she was ashamed of.

She found her afternoon dress and got into it. She knew no one would notice. Maybe Ned, if he came by again tonight, but that would be the only one.

She put on short high red pumps, with a little flower at the heel of each, and she did her face and mouth. Like a fool, she thought of panties and Ned at the same time. She certainly did not need one, and she could never use the other. No, she would not let herself do this to herself. What could she ask of Ned? What could he ask of her?

She rolled her lips together and at the same time became the whore she was born to be. Her mind remembered the clients of Tuesday nights and those clients' movements and eccentricities, and she figured out the best way to hurry both. Her little fingertips moved mascara in the right place.

She turned before the mirror in the green light. Her hips were high and much rounder in the dress, and she wondered who would come from the convention at the hotel tonight. Perhaps no one, but there always seemed to be something different about a convention night, something that made her blood rush and boil and pull at her and tug where she had never been tugged before.

The sale.

Where did this feeling come from?

She smoothed her dress down and made her fingers feel the flesh underneath. Bouncy, like a little tennis ball, that's what someone said about her – and she knew now that she had been thinking Ned had said it, but it wasn't him, after all. It was someone named Danny, a long time ago; it was all misty, frosted, in her mind, and she was permitted to remember only those solid, icy fragments which her will could not destroy.

She liked to feel her life was made of single shots of rye, that it was to be consumed and altered, and that she should go along with anything. And now she was beginning to see that it wasn't like that at all, that there had to be some other plan.

Someone came and knocked again, and she knew this time it must be Mama.

'Girl?' a voice called out, and she knew for sure it was.

'In a minute,' she said.

She thought of thirty-four years of not knowing.

If Ned would only lift his head, he'd see how wrong it was, and then he could make it all impossible. Why had she acted the way she did? It seemed so irrevocable, so irresistibly did she yield to the thing she felt, like that feeling she had a moment ago which impelled her to copulate immediately.

She stood in front of her bed and lit a cigarette from her dressing table. The room began to close in on her, and she almost didn't know it at first. When it saw she was noticing, it stopped the moving inward.

She went back to the mirror and sat in front of it. She watched herself smoking the cigarette. And she thought of Danny.

Danny had been her mother's lover, fifteen years ago and more, in a place something like this – although they all seemed to be like this place, even since she was a little girl and found out quite early that men stuck it in women. Danny had been her mother's lover, she thought again, and perhaps if he hadn't been, she'd be something else right now, maybe even a woman with a husband and children.

Danny was her mother's lover, and sometimes she watched them loving – so professionally they did it – and she knew that Danny knew she was watching through the upstairs doors: when, knowing this, he became more ardent. Then it all became freakish, and her mother and Danny became freakish, their bodies, black and yellow, became a wet, cushy merging-in together that produced wild animal cries of passion and the fetid stink of bodies mating, squashed together, monstrously something other than what they were.

Sometimes they clashed, Mama and Danny, because she was too old for one thing, and she was becoming impotent for another, and Danny lusted after flesh – that was the other. Flesh that he could taste and know with his tongue, flesh that followed after him through the maze of countless animal delights he could devise.

She wondered, afterward, whether there had been other 'Dannies' for Lorraine and Denise and Terry; it seemed too easy for them to be the way they were. Mama was behind it all.

If it hadn't been for Mama's finding out, maybe she would have never guessed, then she wouldn't have been infuriated and vengeful, and she wouldn't have killed Danny . . .

Wanda felt herself jerk, because she hadn't been expecting to have that thought, and she looked around the room suspiciously, to see if anyone else had heard. She was alone, and yet she was not alone.

Kill. Kill.

No, but it hadn't been that way, Mama said so herself; she said it was an accident. Remember? Wanda came in, and she knew Mama had found out because of the way her eyes had swelled in her head and her hair was standing on end like a cat's and she was spitting, spitting her words out, and even as she slapped Wanda hard across the mouth, she screamed at her, 'I didn't *want* to hurt 'im – but you don't know why I just HADDA hit 'im! You don't know!'

Danny was her mother's man, that's what he was there on the floor of the place that looked a lot like this place and all the other places they had lived in, had whored in, had bled in, like monsters, mummies, on display, to be fingered and touched and entered.

She looked at her bedroom floor, and it was all she could do to squeeze the gasp from her voice. It seemed like . . . it looked like . . .

But here she was, herself again, the cigarette burning down in her fingers.

Mama blamed her for everything. She had found out what he had done to her, Wanda, and it was more the fury of jealousy than the indignant wrath of righteousness. Lorraine and Denise were already whores. It wasn't long before time ran out on her and Terry.

Mama said she would never forget it, and she never did, not yet, and that being almost sixteen years ago.

Wanda lowered her head, wondering how it had all happened. She could remember little of it, why she had to be like this right now. Slave of sale, slave of Mama, and now this new slavery to Ned Land – the worst kind.

She remembered the outline on the floor.

Mama said he was sick. That she took him to a hospital. They would take care of him and he would be all right in a while. But he wasn't coming back there, that sonofabitch. That dirty black bastard. That jelly-roller.

And her, Wanda, she was getting it right up the ass, like what Danny did. And she was going to hoe it. She was going to hump it. She owed it, and she was going to give it. She would never be free now if she ever had before.

Nobody ever saw him again.

And sometimes now, she caught that great black face watching her, as though it suspected that she knew what had actually happened after all, and as though it expected her to tell someone soon – and the fear that it would not be there to stop her.

Mama would never forget, and neither would Wanda.

She used to count the men at first, but then she got tired after ninety-something, and it had only taken a little while to get that far. They had a place in Brooklyn once, the time she thought she might get away with a fella whose name she couldn't even remember now – a fella something like Ned, but not *like* Ned, not what she felt for him. That time she hadn't cared, and she was full up and sick of a lot of old men – she was only using the fella. And Mama knew it all the time, but she didn't say a damned thing, not before or after. She was on an Ellington kick then, and all you could hear was '*Take The A Train*' all the time. Mama dared her and won out.

When the guy came to see her again, Lorraine told him Wanda didn't work there anymore, and she made the guy pay ten dollars for a lay so bad he never came back again.

That was when Denise decided to stay on in New York, when they thought of Pennsylvania for a while. Denise hated her, Wanda, for no reason at all, it seemed. She had promised Wanda when they were children, 'I'll kill you some day. Black bitch,' she could call her, for Denise was lighter, with raw bones like a hunky, 'I'll kill you some day.'

She could never understand about Denise. For no reason, she had wanted passionately to see her, Wanda, dead. From childhood, almost, since Denise was only a year older than her – she could remember their coming up together. Always, when she got a chance, she would hurt Wanda physically. Or maybe they *all* hurt her, she thought, going back over it. All her sisters.

But Denise more than the others, that she was sure of. Denise would jab her with a pin, just to see the blood run. No one else did that, not even Lorraine, who hated her too – not to see her blood that way and be glad because they were seeing it, the way Denise was glad.

It was so *unreal*, being a whore with sisters who were whores. Mama and all the others were dream figures – yes, even the men who would come tonight. It was a realization that she never had before, and it was caused by Ned Land, the painful reality of him. There had been reality in Danny, voluptuous, sucking, stinging reality – but nothing like this, this feeling of pure woman-breath that enveloped her and made her want for the warmth, the strength, the muskiness of a man's arms.

No, she could not bare this – this yearning for relief. She had to be satisfied, and in so many things she'd never even considered. But she could not afford the risk. Not for her –

she wasn't thinking about herself. But Ned, most of all. She felt guilty in taking this thing from him.

He was twenty-seven.

Wanda began to brush her hair. It was that thick, curly sort of stuff, black, with new grease, soft and warm, alive with depthness, slivering over her fingertips. She let her fingers stroke it and pile it, until it hovered over her face like a great black cloud, catching glimmers of the green light that looked like flashing lightning just beginning, in the mirror.

In a few years she would begin to sag. It wouldn't be like a woman who had borne a child, though Lord knew she had carried many tags of men within her. No, it would be another kind of aging – that which went on inwardly instead of outward. It would pull her down, toward the pit of herself, converging on her crotch, as though that mouth there would swallow everything eventually and make her a thing that had never existed at all. That would be the way in which she would be. And then, without her youth, and this death preceding, only then, would she be free.

She put down her brush. She turned her head about the room. Her eyes caught bits of light from the window by the street.

She couldn't wait that long.

She didn't dare wait – and at the same time, she didn't dare attempt to make it any other way. What could they count on, her and Ned? Thirty-four lost years? What would he eventually think of her? How much would he hate her then?

She checked her packaged syringe in her bottom drawer and looked to see how far the night had advanced. A tension rose within her.

She had never believed in God before, not really being able to. But now she prayed with all her heart that God would find a way out for her. For them.

Her hands clenched together on her dressertop.

He needs me, and I need him, that's what it means, even more than life, and please, God, bless us.

She began to cry a little, and she felt good because of it, because crying was something she hadn't done since the last time Denise stuck her with a pin.

Wanda rose again and felt her body. It was a good body. It needed a man like Ned to tell it it was a good body. It needed him to manipulate it with that queer hunger he had, to suck its breasts like a little child, and enter it with fear like a crushing Bunyan through the forests. She felt her body thrill a little bit. She paced across, slowly and wiggly on high heels, her body trembling with her movement. She tasted a tobacco chip in her mouth, and she blew it out with a quick neat sputter. She found her pack and lighted another one.

The promises she made to him, and he to her: too much was all they said and couldn't fulfill.

But didn't she deserve a chance, despite all else? Even if it meant Ned would destroy himself because of her, sooner or later? She wouldn't have to love him at all, to do that. She was caught, and she couldn't turn or cry out, snagged inexorably. She did love him, she knew that – if she could call this thing love: this tearing away at her insides as though she were a jungle animal being disemboweled by other jungle animals. Still alive while they were doing it. That's the way she felt.

She felt painted on a wall, like murals she had seen in some of the fine houses she had been within, with some of the many fine men who had done so many unfine, unmanly things to her – just something on the landscape that is alive but the artist and the viewer don't know. Just the pain of pain was unbearable.

That's what it was: her being torn away from it all by Ned Land, and him not caring how much he hurt her in his tearing: her screaming with the pleasure of it all the while.

Mama turned up the volume from the outside, and the music came uninvited into her room, filtering through her with jazzy obnoxiousness.

She caught herself waiting and praying. She called herself the most nasty thing she could think of, but she was glad that the name was probably the sort of woman she was. That sort of a girl with Danny. A piece of murder. A stain of blood on the rug somewhere.

How *could* she justify herself to Ned?

Thirty-four.

She twisted around, the cheek of her palm coming against

her hip, trying to reassure her. She was flesh, and warm, flowing blood from a hurt wound. She had a right to own herself for a while. Mama didn't matter – none of them. Not even the sale mattered.

She puffed out smoke from the cigarette. Again she felt her mind whirling, and she set out to defeat its effect. She leaned against the iron railing of the bed, holding the cigarette down so the smoke wouldn't get into her eyes. But it was still there. She came forward quickly to the door, feeling herself wiggle on the high heels. Still, her mouth felt dry, and she went back to put on fresh lipstick.

She wasn't strong enough. Could she *be* strong enough? Maybe she could raise her head this time, stop drowning like she had been, look up and see a light that wasn't green or red.

That's what she had to do – but still she felt too weak.

It would take Ned, and she did not know if he was strong enough. Not yet. Maybe she would never know.

The music ended and a man's voice came to her from the outside. She waited, but her heart seemed to lodge in her throat and she had to cough. The music started again, but still no one came. She hoped it was Ned, and in a way she hoped it wasn't. He would only trouble her tonight.

She thought perhaps it might be Cullen – he would be the only one to come this early. But still no knock. She heard someone move over her in Carla's room, a sickly moving about. Wanda had been able to see it in her eyes lately, a giving up to death. Carla was a loathsome thing like that.

The man had wanted someone else. Wanda began to breathe again. Some of them got to you, early like this in the evening. And then you found it hard all night. She wasn't prepared, and it was so important that she should be.

Another record clopped down on the turntable from the outside. This was one she particularly liked, Billy Eckstine and a band that sounded like Sauter-Finegan. She listened to the velvet voice, so deeply precise and imploring, but it could not keep out the vibrato of pretentiousness.

Wanda went over to look out the window and see the clock in the window of the pawnshop across the street. Ned's place was still open. Eight-thirty, and the night becoming blacker.

Where was she going from here? She had to make up her mind to that, sooner or later. With Ned? – thirty-four, and with Ned? It was a bet with the odds against her. She could *make* him love her, if he didn't already. She knew how to treat him, she knew how to touch that tender, responding thing in him: she could find it writhing like a little nerve end and fondle it and squeeze it until he knew that he was a man and nothing else. That she could do, and this much nature and life had given her an ability to do. But when she began to change and he saw it, when he became used to her and knew the days on which her menstrual cycle would begin and end – with that familiarity, and the passing of years – what could she do to keep from dying?

Especially when the cycle stopped?

These things she would never know. This was her gamble. This was her chance to do something right for a change, and not worry what Mama *had* done that night.

The knock sounded. She knew she could put it off no longer.

She went over and opened the door. Lorraine stood there, her face freshly painted.

'Ned's here,' she said.

'Thanks,' Wanda said, but Lorraine didn't go away.

'I'd sure like to know what it is you do to Ned,' Lorraine said in a soft voice.

She came past Lorraine into the hall.

She was becoming more and more afraid of Lorraine.

She walked quickly to the living room. The stereo blasted out mad, inventive music.

The first thing she saw was the big, black, grinning face of her mother.

And then she saw Ned.

9

David shifted on the kitchen couch. He had on new shoes his mother had bought. His hair was combed and his mouth was clean. His eyes were bright and targetlike. He shifted again and scratched his leg. He watched his mother moving about the apartment. She set a dish down on the table, too close to the edge and almost where his birthday cake was.

Behind David's eyes, a thing began to work, a beautiful, childish thing of pleasure to come, of experimentation and spite at the same time, with a kid-like knowledge that two and two were four even if it didn't seem like they were. It circulated all about in him, like ring around the rosy, and it didn't feel bad, because it wasn't bad to him, not doing what he planned to do: he was what every child is, a careless motion, a comic action that reiterates itself because it is being forced through the groove of the thing that made it.

'David!' Doris shouted at him, but it was too late.

It was like vanilla flavor, the way he did it, creeping over to the table like that, on tiptoes so she wouldn't hear him, and, this way, on tiptoes, reaching out toward the table edge with his little fingers pointing, then, with a quick snip of his forefinger, flicking out against that dish set too close to the edge and almost where his birthday cake was.

He watched it fall. It flipped over itself twice before it hit the floor squarely. Then it smacked down, hard, cracking into two, then three, then, as his eyes watched it destroying itself against the hard floor, splinters of plate split into more splinters.

Of course he said it was an accident, but his mother knew he was lying, and so did he. She made him sit on the couch again, and he looked injured in a way that, under other circumstances, would have made his mother think he was being persecuted.

'I'm just like Christ,' he said to her, pouting across the room.

'What are you sayin?' she said at him angrily, trying to get the plate up from the floor.

'I said I'm just like Christ. That's what Grandmommie said. Christ was crucified on the cross for something he didn't do on purpose, too.'

'David,' Doris said, 'I'm just a few seconds away from whippin your ass. Now you just keep quiet after what you've done.'

'I bet you wouldn't say that if we was home in Grand-mommie's house,' he said. 'You'd be scared then to blame me for something I didn't do on purpose.'

Doris started to say something but David began to sing a song he had learned in school and could sing so well in class, where he would like to be right now because he liked his white-skinned teacher so much, so much better than his mother. And his voice rose an octave higher than she could make hers go, with the singing school words, and he drowned her out: it was like a siren screeching out in a black sky, even worse than that in the small apartment.

'David! You shut your mouth!' Doris hollered at him.

'Granddaddy sings at home. Why can't I sing?'

'Because I'm tellin you to shut up, David, and if you don't, I'm going to beat your little ass until it's red. I've gone to the end of my rope with you. You're not at home now.'

'You sing sometimes,' David said. 'Why can't I?'

'Because I'm your mother and I say you can't. Your Grandmommie can't protect you here.'

'I wish we were at Grandmommie's house,' David said wistfully. 'I don't like it here. I specially don't like him.'

He placed his feet on the floor, under the half-man new pants, the little cutaway coat above, turquoise was the almost color, and the three neat buttons with white thread. She was looking at him in that way she said he looked like his father sometimes, and her eyes were burning him, which made him know that she was thinking of him like that. But he could see something else, something that gave him a clue to what she really looked at, and he saw love and hate and resentment, felt it with his child's mind, and he knew as always that there wasn't anything she could make herself do to him right then.

He bent a head that was shaped like a walnut and tapered toward the base of the neck. His hair was curly, but it lay curled close to his head, with a little widow's peak at the front. His forehead ballooned babyishly to a snub nose in the center of two round, selfish eyes. His small mouth puckered outward, open most of the time, with two big but beautiful white teeth. His chin was silent but stubborn.

David gnashed his teeth and made them talk squeakily, the two big ones against the lower ones, like the screaking machine his grandmother had that could sing 'Three Blind Mice' while it was washing; screak, screakee, skree.

Rising to empty the last bits of the plate into the trash basket, Doris watched him doing this. She watched for a long time. He saw her watching him, and that was what he wanted her to do. The screaking grew louder. She watched him. He saw when she got to the place she could stand it no longer, and he tensed, waiting for her. She came, and he saw her coming. She grabbed for him, but he dodged out of the way and ran into the only other room, the living and dining room. He ran around the furnished table, but she didn't follow him.

She said, 'David, come here.'

He screaked his teeth at her.

'David, I won't hurt you, baby.'

He screaked again.

'Come here, David. I'm going to tell your father.'

'He's not my father.' Another screak.

'David, don't do that. You know it makes mother's skin crawl.'

'I didn't mean to knock the old plate off,' he said. 'I apologized for it. I said it was an accident.'

'Sure, it was an accident, baby.'

'You just wanna spank me,' he said.

'No, I don't, David. I just want you to come here to mother and stop doing your teeth like that.'

'I haven't got any birthday presents.'

'Mother's got you some nice presents. Just come here, David.'

He made his teeth cry.

'You don't care anything about me,' he said. 'Nobody but

Grandmommie and Granddaddy do. That's who. That's why I know.'

He screaked his teeth.

'You said a nasty word,' he said. 'You said ass.'

'Come here to mother, David.'

'You said you would beat my little ass. You got to promise you won't.'

'I promise,' Doris said.

'I don't believe you; you tell stories.'

'I'm not tellin a story this time, baby.'

'If you do spank me,' David said, 'I hope you die.'

'Don't say things like that, David.'

'I wanna go home.'

'We're goin home, David. Come on out, now. C'mon, Dave baby.' He wouldn't. 'All right then.' She went back into the kitchen.

He lay his face against the furnished table top. It felt cool to his cheek. He stretched his hands out, palms down, and they felt cool, too. It felt like the sun had suddenly gone cool on the table. He warmed and spread against it, all of him, his face, his brain, his foot kicking up under the table. He became the table for a moment, with four big furnished legs, indestructible through all tenants and little boys with their faces against the finish, and their hands too, and a foot kicking up under the bottom.

'David, come on and eat,' his mother called.

He swung his foot and gnashed his teeth against the table top. He leaned the tip and side of his head against the table edge and began to trace it with his head, to the short flat slanted side, then around to the long side, walking slowly, until he was there at the door of the kitchen.

'I'll bring it out here, then,' his mother said.

He turned around and faced the other end, and slapped his hands down hard on the table, smacked them again, till they sounded like the horses' hooves on Grandmommie's TV. Kit-top kee-plop, kit-top kee-plop.

He wished he was a superman and he wished he had long hair like the kids on TV had. And a light skin too. And nothing but a Grandmommie and a Granddaddy, on a great big ranch, and a big six-shooter for him to shoot his mother and specially him.

That's what he wished.

He wished for it pretty hard, too.

'Now here's the cake,' his mother said, 'with eight pretty candles.'

He watched her coming in with it. She set it on the table, too close to the edge, he saw.

She looked like a good mother, but she wasn't. She looked pretty. She looked so something he didn't know how to think of. He moved around to the other side of the table, grinning back at her grin.

'Eight big candles,' he heard her say.

He screaked his teeth.

'Isn't it pretty, David?'

'I wanna go home.'

'Sit down in that chair, baby, until mother brings the chicken and other stuff in. I guess we'll have to start without your father.'

She went into the kitchen.

He watched her bending to look into the oven. Her dress came up a lot. He saw a lot of her. In the front she was nice, with her little breasts – but she wasn't in the back. It was like she wasn't being good. He thought about Jesus on the cross, being good.

His grandmother took him to a sanctified church, and grandfather went there too. They jumped around and sang. They ran all over. They were happy because of God. The trumpet said it, the guitar said it, the piano said it, the drums too.

'Grandmommie says we should love Jesus,' he said to his mother bending to look into the oven.

'Yeah, but Jesus don't love us,' Doris said wearily.

'Grandmommie said you gotta love Him.'

He knew his mother was getting mad again.

'I don't give a damn what your Grandmommie says, David.' She came back in. She grabbed him before he could get away. 'Now, I've got you! I'm gonna beat your ass, David.'

He struggled, but she held him, coming around to where

he was, and too late he saw the ironing cord she had detached from the iron on the board in the kitchen.

'You tell Jesus to keep you from getting your ass whipped good right now!' Doris said. 'You're too much for me, David. Of all the days I have to pick to show you I'm your mother and you're going to do what I say, it has to be on your birthday. But, David, this is *just right!*' She came down with the cord, and the electric pain coursed through his thigh and nice new suit. 'Can Jesus save you now?' Again, too hard this time, he felt the pain explode within his little flesh. 'Jesus never gave me what *I* wanted!' He began to scream; wildly, he lashed his arms and began to punch at her belly. But the cord never stopped, and he began to get frightened with the continuing pain. 'Your Grandmommie's not your mother, David – I am! If I have to beat that into you, then you're gonna get it!' Her fingers tired at the nape of his neck in the new suit, but David never did. She relaxed her fingers for a moment, and in that moment he was erupted from her and the cord and dashed free to the other side of the room.

'I hate you!' he cried wild words. 'You're a damn old witch and I hate you!'

She came around, and he came around the other way.

'I'm gonna tell Grandmommie about what you did, you fart you!'

'David!'

'That's what you are, just an old fart and a damn old witch!' he screamed. 'Grandmommie's gonna beat you up for this! Suppose she whipped you like that? Wait till we get home, I'm gonna make her do it to you, you fart! I don't want a fart to be my mother I wanna go home! I wanna go home! I hate you, I hate you, hatecha!' He started spitting at her, and a bit got on the hem of her dress.

A sound of music came into the room where they were, tentative and apologetic at first, then growing a little in purpose, till it was too big about them.

He saw her trembling with the cord still in her hand, and he sniffed a salty tear up his nose. He could see his nose was red by bending his head and looking down the little slope. He always got cross-eyed when he did that; he knew because he'd seen himself in the mirror a lot of times. He wished he had natural cross-eyes. Then he could look at people, and they'd be afraid because they wouldn't know whether he was looking at them or not, or whether he was going to do anything to them. He might be getting ready to kill them, and they wouldn't know because of the way his cross-eyes were looking.

He tried looking cross-eyes at his mother right now; he saw how strange her face looked when she saw he was looking at her like that with his eyes.

'David, you've got to understand somethin. I'm your mother, David. I had you; I made you, David. Your Grandmommie and Granddaddy, they don't count as much as I do.'

'They do to me,' he said.

'But they *don't*,' she said, while he watched the funny pain on her face that made it look crooked and ugly. 'I'm more than they are. They're just my mother and father. That's the only way they can be important to you, as *my* mother and father.'

He kept watching her cross-eyed.

'This is got to stop, David,' she said. 'For eight years you've had your run, just like Ned, and I'll be damned if I stand for any more from both of you! I'm important! I don't care what you say or think, I'm as real as you and I'm as important as you, David – more than that – because if it wasn't for me you wouldn't even be here!'

'I wish you *hadn't* done it and made me, so I'd be here now!' He saw two faces begin to cry through his cross-eyes. 'Anyway, Grandmommie says an elephant brought me to her house.'

'That's just the same old lie like the lies she tells about Jesus,' Doris snorted.

'Jesus didn't tell lies.'

'Maybe He didn't, but your Grandmommie does.'

He uncrossed his eyes and took a testing stance toward where she stood by the table. 'When are we going home, Mommie?' He knew he could maybe fool her if he said that.

He saw her eyeing him closely. 'David?'

'I wanna go home, Mommie, after the birthday party is over.'

'That's what we're gonna do, Davey. Tomorrow, we're goin home. Will you please try to wait till then?'

'Okay. I'll wait.'

He could see she was still unsure, but she went and sat down anyway, and he came around with confidence and sat in the chair next to her, while she began to fill their two plates, looking at him all the time she was doing it, as though he weren't really David at all. 'Chicken, honey?'

'Okay. And I want some potato chips and ice cream.'

'Not right now . . .'

'Grandmommie lets me,' he said.

'Well,' she said, 'all right,' and filled his plate.

They began to eat. The music, from outside the apartment somewhere, came through the window opened against the heat in the tiny rooms.

'Your father might stop by,' she said over a spoon of potato salad. 'I've got some cookies in the oven.'

'I don't want him to.'

'You like cinnamon cookies, don't you? Remember when I made some before?'

'Grandmommie makes the other kind that I like better.'

'You'll like these, David.'

'And I don't want him to.'

'He might bring you a pretty present.'

'What kind of present?'

'I don't know, but suppose he did bring you one?'

'Well, maybe I'd let him stay for a few minutes but then he has to go home to his own home.'

'Will you be nice? You won't be like the day we stopped by his record shop?'

'Okay.'

'David?'

'Huh?'

'Baby, where did you learn words like that? You know — what you called me?'

'In school.'

'They're not nice words, David.'

'I know it. Everybody else says them.'

'Do you know what a fart is?'

'It's like breaking wind, like Granddaddy does sometimes.'

She had stopped eating, and he put himself on his guard.

'David baby, you mustn't use those words, I don't care whether everybody else does say 'em; they're dirty, and I don't ever wanna hear you say 'em again, and if you ever call me anything like that again, David, I'm gonna try to beat your living brains out!'

'Your boyfriend said somethin worse; I heard him say it myself. If he can say it, why can't I?'

'When did you hear Jack say anything like that?'

'At Grandmommie's house,' he blahhed at her. 'Grandmommie and Granddaddy were gone to the show and you thought I was 'sleep, but I heard him ask you why didn't you give him some before they came back.'

She stood up from the table like something had sprung her up, like a Jack-in-a-ball that he used to call Jack like her boyfriend, that Grandmommie bought for him one time. 'You!' she shouted at him.

He moved out of her reach. 'And I watched you while you did it, too!'

He made his eyes cross-eyed and screaked his teeth at the same time. She became four zig-zaggy people in his sight. The music from the outside swelled around them again. He dragged his plate away from hers and took a potato chip with cross-eyes, which was quite a feat, since there were so many of them to choose from.

His mother couldn't say anything, he knew, because he knew she knew he was right, and had heard Jack say that, then she probably remembered that if he had saw that, he saw what she had to do with that man, with her legs all split open and like a bear's face deep within, and he even saw pink colors, which had terrified him the most.

But what he saw then: he knew she didn't want to be thinking that he saw the way they did it, almost like two dogs he had seen do it before, but not from the front like that, the dogs, which made them have to look into each other's face like that, and see the ugliness of each other's face. It didn't seem possible, the way they did it, and, as David had watched, only the movements of the half-naked bodies meant anything. They had stopped almost right away after they started. David had wondered why anything so important to the two of them should end so quickly: it should go on for a long time, he had thought.

And that's what doing it was, and this time he wasn't telling a story, for he knew what it was his mother had that Jack had wanted. And even the man, his father, wanted. That's why he didn't want him to come, to take what she had to give again. That's why he was screaking his teeth now and looking cross-eyed and munching a potato chip all at the same time.

His mother couldn't say anything.

The music got louder, someone's fingers turning it up.

A knock sounded on the door, and Doris jerked her head. She went quickly past him to the door. He had to uncross his eyes now to turn and look. He still ate potato chips. He saw the door open and the man standing there, the black man, him, blacker than David, with something in a package under his arm. He looked funny with an open white shirt and the top half of a suit. David didn't like him. He didn't like the way his eyes looked at him, sometimes all blank and guilty-like and red-flecked white in his black face. He didn't like his mouth that opened, like David's own, showing two big teeth, and the way the mouth always looked as though it were going to say something. He didn't like it. He didn't like it because this was his father, because he *had* to be his father coming here this way, even though David didn't want him to be – and there was a something like jealousy in his big eyes as he watched the look on his mother's face and knew then *how* important she was.

His father came into the room, smiling uncertainly at him. 'Hi, kid.'

David didn't say anything. His mother was taking the package and his coat from his father. His father couldn't watch David all the time, and neither could his mother. He pushed an arm against the birthday cake, which sat too close to the edge anyway. It went over, flipping once, then plopped, candles and all, in pulpy destruction on the floor and he felt some of it gush against his new pants leg.

He looked up at them and their not-understanding faces.

'It was an accident,' he said.

10

The night had turned blacker than the inside of Ned Land's soul. He tried to walk faster, shamed with an unidentifiable demand on himself, impaled on two prongs of his own making. People were beginning to crowd the street, there were lights at the farthest end, but he paid no attention to this.

Too late he had seen the look on Doris' face when he had to go, when she saw that it was really no use – and that look had frightened him.

A cloud of black began to form in the outer sky. Little green, gray, red, silver lights of the little city worried him as he walked fast down the street.

Music from the *Three-Penny Opera* came to his ears. Then ahead of him he saw the man with the monkey and the box he wound. He was arguing with another old man as Ned approached. They looked Spanish, but the language they spoke, intertwined with familiar but distorted bits of English, was not.

'I'ma tellin you,' they said, and Ned watched their fingers waving in the air.

'Mysa nah,' said one, the one without the box, 'my dog, he eat you little man up!'

'No dogga, *any!* Pietro kill all; he kill all he meet!'

'Hah!' the other said. 'We bet!'

'Bet! Bet!'

'Bet!'

Better than living and doing nothing, Ned thought, better than anything else. Better, as he walked ahead, thinking of what he had to do.

He passed the park and lighted a joint. He had finished it, and made a roach in a cigarette, before he got to the other end. He met a patrolman, swinging his stick, doing tricks to amuse himself. Ned went on through the night, to where he had to go, with not much time left.

The walls of the buildings grouped up against him. He

squeezed his way between them, and sometimes they had begun to close on him before he got fully through the little spaces. The weed was doing this, making everything seem smaller than it was.

He was almost crushed by a laundry truck, with two grinning eyes in the night.

The buildings rushed by him.

His feet touched the other side of the street, and he looked up at the sign. He hesitated, coming down from the other side of the street. Across from the Brazilian's apartment.

He felt funny here every time he came, and the only other times he had come, two, were with Ruckson. His foot touched the curb edge.

It was Velma more than anything else. That way she looked at him. That way she stood sometimes. That way she raised her eyes and mocked him. And it was the whiteness of her and the foreignness, that was the other thing. And him trying to deny he wanted her.

Until Wanda, women had tired him out, dragged him down, sucked his blood; they were sucking orifices with lower and higher degrees of inner warmth. If he began an act with one, she usually ended it. Yes, this was the way it should be. Until Wanda.

Ned stood outside and sucked on another joint, since no one was coming. He was beginning to get afraid. If it wasn't for what he *had to* do, he wouldn't be. He looked around and turned, a nightlike thing in the night, then raised his head and turned his eyes toward the blackening sky, then down upon the lighted shades and windows of the upstairs room.

He stepped into the street. A car tried to kill him. His hands were sweating, and his heartbeat tight. He tried to rinse his mind of fear and desire for the unknown. I've got to be strong, he thought through the high winds of weed.

That kid was something else. He hated the little snot until he realized that he was hating himself, himself inside that kid. He hated Doris, that's who he hated, for even bringing him here.

But he stopped, and here a different feeling came on.

He wondered what would happen if he didn't go up to

the Brazilian's apartment and pick up the stuff and went to Detroit and come back and got three hundred dollars so him and Wanda could get away.

It was something to think about, and although he didn't want to, he had to endure the pain of such a thinking. What if it didn't come out that way? What if he went back to Doris and took that kid and began to whip that kid's ass the way it should be whipped? Should have been whipped a long time ago? And try to do something else, maybe?

Like what?

... Like thinking of Wanda now, and the other woman above, and knowing that they both had something to give him.

He went through the apartment doors and took the self-service elevator. The elevator was quiet, and the place was nice. He waited while the machine made the box rise, and it seemed he rose twice as high because of the Pot and how high he was.

It stopped, and the doors clicked open and Ned Land came out. The floors were padded and soft with a very old carpet, and the corridors were quiet and warm. Maracas shook from inside the room he approached.

He raised his fist and let the knuckles fall twice. It took a year for the door to open. A night-latch chain divided her face: Ned could see the upper hazel of eyes and a careless, all-night bush of black above the white forehead. Below, there was no mouth; it was in shadow. But a pip of light shone on her nose, smooth, like alabaster. The upper part of her bosom through the door watched him with a straight-up smile; it told of Velma's heaviness.

He nodded his head.

The door opened, and he came in behind Velma in a spangled black thing, off the shoulders, that made her look too wide on small legs and stilted heels.

'C'mon in and have a seat,' she said, ahead of him.

He closed the door. 'Ruckson—' he started.

'He ain't here. He won't be back soon. He told me to tell you he'd see you after you got back.' She turned and smiled at him, and this time he could see her full red, laughing-at-him mouth. 'I'll take care of you, Ned.'

He didn't know how to feel, and Reefer, at that second, didn't let him. He began to see things that weren't there. He saw her smile at him in an inviting way that couldn't be. He saw her eyes lower, almost a wink – and that gesture she made toward the bottom part of him.

Ned knew he was higher than he should be. He sat in a little sitting room, just by the door, with web-footed Chilean rugs, while she went away. There was a big couch, and a console phono in the corner, from where the maracas and Cuban bongos swung out in slamming tempo.

He relaxed on the sea of the driving drums and imagined Africa for a moment, those thumping jungle sounds that, underneath the skin and blood, pulsed toward the heart and drove the body into black pits of horrors and the freedom of excruciating delights. He listened to the drums. The drums drove on. They spoke of John, a nameless jungle man, they spoke of John and his woman; they spoke of John and his children; they spoke of John and his dying; they spoke of John again, created in his own image.

The drums rolled and lubbed at him; they punched his flesh like fists.

The drums said Ned, Ned Land. Ned Ned Land Ned. Ned Land said no, because the power was too much all at once, and it was a thing that made him ashamed again, this heathen drumming, that aroused his own jungleness and pulled at the fiber of his body; pushed, crushed, against him, because Pot had served to make him aware of this kinship instantly, made him know that he was *not* removed, however much he thought he was. That this was the source of him, like an exposed nerve.

The drums beat, thudded, bombed away at him.

Velma came in like a white sacrifice. She held the package in her right hand, held it out to him, a virgin-like gesture that made Ned look her all over. The raciality of them was accented by the drums beating, accusing him, cajoling him into a sort of vengeance.

He had never had a white woman before. Of all the women he had had. Not Her. Not Her of the white and lusty thigh, of pink-tipped tit – not Her of What Every Woman Should Be.

He had known men who had, but not him.

He took the package, rising toward her.

'Wanna drink?' she said.

Ned looked at his watch. 'I've gotta be goin in a little while.'

'Ah, hell, don't be in such a rush,' Velma said. 'Have a drink.'

'Okay,' Ned said.

She went back out. Her butt was almost flat, but it bounced beneath, where he could almost feel his hands were. She turned at the doorway and looked at him as she went out.

Ned listened to the drums. It was as though they could help him know what to do; they gave him a strange sort of strength; they jogged him with their power.

Velma came back in with the drinks, with a drink for herself, and she was wiggling this time, barefoot, jiggling to the music as she came toward him.

'Here you go, honey,' she said, and handed him the drink.

Ned sipped and watched her spread up above him.

'You like that music?' she said. 'It's Pancho's. Doesn't it do somethin to ya?'

'Have you ever been in Brazil?' Ned asked.

She closed her eyes dreamily above her luscious lips. 'Brazil is nice, ya know, Ned? I like it. I dig it. Everybody's happy there. Sometimes I wonder why I'm here, ya know? When everybody's so happy there? It's a puzzle.'

'It's probably money,' Ned answered for her. 'A lot of it.'

'Pancho's got enough already,' she said in a lamenting voice. 'He ought to get out.'

A drumming thump brought blood to his ears, as though he had suddenly been struck with a folded fist. It even made him reel, then right himself, because he had to, to listen at it again – and again it struck his brain hard.

Velma danced barefoot.

'C'mon, Ned honey.' She stretched out a hand to him. 'Dance with me.'

Ned rose, illogically thinking how hateful the kid was, and went to her. But the way he went to her was not the way she had invited him, and Ned came to her a man aroused. And when she saw this, she laughed. He didn't know whether it was a laugh of derision or amusement. Whatever it was, she came against him and that part of him. With a thing like fear, he moved away from her. He knew how weak he was with the movement.

'Get that sirupyness,' she said, her eyes looking up at his mouth, her warm, fat flesh in his hands. 'It's like sirup, so smooth. My old man had a sirup farm in Canada, with big trees, Ned. Aw c'mon, Ned – dance. It's easy.'

Ned tried to dance with her.

'I like to dance with Negroes,' she said. 'They're not like white, or even Pancho, the way he dances. It's like dancing with an animal.'

Ned tensed against her.

'I don't mean like you think,' she said. 'It's another kind of being free. That's the way it is.'

She wiggled against him with the drums.

Don't, Ned almost said. But it was too late to stop her, and she began to explain what she was trying to say with her body. Her body said that they were two people listening to the father of Ned Land, and she was a white woman who had no business being this close to him *because* she was white.

Ned didn't know what made him frightened. He wasn't afraid of Pancho, that big-small man, and he didn't care what Ruckson would say, with his talk of 'the game', or what life ought to be.

The father of Ned Land said, Harken to woman. Listen to the drums crying, listen to the tale they tell of a thing that has happened a million times before, listen to the silver and gold of living.

'Pancho had a farm,' she said, in time with the drums. 'He used it to grow pot: that's how I met him: through a Chicago connection. He used to smoke his good green pot and make a couple of guitar boys and a little drummer kid play for him on the front porch.'

'I bet it was hot,' Ned said against her, his voice rising with the words.

'It was hot as hell,' she said. 'But it was *living*, Ned baby, you believe it. That's where I'd like to live all my life.'

Her eyelids seemed purpled yet flame-flecked. Ned's bold arm pulled her toward him, and she didn't try to stop him. She looked up at him, while the phono began to shriek.

'Want a joint?' she said.

'I'm already high.'

'Have another.'

She came away from him and went into the other room. Ned remained to weave with the compulsive sounds of the drums. He was a part of it now, and the longer he stayed here with Velma, the longer it would be before he did what he had to do. But somehow, this too was important above anything else. This he had to do and didn't know what it was. This that had something to do with Velma and the way she liked to dance with Negroes, and the way she laughed with derision, or amusement, at a part of him that was no laughing matter.

He waited for her return, beginning to sweat.

She came back in. It seemed the sounds of booming pressed her in toward him. Her head was high and her eyes were not a secret. She was an S mark on a map, which beckoned him, the unfamiliar driver, along the curves and indentations of its skeleton, taunted him with slopes he should take at thirty miles an hour and those that demanded his full foot on the gas. He drove down her mountainside, as white as snow, felt himself plunge over the bulging hillocks and skirt the belly button beneath a spangled forest, and catch a rounded rib at the bottom, then continue down around the rounded mound of joy and inception, then down to the triangle of life, the wooded area that hid the sky. He plummeted out of control down one long leg.

'Hava joint, Ned.'

He lighted up and escaped through the shadows of mist in his already-high.

He went over and sat down and smoked the joint. The record on the phono continued as though it would never end, growing in intensity. Velma danced alone, her body imperceptibly moving.

'You'd like Brazil,' she told Ned. 'You could pick your own pot, all free. Nobody bothers you, Ned. And the girls – there're some beautiful girls there.'

'There're some beautiful girls here.'

'Not brown-skinned and ripe like that,' she said. 'They'd make you think they'd burst if you touched them. Come dance, Ned.'

He rose again and felt her body in his hands.

'I've got to get on to Detroit,' he said. 'It's after nine.'

'Did Ruckson give you the ticket?'

'He stopped by the shop.'

'Then what's your hurry?' she said. 'You've got plenty time.'

'I've got another train trip to make tonight.'

'You're going away?'

'Ruckson and I have a partnership now. I think maybe I'll go to Detroit.'

She gave a half-serious squint. 'How do I know you'll come back from the first trip?'

'Trust me,' Ned smiled.

'Sure, Ned, I'll trust ya.'

It was at that moment that the drums did it. They made him do what he didn't want to do but had to do. He felt the forearm of his coat about her come toward him until she was there all the way, plastered with his strength, and he saw her mouth, and eyes, looking up at him, as though she had a mind to cry out.

The drums pushed them on in their steps. They roared and rumbled and sank and rose, and Ned and Velma were on each crest. The shoulder of her dress came down from the motion and exposed the topmost part of her breasts, with the grinning upward smile. Ned pulled her face into his throat, where it was smooth, and he could feel her forehead, hard and actual, a white thing under his black, against his black.

This seemed the endless end to him. Her body was his, with a resistance he could feel – really his, though he forced it to be. She was against him hard and soft, with her secret most parts, and yielding because he made her flesh yield.

The drums surged upward while he heard her say, 'Ned . . .' in a long way that held no sense, and for a moment he was allowed to look in on her indecision, the hurdle of a thousand years.

He wasn't strong enough, and yet, still knowing this, he grappled like a boa of insecurity about her. She began to lose her breath, but Ned lowered his mouth on hers, his mouth throbbing, tomming, to take her breath into himself rather than the air, where it would become nothing. In him, it became his name, and her flesh, and a thing of him that rose against her with a command. Not a thing of lust merely, but a thing of suppression set free that knew no bounds of reprisals. He made her feel him, made her feel the man of him.

She pulled away and yet could not pull away.

Ned lost his mind.

Behind her flat behind, his hands came down and grasped the all, the pit, of her. Ned Land became a cry of motion against her belly. She could not help but respond, because the plea was so human, and this was why she became warm and into him for a moment.

The drums rose and roared and thummed like an old man's death dirge.

Ned gasped and cried out softly. He made his hands come up and around her wide breasts in front. His fingers sunk into the soft meat.

Velma turned away from him, crying, 'You hurt, Ned,' but not in a hurt way, crumpling under him to the soft floor, where he still bent and held her breasts in both his hands, this sacrifice. She held her head straight up at him. Her eyes were clear, yet dulled with Reefer, and he saw her looking past him, to something else, and he had to turn because of it.

She pulled away.

His hands followed her and found her, and she said, 'The train, Ned, you're going to miss the train . . .'

And the words somehow released him. He felt his fingers rushing up her dress tail, and then the soft upper thigh, but further still, the moss bagful of warm hair and warm, lubricant flesh filling his hand.

'Ned . . .'

He kissed shut her mouth, because he was afraid she would say this was what he shouldn't do, or he was a nigger, or something like that; knowing he couldn't bear to hear this, not now, not after what he had done.

She pulled away and sucked her breath in.

Ned was like a man knowing his reason is gone and being unable to do anything about it. He pressed her body down against the floor.

'Ned . . .'

He pasted his mouth down against her throat, black lips against white skin, and traced it upward with his tongue, to her ear, and he heard her gasp because of the feeling. Her fingers pushed and pulled at him, and then they stopped.

She waited until he realized she was waiting.

When she sat up, she pushed down one round, white, red-tipped breast that had escaped outward from her dress and brassiere.

Ned's hands had gripped her wide, flat back.

It was a mistake, and he felt that he was glowing as red as the tip of her breast because of it. Velma's eyes looked up at him as she put herself together.

'Get off me, Ned baby,' she said.

He pulled himself from over her. He saw her laughing look again. She had been trying to make him do this – even through his high he saw this – but he didn't know why. She looked satisfied.

'Up, baby, huh?'

Ned dragged his last from over her. He got to his feet. She still lay there under him, white woman under black man. She smiled up at him, openly, like a snare.

'Boy, the things pot does to a guy,' she grinned up. 'I said I like to *dance* with Negroes, Ned baby.'

As he left, he heard her laughing softly, the drums dying.

He hurried toward the train station with his package, trying to escape a horrible ghost.

11

Going to Detroit. Going to Detroit.

He was too high.

Outside the train windows.

Mountains of passing things he couldn't tell whatthehell.

He still burned because of Velma, but he'd succeeded in shoving her away a little and trying to concentrate on what he had to do. But why had he got so high?

One thing Pot couldn't do was hide you. Sure, he knew better than that. That breathlessness it leaves you with. He tried to fill his lungs and found he couldn't, and he found that the other passengers seemed to be watching him: this was an illusion Pot always induced in him. He knew, really, that it was only his conscience working overtime and overhill and overunder every goddamn thing he'd ever been afraid of.

Going to Detroit. A place he last said he'd never return to, but here he was going again, and glad in a way that he was going now. He didn't know what it was, but there was something about Detroit, his home city, that held an attraction no other city had for him. No matter where the hell he went, what the hell he was doing he could never quite lose sight of the twisting streets, the boxy unobtrusiveness of the million buildings, the gray gladness of Friday, end of the working week, and Everyman, the way he rejoiced at its coming.

From the train windows, the tall expanse of countryside rose up like a long, black prehistoric animal, mired inextricably in potbellies of suburbs, townships, principalities and the rest. It wouldn't be long now.

And he was glad.

Glad more so by the simple fact that he was finally here, as though this was a trip he had planned and put away for many thousands of years, and that, finally, he had scrounged up the power to make it consummate at last, despite the horrors that may have been awaiting him.

'Michigan Central!' the conductor said, coming quickly

through the car. He said it as though it were the last place in the world, '*Michigan Central!*'

Ned winced with the words, for they were aegis of all he expected and all he could not possibly have way of knowing. He stood as the train slowed perceptibly. But, what he didn't know, was that they still had a long way to go before entering the terminal, and he was left standing there uselessly, like a tool of indefinite purpose, or a man with an ill deed in mind.

And then they were there, of course, and he had a legitimate reason to move down the aisle, glad that he'd thought to bring a small bag, anyway, so that no one would look in that funny way people looked when you did something that was out of the ordinary.

Outside, it bubbled. It couldn't help being turmoil and too many bodies, and he became a seething mash in the press as he made his way to the front of the huge terminal and the outside doors. A cab was waiting, and he got right in.

He gave the address. It was a place on Adelaide, right on the corner of Russell, an area in which he used to play as a child; this was the land of whores and pimps, and street hawkers with abundant notices of fresh limpid fish in the summertime – where playland was a condemned building and Aladdin a black peeking face somewhere in the rotting recesses.

Ned remembered this kind of spot well, particularly from the urgent perspective marijuana gave him.

It was late as he paid the cab driver and stood alone in the empty streets. He knew he had only a little while before his train left again for Westphalia, but he couldn't help reviewing a past life in darkness not quite dark enough and eyes that refused to forget.

Then he remembered Wanda, and his task. He had only one reason for being here now, looking at these ghosts, and it had seemed for a moment that he might become ensnared by them and unable to return.

He walked quickly down Adelaide Street, keeping his eyes turned from the vacant, empty hulls of buildings that now belonged to the City.

And he trembled as he almost heard:

'Hi, Ruth!'

'Hi, Sister Land . . . how you today?'

'My Ned's got a cold . . . cain't go to school . . .'

'Aw, hush, that boy's strong as nails.'

'Don't God wish it was ture, makin life so hard for us.'

'Don't blame God, Sister.'

'No, that's true.'

'That's true.'

'Got to give thanks for livin, at least.'

'And give God His due for yo little Ned Land . . .'

Ned Land was running when he reached the corner, heart thundering in his chest. He made his lips move over the number Ruckson had given him, made them shape the little vowels so that they seemed like pebbles in his frightened mouth.

The house was old, as he knew it would be. A two-storied dwelling, it had a gutted face and double entrances, for both the lower and upper apartments. Upstairs, where he had to go, a porch bellied out the entire length of the structure, and on the lower floor an old washtub hung near the windows, the upper sections of which were antique stained glass, so popular in construction during the turn of the century.

The steps cascaded down crookedly on either side. He went carefully up the ones to his left and knocked hard on the thick plate glass of the front door. For a long time nothing happened, but when he knocked again a light clicked on at the landing and, through the faded muslin curtains, he could see a heavy-set woman start a torturous journey downward.

'Yeah?' she said in a harsh frog's voice, opening the door.

'I'm here for Ruckson,' he said.

'Why didn't he come for hisself?'

'He said you'd know why if he couldn't make it this time.'

She stood for a moment longer, looking him over, then she swung the door open for him to enter. 'You got some money for me?'

'As soon as I take care of Ruckson's business,' Ned told him.

He followed her up the long steep stairs to the top, where they entered a large dining room, furnished haphazardly, it seemed, with discarded relics of past opulence, and a large dining table, where two women sat, one, the eldest, with her head on the butt of a palm, nodding, and the other anxiously intent on his face as he entered.

'Did you see the whore car when you come in?' she asked him.

'I didn't see any cars,' he said.

She licked her mouth. 'It's gettin so, everytime you catch a trick, you have to run five miles after you get the lay over. The goddamn police. The bastard police.'

Now Ned turned to the larger woman, a yellowish, staring rock with blue around the portholes of her wide, vein-scarred eyes. Her mouth was thin and whitey-like, he thought, and there was too much jaw on either side of her face.

'Gimme the cop money and sit down here at the table,' she told him in the same harsh voice.

Ned did as he was told. The big woman went to the rear of the house. He looked at the two women. The one who nodded had not yet opened her eyes, and he figured she had just copped a blow somewhere and could not help nodding under the powerful press of heroin.

The other woman turned on him, actually incorporating him in her problem. 'You gotta see how it is. Do you see? How can I turn a trick with the goddamn whore car runnin up and down all the alleys? But do you think Larue will care about that?'

She licked her mouth again and crossed her knees, suddenly noticing the abrased, dirty tops of them. 'Look at this . . . goddamn . . . *goddamn!* Do you know how I did this? Please, look, do you know how I did this? *Runnin* – running from the goddamn whore car!' He saw a vapor at the corner of her eye as she whirled on him. 'You know how much money I made tonight? Nine dollars for three fuggin tricks! But what can I tell Larue? I been busted twice already for accostin and the next time I fall I'll have to do a bit – but I can't tell him that. What am I supposed to do?'

Then Ned, still one in a realm of tricks, looked about the place and saw it was a trickhouse, where the whores brought their customers. The front room was dimly lit, but there was a rumpled one-sheeted bed there behind a pair of dirty curtains. The rest of the place, a hall he could see, housed doors and, he knew, many other beds like the one in front.

'It's like this,' the whore said, and for the first time he saw that her face was smooth and almost bright under the garish make-up, like someone's little sister playing at being a woman – but the eyes: they sent a thrill through him, for he became a part of their pleading with a certain knowledge. 'I've had Larue for five years. And I been good to him. He's drivin a Caddy, and there ain't many whores can say that – like that junkie bitch there. All she's got is a ten-year itch from usin stuff all day. But I been good to my Daddy, you know, baby? Three hundred a week ain't nothin for me to lay on him. That's why I wanna know why he don't understand. Oh, goddamn . . .' She became intent on her stockings again.

'Do you know what I mean?' she asked Ned pleadingly. He nodded.

'Five years, and it ain't ever been like this, not this kind of pressure on me, the kind of pressure he's puttin on me, and I never bitch with him about the other broads in the stable, because I know there's not one can touch me, and Larue knows it, too. So that's why I don't understand.'

The whore who nodded seemed to laugh in her sleep.

'What are you laughin at?' said the little sister whore, but the other did not reply, silent and still with head on hand.

'That goddamn junkie bitch is out of her mind,' the other said viciously. But not vicious, really, in a vicious way – more a spontaneous self-evaluation. 'I try to do my part, you know, baby? Do you know Ted or Nero? I mean, those pimps don't even touch Larue – it wasn't the stable put him on his feet that way, it was *me*. Do you understand? Baby, I been kickin mud for five years, I mean really kickin it, and it seems like he should have a little consideration for me!' She began to pout again at the ripped knees of her stockings.

Then, as Ned watched, her face softened and he knew her thoughts were lost to the reality of the moment.

'I know I won't have to suffer much longer. Larue said so. He said, right after I build this last grand. To the coast. I never been out of this fuggin city, you know that? I feel like I been cooped up all my life with nothin but tricks and next month's car note. But it's gonna be different. I deserve somethin, don't I?'

He watched her face return to normal, feeling a small chill as he witnessed the relapse.

'Let me tell you somethin,' she said, looking at him squarely. 'Do you know what's gonna happen to me?'

He shook his head.

'Do you realize one thing?' She nodded her head violently with the words. 'Larue's gonna beat my ass for the kind of money I bring in tonight. Is that fair? I ask you, goddamn it, is that fair? After five years? And all I done? You saw my knees – do you think I got that hangin out in some reefer pad all night?'

Ned was silent.

There was silence all about, only her eyes accusing him.

'It ain't fair!' she finally cried.

He wanted to reach across and touch her, but he stayed his hand for he knew it would be like touching dead flesh.

'It ain't fair!' She pounded her tiny fist against the table, then turned to cry for a moment into her clenched hands.

'Well . . .' she said, looking up, but didn't go on just then.

He turned his eyes to the blankness of a wall, not able to look at her any longer.

'Well,' she said, 'I guess I better get back out there for another hundred-yard dash. And you know one thing? Some of those same cops who run the hell out of me have been my best tricks! Ain't that somethin?' She made her eyes wide. 'Oh, I could tell you somethin about the way a cop turns a trick. It'd turn your stomach if I told you . . .'

The woman who nodded lifted her head to look around and mutter half-audibly:

'You don't know who's the biggest trick . . .'

'Whadyou say?' said the young whore.

'I said, the biggest trick is you, baby, and you just don't know it.'

'Why don't you shut up?'

''Cause the truth will set you free, even if you don't wanna hear it.'

The young whore looked impatiently over at Ned. 'Don't pay any attention to her.'

'You know why you're the biggest trick?' said the nodding

woman. ''Cause what you're buying don't even exist. At least the trick gets somethin for his money, but you, you whore, you don't get nothin but a promise from some bastard who only wants to work the livin shit outtya.'

'You shut up, you hear me?'

''Cause what? – 'cause I'm a junkie?'

'Yeah, 'cause you're a junkie, that's what, and *you* couldn't pimp a man if he was blind in both eyes and deaf and dumb besides.'

The other woman laughed, slowly, nodding again. 'I found the best pimp of all, baby – my senses. Just what your lucky Larue and all the rest found. When I whore, I whore for my habit; it don't need no Cadillac or pretty clothes.'

The young whore stood, slamming her hand against the table. 'You can't talk with your stinkin mouth! I'm just a whore for right now, just for a minute, and if there's anybody I can trust it's Larue. Now, who have you got? *What* have you got, you lousy bitch? You know what they say – once a junkie, always a junkie.'

'Yeah, honey, you're right,' the nodding whore said, blinking up. 'But here's somethin you didn't know: once you're a whore, that's all you'll ever be.'

The young whore stood speechless, then turned quickly and went out. Ned heard her hard heels clicking sharply on the ancient steps.

The nodding whore laughed, and began to nod again.

It was a while before the large woman returned, but she brought a package the size of a brick with her and handed it to Ned.

'Be careful,' she warned. 'It's hot around here.'

'I will.' He placed the package in the bag he'd brought along.

After he'd been let out, he looked up and down the street both ways, but he saw no sign of the young whore.

Then, as the mass of dead buildings closed in on him once more, he thought of what the nodding woman had said about there being no return from whoredom.

And he thought of Wanda, and wondered about the fiber of his resolve.

12

It hadn't taken Burris long to make his mind up, after talking with Cullen. There didn't seem to be any other way out of it, not with Coral acting the way she was.

He closed the shop tonight without stealing a bit of meat and walked down the main spread of street in the direction of Ernie's Bar. He knew she wouldn't be there, not this early. And, anyway, he wasn't coming. He wasn't coming for a long goddamn time, Burris'd see to that.

As he walked down the street, he made his long fingers, still blood-grimy from their work of the day, curl into big hard fists, thinking of Ned Land and wishing. Wishing. Wishing he could take a cleaver and not release it till Ned no longer had a head, like the carcasses on hooks in the freezer at the shop right now.

All because of her.

Prison had made him able to turn his eyes without the use of his head; this he did while he walked, pausing in thought only long enough to glance over at the warm lights of the record shop. But he wasn't there, not where he could see him through the windows. He felt his heart flutter a little.

Well . . .

It didn't make much difference which day Cullen did it on, but he sure as hell wanted that Land to be in his rightful place when it happened.

All because of Coral.

The night seemed to be warming up as he strode determinedly on, and a faint thin sweat rose up under his collar.

At the next corner, and to his right, he saw the neon flicker of Ernie's place and quickened his pace a bit.

The inside of Ernie's was a small obstacle course of matted table tops and too many people, but he saw her at the end of the bar, and she, expecting him, saw him immediately. Pushing through a group of laughing people. Burris went over to her where she sat.

'Hi,' she tried to smile.

He sat. 'Hi, Doris.'

The bartender, Ernie himself, a fat little yellow man with an all-business face, quickly made himself available. 'Hi, Burris?'

'I'm all right,' Burris said. 'Let me have a beer, huh? A Black Label – and give her what she's drinkin.'

'I'll have the same,' Doris let him know.

When Ernie went away, Doris said, not looking at him. 'Ned's givin the shop up, he told me tonight. So you don't have to worry.'

'How do you know for sure?' Burris said, suspicious.

'I had a party for my son, and he told me.'

'Maybe he was just lyin, just to make you think somethin while he does somethin else.'

'Ned don't lie,' she said, looking at him with sharp defensive eyes. 'He may do everything else, but he don't lie to me. If he goes away, you don't have to worry about your wife.'

Burris was thorough in the privacy of his thoughts before he answered again. 'I thought you told me you wanted to see him get what he's got comin, and that's what I wanna see, too. You don't know what he's done to me – how do you think I feel, a guy playin around with my wife. Don't you think a guy who plays around like your husband does is got somethin comin to him?'

'He's not my husband . . .'

'Well, he might as well be, and that's what he *should* be, and that's the main reason you should feel like I do about this thing. Look how he deserted you and your kid . . .'

Ernie returned with the beers, and Doris sat silent, sipping slowly from a long-stemmed glass.

'I think you give him more than enough time to act like a man about what he's done to you,' Burris said. 'It don't seem right to me that a man like that should put us in this kind of predicament.'

'Listen,' Doris said, eyes angry for a moment. 'It's all through. That's the way I feel. I've been tryin to make Ned see that for a long time – not through. But how I'd feel once it's over. You don't know how much he took from me, even before the baby, and how my people acted.'

'Drink your beer,' Burris said.

'Now he's goin away,' she said, sipping.

'How do I know he ain't comin back?'

'He said he wasn't comin back.'

'But how do I know?' Burris said. 'I got a lot of pain, too. All right, so I know she ain't no good; she's a bum bitch. But don't you look at me like that, because he's just as bad, and you know what I'm talkin about: he probably said he wasn't comin back just to make you think that so he could just keep right on goin with my old lady.'

Doris listened strangely quiet.

Burris shook his head. 'If we just let him go, just like that, what are we gonna get out of it, specially you? All these years, and he don't wanna act like a man and stand up to his responsibilities. I think that's a damn shame.' He shook his finger at her. 'He's gotta pay for it, Doris, you know that.'

'You mean,' she said, looking at him steadily, 'that we should hurt him.'

Burris shook his head quickly. 'No, I didn't mean that. What I'm sayin is, we should do somethin to make sure he don't hurt us anymore. We gotta insure ourselves. When you tell me he told you he was goin away, I know this is a damn lie.'

'I don't know,' she said in a defeated way. 'Maybe it is. Maybe it's all been a damn lie, right from the start – me tellin me about the way it should be. You know . . .' She set her glass down and began to trace rings of moisture on the bartop. 'For as long as I've known Ned, I been tryin to *make* him be my man. Ain't that funny?'

'No, it ain't so funny,' Burris said, thinking of Coral.

'Some people want a house, or new car, or clothes to make your eyes pop – but I've just wanted this one man. The night I met you, I guess I wanted him so bad I didn't know what to do. I ain't never wanted to hurt him – I just *wanted* him.'

'But he ain't wanted you . . .'

'I know that.'

'People like him, I know all about. They just go on,' Burris said, 'thinkin the whole world should kiss their tails, but they don't know when to stop – they don't think other people got feelins, and they don't care how much other people care about 'em. That's why somebody's got to stop 'em – not hurt 'em – just make them stop their hurtin.' He was silent for a while, then called Ernie over for a repeat.

'What do you want to do?' Doris said, in a voice that was suddenly resolute.

Burris waited until Ernie brought the beers and left. 'I want to let Detective Cullen take care of him.'

'What are you talkin about?'

'You know . . .'

'About what?'

'About the reefer he gets from Ruckson.'

'But then he'd have to go to jail!'

'Listen, how can we make sure any other way? He wouldn't get much time, and we'd both be sure about him, wouldn't we? See, I don't want to hurt your man – I could take him in my two hands and kill him. I just want him to leave my woman alone, and I want to help you. I gotta hunch: Guys at the poolroom tell me Ruckson's outta reefer. So he's gotta get some, and—'

'You think Ned . . . ?'

Burris became animated. 'Suppose he does it for Ruckson, or suppose Cullen finds him with some weed? You know what I mean? Like I say, I just got a hunch, but suppose we call a shot like that? He wouldn't get much time, and it'd make up for somethin, wouldn't it?'

'I don't know . . .'

'Look,' Burris said, and his face became a bit fierce. 'I think it's better if it did happen like that, because somethin's happenin to me that'd make me do somethin else that wouldn't be so pretty. You don't want him to get hurt?'

'No, please don't hurt him—'

'Then let me take care of this . . . I just want some peace, peace with Coral, and I can't have it with him here in Westphalia. You just let me take care of it.'

'You gotta promise he won't be hurt.'

'Just let me take care of the whole thing.'

Doris stood and smoothed her dress tightly down over her small breasts. 'Me and my son are leavin for Detroit tonight.' She stopped and her face was confused. 'Sometimes I feel like

I'm crazy, like somebody big arranged all this to happen to me. When I go home, I know I'll come back and . . . try to see him once before I go. I don't wanna talk to him or anything – I just wanna see him.'

'I'll take care of it,' Burris said.

She drank her beer with a sad flourish. 'I'll almost forget,' she said, and turned to make her way slowly through the doing-nothing crowd, which soon absorbed her from his view.

He sat and drank beers for the next thirty minutes, then finally stood himself and went out. At the corner, looking down to where he would have been unable to see a few yards further, he picked out Doris on the opposite side of the street from Ned's shop. He strained to see the lights in the front window of the place, then went on down the street till he came to a public phone. He stopped and dialed the number Cullen had given him.

'Yeah?' a police voice said.

'Let me speak to Mr Cullen.'

'This is Cullen.'

'This is Burris, Mr Cullen.'

'Burris – good boy. What's up?'

'Will you meet me in an hour, the corner on the south side, near the record shop? I got somethin to tell you.'

Cullen's voice was hesitant now, no longer brewing a police tone. 'Is it about what we talked about?'

'That's right.'

'Look here, are you sure?'

'Just meet me in an hour and I'll explain everything to you.'

'Okay,' Cullen said, 'I'll be there.'

Burris hung the phone up and started home, imagining an odious scent about his body that he had never smelled before or had not noticed: a fear smell that wavered in the night air and accusingly hung about him.

He turned off the main street and walked quickly downhill, the heavy business area composed of a block-long salt mine and two wheel bearing factories that had plunged their tails into the face of a small mountain. He crossed several railroad tracks, thin arms jutting out and into the black bottom of the night sky, to the other side of town.

His house was one of a string of others that embraced each other ineffectually, like a group of drunken old men, wobbly in their stance, three stories high. On the other side of the street pavement, wild bushes grew.

He stopped and looked up to the top floor of the place they lived in and saw a light was in the window.

She was home.

He suddenly felt weak as he opened the front door with the key on his ring and started up.

When he came in the tiny apartment, she stood in front of the dresser mirror, dressed in a tight sheath from last week's pay, applying lipstick and powder, oblivious of his entrance until he slammed the door.

'Oh, goddamn,' she said, 'do you have to scare the hell out of me everytime you come in?'

'Where're you goin?' he said, coming over to stare at her face in the mirror.

'Out.'

'You're not goin anywhere, Coral.'

'That's what you think.'

'No, that's what I mean,' he said. 'He's not gonna be waitin for you.'

'Who, Burris baby?'

'You know who I mean – the record shop man.'

She threw her lipstick on the dresser. 'Here we go.'

'He ain't ever gonna be waitin for you again.'

'Are you crazy?' she said, turning to him. 'You got record shop man on the brain, and it's eatin right through.'

'Take those goddamn clothes off, 'cause I mean what I say, Coral – you ain't goin out tonight, or any other night.'

She stood, eyes simmering. 'You get out of my way. I'm so goddamn tired of you, I don't know what to do.'

She tried to come around him, but he pushed her back to the chair in front of the mirror.

'You listen to me, Burris,' she said slowly. 'I'm gonna get the hell out of here tonight, one way or another. And I ain't gonna let you push me around, you stupid bastard.'

'I'm not gonna let you meet him,' he said in a loud

voice. 'I told you he wasn't gonna be there – tonight or any other night.'

'What are you talkin about?'

'Your record shop man – Ned Land.' And now he grinned at her. 'I told you that dope he was usin would get him in trouble, and you don't know how lucky you are you didn't get mixed up in it.'

She stared at him. 'What did you do, Burris?'

'Yeah,' he said, still grinning at her. 'You'd like to know, wouldn't you?'

'Burris . . . what have you done?'

'I done what I needed to do a long time ago,' he half hollered at her. 'You think I'm gonna be a fool for the rest of my life? You think you can step all over me any damn way you like to, huh? Coral, goddamn you, you just think I'm somethin good to play with, but I'll show you and him, too. I made up my mind I'm not gonna be stepped on anymore, and anybody who tries it is gonna get their burly heads caved right in!'

'Burris – *what did you do?*'

He tapped a hard finger in his chest. '*I* turned your lover man over – *I* got that woman had a baby by him to help me send him off to the big house, to Jacktown, that's what I did! I fixed it up so when he sees the sun every day, it'll be twelve o'clock, just comin over the wall – *I* did it! I gave him three meals and forty cents a day and a movie on Sunday – I gave him plenty time to think over what'll happen to him again if he messes with a man like me! Now, you just take off that hot-pants dress and whore face and set your tail in the right groove before I cut it off. Ned Land is your fault, you evil bitch, and I'm not sorry for one thing I did to him!'

Coral tried to burst past him to the door, but he grabbed her by the arms and sunk his fingers in deeply. 'I said you're not goin anywhere, Coral, so you just make your mind up to it.'

'You goddamn fool, you,' she snapped at him. 'Ned Land don't want me any more than I want you! And I won't tell no lie – I tried to *make* him want me.' She twisted in his hands. 'Let me go! There's nothin you can do to stop me from tellin him what you've done!'

'Coral, listen to me . . .'

Her eyes blazed at him. 'Get your hands off me, you lousy pig – you jealous-hearted dog! Do you think Ned Land is the only man in the world? There're others, just like him – and I'll find them, whether it's in Westphalia or Africa, and I'll have him when I find him – I'll give him all I've got and all *you* give me.'

'Coral ...'

'Let me *go*, Burris, goddamn you!'

'Coral, why don't you try to understand that I *love* you? That's why I do what I do – that's *why!*'

'That's why you're crazy!' she screamed at him. 'Because I *don't* love you! I hate you to touch me. You can't send every man I go with to the penitentiary, don't you know that? You, with your stinkin, jealous mind – I'll make you suffer if you don't let me go!' She spat viciously in his face. 'I'll have a different man every week if you don't let me go!'

'Coral, baby, Coral!'

'I'll have a different man every *day!*'

'You dirty whore!' his voice exploded. 'I'll kill you!'

'I'll have a different man *every hour!*'

His hands came up and around her soft throat without his knowing, for his eyes were clouded with rage and tears and he could not see past the snarling red page of her mouth, which seemed somehow to devour him and his frustration and spit the juice of him on the remains of his pride. Outside his broiling, blue rage, the operation of his hands and thumbs were automatic and filled with superhuman strength, encasing her lovely neck in a band of chiseled flesh that cut off all woman sound and left her dangling grotesquely full and fine, breasts and buttocks jerking as her death-new fingers dug their nails into his unfeeling, furious face and gouged out blood and hunks of bitter meat from lips and chin and upper brow.

Her neck lengthened under the crush, and her eyes bulged, overlapping and myopic from the terrific constriction, and soon death laughed over her mouth and swollen outward pucker of tongue, and her jaws swelled from within until her face was a child's balloon of impish disdain.

And then, she was emphatically dead.

Dazedly, he let her slump to the floor and stood over her

quiet body for many minutes, looking ahead of himself and not yet aware of what he had done.

Then he said, 'You'll make me hurt you, Coral, I swear to God, you will.'

Amazingly he did not comprehend – his consciousness did not allow him to. He stepped over her body and went to the doorway, remembering his appointment with Cullen.

'I told you you wasn't goin nowhere,' he said, but refused to look at her body. 'Now, damn it, you remember what I said.'

He did not look.

And she lay curled atop, her face a-bulge, but below her torso, her thighs and legs were sexually awry, revealing panties and garter belt and fish-white inner thighs.

'Now, damn it, you remember,' he said, going out.

When he was outside in the night, going to meet the policeman Cullen and hating Ned Land in a way that defied his reason, he looked up at the lighted upper floor where they lived and left these words alive on the empty street:

'And you better be home when I get back.'

He walked on, then said to himself as an afterthought:

'I never loved a woman so much.'

While the light in the upper room awaited his return.

13

In the dark and red of the room, Mama Harper looked like a white-capped mountain sitting outlined in front of the big window with the candlelight. It was late, but there were lights at the other end of the street.

Behind her, some man on the record in the stereo blasted out solemn, dubious, deep sounds on a tuba, to three-quarter time. The violins flowered at intervals in accompaniment. Mama had forgot the name of the piece, but it was one she liked, one that fitted her, oomphahed her dying flesh and made her fit a purpose.

Mama sat smiling with the music and what she saw going on outside. She had seen traps before, man-traps. First it was the woman, and no one else for a while. Then, after one o'clock, Ned, the boy, came back and opened up the shop. Mama saw the woman watching in the shadows. Then she saw a tall man, that much she could tell: her eyes were getting worse and a sac of transparent crust was growing over them, but her eyes were good for watching shadows.

Mama saw the tall man see the woman and go to talk to her for a long time. Together they watched Ned's lighted windows. Then she saw Cullen come and stand across the street, then this big man go over to talk to him.

A little black man, heading for Ned Land's shop, saw them and turned around.

Mama was puzzled, because tonight wasn't the night Cullen usually stopped around. Then she squinted her eyes, white things, unearthly, under the white hair – and knew that the woman, the man, and Cullen, were seeking to trap Ned Land.

Cullen came away, over to Mama's front steps. He came up to the top of the steps, but Mama knew he couldn't see her because of the red light and shadows. He rang the cow-bells.

Mama got up torturedly, three-hundred and seventy-five pounds of her, and rumbled slowly across the room. The room shook because of her, it wavered uncertainly and shrieked with a woodlike scream of almost unendurable stress. She finally made it to the bar, where she made the huge rear of her, the monstrosity of her butt, put down its heap on the reinforced stool.

Bala is good, she thought.

She felt herself settling with the exacting toll of gravity.

Carla went to answer the door. Mama saw her frail hips go past the doorway. Mama knew she was dying, because Mama was praying her dead, killing her because she wanted to will Mama. She had done it before, and she was doing it to Ned Land, too. Mama liked the way they were dying, the way she was making them die. She enjoyed this sensation above all the other pleasures she had experienced during her long life.

Mama prayed to the god of Evil, who had used her. She had paid in many years of flesh. Look at her sacrifices, the girls, the human sacrifices. She had a right to a power of her own – and the best of all was the power of death. This was the only thing that would suffice: no longer could she hope for beauty, or passion, or desire for the phallus – these were swept-wind things that momentarily paused in unsure flight.

Now it was creeping death seeking a climax, that obsessed and possessed her black flesh, wrung out the thousandth physical delight.

The solo tuba rose to unexpected heights.

Cullen pushed through the Chinese curtains. She thought his face was pallid and a little frightened.

'Hi, boy,' Mama said.

'How're you, old woman?' Cullen said. He came closer to her.

'Drink?'

'Not right now. Is Wanda in?'

'She's never out,' Mama told him. 'Yeah, boy, she's never out.'

'Tell 'er I said I want to see her.'

'Carla'll tell her.'

He placed his hands on the bar.

'Have a drink,' Mama urged him.

Cullen looked at his watch. 'Okay. Bourbon straight.'

Mama poured him one and watched him drink it. 'You need another,' she said, pouring him one.

'Thanks,' Cullen said. 'That really hit the spot. I'm in kind of a hurry—'

'You can't hurry things like this, boy. You just take your time. Sit down and warm yer pants.'

Cullen sat on a stool in front of the bar.

Mama looked at him hard before she spoke. 'You got somethin goin, aincha, boy?'

'Listen,' he said confidentially, 'what do you know about that guy across the street with the record shop?'

'Some things I know, some things I don't.'

Cullen leaned forward. 'Old woman, I think he's involved in something I've been working on a long time.'

'What would you call that?' Mama said.

'Dope,' Cullen said heavily, his wind rushing out with the word, the thing of it too big to contain in his smallness – the threat to him. He didn't want to see it happen, she could see. 'These people have got no right, coming here to Westphalia, old woman. White and black, we work hard together. We like each other. You know how I like Wanda.'

'Sure, yeah, I know,' Mama said.

'Then why, old woman?' His hand came out toward her, with no confirmation of strength. 'Isn't Westphalia a nice place? You know how I treat you and the girls, you know that. Then why? Why do they have to come here at all?'

'Don't worry,' Mama said.

'They're big operators,' Cullen said with quiet conviction. 'I've always been proud of Westphalia, old woman. The way we work together. It was like the rest of the world didn't matter, my old man used to say, him being a preacher. He used to say Westphalia was like a terminal with so many people coming and going, they didn't have time to do any harm.'

'Dope,' Mama said, as theme of what she intended to say. 'I've seen a lot of dope, boy, black dope you never saw before. I know how you're scared—'

'I'm not afraid,' Cullen told her unafraidly.

'I was a cab'girl on a schooner,' Mama said. 'Bet ya never heard of a somethin like that, did ya? I was cab'girl for the Englush upper lords, on the way home from India or Singapore. Ah, boy,' Mama sighed, 'ahhh, boy. Such times I had you'd never think would happen – all them young white fingers a fingerin me 'cause I was black and unusual. And dope!' She winked her white eye at him. 'Cocaine was their bowls of soup, and as many a hard peter you never saw at one time alone in yer whole life.'

Cullen sighed too with the vision.

'You never been whipped by that salt wind,' Mama said, with her creaking mind pulled to the past. 'And once in Manila, we saw the sharks chop at the pilins, that hungry they was. And all the while the pink gods was sniffin they cocaine and pushin me down to the bottom of the boat. One said it was like doin it to a dog, but I didn't mind, 'cause I knowed how they needed me. You ain't never seen dope before, you, you boy, like I seen dope in those days.'

'It's that record shop fella I'm interested in.'

'Ahh—' Mama propped big white head on fist. 'What could I tell yer 'bout him? 'Cept he's a bad man.'

'How do you know he's a bad man?' Cullen said.

'How do I know the way to make you spout yer last drop?' Mama said. 'How do I know the sea is a woman, always givin birth? How do I know? I *know*, that's how I know.'

Cullen looked impatiently around for Wanda.

Mama poured him another drink.

'Lissen,' Mama said, and evil music began to come out of the stereo, balling, brassy, bold.

She could see Cullen listening and not hearing anything. She made her eyes into tiny slits. 'You ever seen a spur tongue cut right off? That's what I got, from the days I was a girl. When you lose that bit, and you have to rape yerself for satisfiedness, that's when you know for sure.' Mama raised one huge fist over her head above him, and for a moment it looked as though it would fall and crush out his brains. 'I know a war's comin, that's what I know, that's what my black vision tells me – I know the evil that makes man live. I know. Don't ask me how I know. Ask me who is God, and I tell yer Bala. This is because I know.'

Cullen's eyes looked at her hard now, frozen.

'You ask me 'bout an evil man, and I tell ya.' She looked about her, and for a moment listened to the waning music from the thing in the corner, then she lowered her voice. 'He wants to take her way from here.'

'Who?' Cullen said.

'The little black man,' Mama told him, 'Ned Land. He wants to take Wanda.' She watched him but couldn't see the little lights in his eyes. 'He's gone take her way from me,' she said. 'From you.'

She tried to see his face change with her words, but could not. In the red light it had a whitelike hue. His flesh of face was almost like the hills she should have remembered a long time ago, but couldn't quite now. The hills of fear that plunged indefinitely, and soared, and tilted, and sung out to the sky with wild, begging mouths.

His new pink coming was a desert aura in India, that turned the sands red in spots, like molten quicksand beds, a painful and consuming heat that was winter there. But everybody said winter was the worse.

His face like that.

She saw his teeth faintly, for she looked for this, since she admired teeth, the strong white teeth, in a way that might have been impossible otherwise. Her faded brain remembered tastes of human flesh.

She listened to the music, the primeval sounds of the eighteenth century.

Cullen licked his lips. 'When is he supposed to take her away?'

'I don't know. Any minute.'

'You know what, old woman?' he said, raising a finger to her black face. 'I got information about that boy. I don't think he would be doing Wanda any good at all.'

'Neither do I.'

Mama slid away when she closed her eyes, but she was still listening to him, and listening to something else, too. She was praying, and she was listening to her prayers. The longer you lived, the bigger the sin got. Good Bala.

Mama weaved her big self about with the music. The magic medicine was Wanda. She poured out some of that magic medicine and stirred it around in Cullen's fear. Wanda's soul was sold, because it belonged to Mama to sell. Mama would not let her be taken, before Bala. And him would die, that one who thought he could.

Mama began to sweat in the canyons of her body.

'What you do for her? You save her?'

'I'd do anything—' Cullen caught himself, yet still couldn't explain what he'd already said. 'If a guy's doing anything wrong, old woman, I wanna catch him at it!'

Mama waited until the record clicked again, till she found out what was coming, and at the same time she took a kind of joy from the pain she could feel in Cullen.

'In the two years since you and the girls, Wanda, came here,' he said, 'there ain't been no trouble, old woman.'

'Trouble,' Mama said on a deep sea of cellos. 'Trouble is somethin bein taken away from you, boy, that's what trouble is.'

'I've had it on good authority,' Cullen said, 'that that guy messes around with dope. This guy who told me wouldn't lie. He said he found out from a woman who's been coming to see the record shop guy.'

'Trouble,' Mama mumbled.

Cullen was open because of the whiskey. 'Listen. Can I tell you something? I mean just us two here. Nobody but us, and maybe I'll tell you this.'

'Sure, yeah, boy,' Mama said. 'What you tells me dies with me.'

Cullen flattened his hands on the bartop, the fingers whiskey-wiggling yet still possessing sobriety, and Mama felt his eyes looking helplessly at her: she knew how a little man could seem enormous and huge.

'My daddy was a preacher,' Cullen said, while his lips were weak for a moment. 'You never had a daddy that was a preacher, so you don't know, old woman.'

'I've been locked up before,' Mama told him.

'But this daddy of mine,' Cullen went on, blending with the sorrowful music, the deep, big-daddy cellos, 'was a funny man among men. And he wanted everyone else to be just like him.'

Mama saw how the carbon couldn't be. 'Yeah, I got this job,'

Cullen told her, 'but I didn't want it. Listen, old woman!' he flared, 'you'd better not tell this!'

'I won't,' Mama assured him, listening to the music, raising her eyes to the highlights, 'I won't.'

Cullen held out his glass. 'Pour me a drink.'

'That's four bucks you owe me,' Mama told him, pouring.

He drank and licked his lips. 'I hated that old man when he died, and everyone said, Look at the poor good preacher's son: let's do something for him. That's what they said, old woman, and I thought maybe that would be the end of it if I had a job like this.'

But it wasn't, and Mama Harper knew it wasn't, and she laughed like a bloated bitch croc on the wet banks of the sands of Egypt. Mama laughed at slavery, of flesh holding flesh, myriad-colored, the capturer and the captured both. She watched Cullen struggling with things arising in him.

'Wanda,' he said in a long voice, which told of an odd love, a fascinated bondage. 'Well,' he said, looking white-eyed at her, 'you know what I mean, old woman.'

'I know,' Mama told him.

'Why should I tell you any more?' he said, eyeing her suspiciously.

'Because I can help you,' Mama laughed at him, her voice and the cellos one. 'You love Wanda.'

She saw his eyes get big and shocked, she heard the inward voice of him say yes and no at the same time, then she saw the anger of shame, then lust and white-hot passion, too.

'Listen,' he told her unevenly, 'your daughter's a whore – that's all she ever meant to me. You've got your goddamned fat black nerve!'

Mama twisted in the protruding dagger. 'You love her.'

Cullen's face twitched in the red light, but he said nothing. 'You love her,' Mama said again, 'and you 'fraid of Ned Land.'

The woodwinds from the stereo said hello, once, twice, and then a third time.

Good Bala, Mama thought, praying.

'He gone take her way from here. You be dead like yer daddy. You gone die and die because of that. You got to stop her.'

'How—?' Cullen began, then could say no more. Her eyes held his.

'He gone take her way,' Mama said. 'You never see her no more.'

'Stop it,' Cullen told her.

Mama said, 'Lissen! Lissen to the music!' Her voice seemed to be a part of it. Her prayer was incessant and growing in her; she began to forget English the way she spoke it. Her voice became a grunting, a piglike sound that was hypnotic with the pulse of music, and her eye, and the great big bulk of her swaying.

'What you gone do?' Mama said. 'What you gone do?'

Cullen looked afraid. 'I don't want any trouble. If he leaves her alone, then I'll leave him alone.'

'But he won't!' Mama said sharply at him.

'He's sold the shop – that's what this guy told me the record shop guy's woman told him. All I want him to do is get out of town.' Cullen said in a whisper: 'I won't let him take her!'

Mama poured him a drink, then lifted the bottle, and she held it like good gold rum over her head, on her way to the Bahamas and the tom-toms there. The tree trunk of her arm slashed the air with the beaker of life. Then she transfixed in admiration to the music and the memory of the glory that had once been hers. She held Cullen now with the force of her power, gripped him with grizzly strength to her will.

'Kill him!' Mama roared into him. 'Mash that little man!'

'He won't take her – you're making all this crap up!'

'Be the man yer daddy wanted, then,' she spat in disgust. 'Don't stand up for the things you got comin. But you got to kill when you cain't do nothin else!'

'I can't,' Cullen said, his voice breaking, split.

Mama's gaze turned lyric on him. She released him, as she released her prayer.

Her daughter had come in – Wanda – sort of tall and straight, with her breasts sticking out, and Mama retired to the shadows. Cullen rose, like a man to the National Anthem, and went over to her with big quick steps.

'I want to talk with you,' he told her.

He followed Wanda out of the room. Mama felt her heart

expanding within her. She put one hand on the bartop, then another, then she shoved herself forward with a fat surge of strength. While up above, the red light looked down on her struggles. She reared against the bar, tilting it with her weight; her feet felt caught and swollen against the bottom part.

Bala good.

Her body shifted in turbulent coils as she forced her feet, to support her; it writhed in blackness and fat and sweat; there was a dying stink from the lower part of it. Her body moved slowly, inexorably, sometimes nearly falling to the center of the earth, to the doorway, then the door, then the hall, then down where the green light was burning under the door. Except for the swaying of the house, Mama was quiet, a great elephant striding soundless, a mammoth concentration.

Beyond the door, she found another door and opened it with a key from the ring pinned onto the breast of the tent that was her dress. Mama came through, her heart panting. This was the den of her thoughts, and the outwardly apparent was a shield on one wall from the krall of a Tagai warrior; the boo-boo god, in a squatting manner on the smaller dais: round, chubby, both woman and man, tit, chest, and the crest on forehead that identified the mother of fallatio, the drought her pleasure left.

On the platform which was wide as Mama, Bala grinned down at the gods of excess and orgasm, a red, heavy mountain, like Mama, sexless and impotent, but practiced wielder of evil's sure, sharp sword.

Mama lumbered over to the wall and an eyeplace under the wall's tassels. Sometimes she had a man make movies from here. She heard the music outside switch to wild bop, and at the same time her fading eyes saw Cullen in the green room, kissing Wanda all over her body, and going wild: Wanda on the bed, almost with him but telling him things he didn't want to hear, her thighs exposed where Cullen was kissing them.

Good Bala.

Mama backed away on trembling legs. She could hear their voices coming. She listened to make out the words. She wasn't afraid, Mama wasn't, not about Cullen.

She backed away and started out of the room.

Bala good, make them die.

With great difficulty and intensity, Mama genuflected beneath the statue of Bala. When she tried to rise, she found she could not. She let her body collapse to one side until she could get down one arm and push back hard with the other. It took her five minutes to get up, and all the while she heard their voices. When she got to the door, she heard Cullen pleading and knew she had to hurry.

Her legs were happy going back. She found the bar and stool and sat back to listen to Dizzy Gillespie's 'Swing Low, Sweet Chariot'.

Cullen passed so fast, she didn't see him when he left. Then a little while later, Lorraine let Ned in. Mama began to pray again.

'Hi, boy,' she said, as Ned came in.

'Hi, Mama. Where's Wanda?'

'Wanda's not here,' Mama said.

Ned came over to the bar. 'Where's she at?'

'I don't know. She went away with another trick. Lorraine'll tell ya.' Lorraine stood in the doorway. 'Tell 'im, Lorraine.'

'She went away with another guy,' Lorraine grinned at him.

Ned's face became hard. 'When did she leave?'

'A few hours ago,' Mama said.

'She just called me at the shop a half hour ago,' Ned said. He watched her closely; Mama prayed harder. 'Where's Wanda at, Mama? I don't believe what you're trying to tell me.'

'My girls leave sudden,' Mama said. 'Terry left a week ago, and you didn't know.'

'I know about Wanda,' Ned said, his voice trembling. 'And I know Wanda's in this house. Please, Mama, I don't wanna get upset with you or nobody else around here, but I'm sure gonna raise a lot of hell if you don't come up with her mighty quick.'

'I'm right here,' Wanda said from the doorway.

Mama's eyes flickered and fired; she tried to command Wanda to silence, but she began to know that she was no longer strong enough, and the fear that came on her then was frightening with the kind of force of energy that plotted an electric storm, or triggered a cataclysm.

'You get outta here, Ned man!' Mama said. 'You gone die, you stay around! You gone kill Wanda!' She tried to rise and couldn't. 'Go away before I make you die!'

The decision was keen on Wanda's face, but she had not packed, and Mama noticed this. Yet the light in her face denied she needed bags; it was a freedom that made Mama push against her fear.

'Go way, Ned Land, go way!'

Now Mama made her feet and swelled behind the bar, while Ned stood glaring back and full of strength.

'I'm takin Wanda away from here,' he said. 'You can't stop me. I think I could kill somebody who tried to stop me.'

'You suck at a whore, you man?' Mama bellowed. 'You want hyena shit? Go, fool, go, *go!*'

Wanda came and stood close to Ned, for it was best their strength was two against the many strengths of Mama. When Mama saw the way they were, she made the bar crash over to the floor. The red light flared with a misdirected flow of current; the music had a destructive sound. Mama's flesh was jammed against Mama's flesh as she moved toward them.

A slatter of Max Roach's drums was all that seemed to be.

'GO WAY!' Mama hahhwrroared, to the introduction of an African saxophone, with drums and reed fifes, but nobody heard it.

On the outer fringes, with scavenger's eyes, Lorraine made herself a part of the room with maddened wishing. Ned Land tensed to fight the giant coming at him. A trumpet scattered and skittered with a getting-away step. Mama bared her strong, blunt-edged eating teeth, coming forward to demolish them and turn them into dung. She would not let it happen, and she knew by the way her flesh moved that it would not happen. Beneath her, Wanda and Ned were as nothing. In her was a thousand black years, in her was the knowledge of a thousand black years, and it made them nothings, little ants, under her ancient feet.

But her daughter of sin, set free with the wish to be free, stood forward, shielded Ned ineffectually but shielding him still, stood forward to receive the rock of ages. And she faced it with a cry of traitorous blood and the genius of fettered flesh.

'You forgot to lock the door,' she said through teeth bared like her mother's. 'I've killed your god! Bala is dead!'

Mama stopped altogether. Her heart began to fail. She rumbled past them to the door. Wavering, slamming against the walls, she went down to the room in which she had watched Cullen and Wanda.

On the floor there, Bala was a coated insides of green moss growing for ten thousand years, with two little snakes and those that were theirs, that existed on that growth. The phallic cross was there on the inside, and something that was once its truthful pattern.

The music drummed away at Mama.

Mama stopped living.

She slammed over in the broken mess, making the whole house roll and vibrate, where her black mouth came close to the mouth of the shattered Bala, and her tongue came out, white with foam, in another sort of dying supplication.

When Ned and Wanda looked down, shocked, on her from the doorway, Mama Harper was dead. And the record ended outside.

But still she laughed out at them from the shadows of the room.

14

An angelic morning sky was clearing as Ned and Wanda came out of the house. It was death behind them that hurried their feet, but the fear of what lay ahead would not allow Ned to commit himself fully.

Beside him, Wanda was warm and clinging to him.

'Please, baby,' she said, 'let's hurry.'

They began to move faster down the night-day streets.

Wanda tried to explain, but she couldn't, really – and Ned, still high from the Reefer he'd used to reinforce himself, didn't actually hear the things she told of Mama and a man named Danny. He could only sense her immense relief, her hand on his arm that said she was his now. His he had to look out for. His he had to get away from the monstrous significance of her mother's death. Within himself, he tried to understand why Mama had been his enemy all along. He wanted to understand Wanda's mouth telling him, but the words of his mind were so loud he could barely hear her.

And Reefer was making things more difficult for him. He kept thinking he'd lose the three hundred dollar bills he clasped in his right hand pocket, and under his arm a few of his favorite albums he had taken along from the shop were extra-weighted with her hand on his flesh.

His feet were too slow and heavy. It was as if they didn't want him, or her, to go. Ned forced them along with a bursting heart. He could still remember the naked, bloody look on Mama Harper's face. For a terrified moment, he imagined Wanda next to him was that great black hulk of a woman, that hell personified in his frightened Reefer realm. But he could not tear himself away from her, even if now that was what she was starting to be. Somehow he kept thinking that he had killed Mama Harper, that that was the reason they were running now. The things he saw in her death indeed had accused him. And all men. But him more than the rest, because he began to suspect how a woman like Mama Harper had come to be in the first place.

'Hurry, Ned,' Wanda said. 'We gotta catch the two-o-one.'

He suddenly noticed a lot of people on the street, and this frightened him, for they were huge and white-faced in his eyes, like arresters after him. Then he remembered that an all-night pavilion had opened for a segment of the city's race, a white-folk, old country thing – Bavarian – that's what Ruckson had told him.

Then he saw the man with the winding box and the monkey. Ned made himself stop.

'Ned . . .'

In Ned's inside coat pocket was a Sir Walter Raleigh tobacco can full of Weed.

The people of the place were suddenly about them, pushing them forward to the outer circle with the winding man and the hideous little man, and a dog on the flank of another arguing man, a barking thing that bared its lips and spat at the quiet watching monkey.

'Nah, nah!' said the man with the dog. 'Adamito eat you little man!'

'Prove!' said the crowd. Ned and Wanda tried to get away, but they were encircled, and the strength of the white bodies would not let them through.

'Prove!' they yelled, and, 'Bet! Bet!'

Monday appeared, green and good like Reefer, like the three bills in Ned Land's pocket. He pulled Wanda with him along the lip of the inner circle, looking for an exit.

'Now,' said the man with the dog, a long smile under his wide black mustache. He bent and unleashed the collar, then hooked his fingers under the collar, and held back the snarling beast. It was a sick and angry animal, with teeth that showed all the time, and a fur that was tattered and red and torn, from fighting other animals like itself. Underneath were hard muscles packed into a short frame, and the anxious beating of a heart that loved to kill.

The monkey was deep red in the pavilion lights, like Brother Red had been – (and yet the dog was like Brother Red, too) – its tail was long and whipping like a cat's. Although the dog snarled aggressively, straining against the owner's fingers, the monkey seemed calm and calculating, like a little banker, twiddling his two long thumbs that way.

The dog raised itself on haunches, trying to get at the monkey. The monkey squeaked and sat there laughing. Littler than the smallest man, it turned beard and eyes up lovingly at the man with the box, demanding a song, it seemed to Ned, so that he could dance and laugh at the antics of the other beast.

'We fight,' said the monkey's leader.

The crowding people hurrawed, and the man with the dog backed away, to give the thing a running start. The man with the box unhooked the box from himself, and bent to the leash of the monkey. But before he did, he took a pencil, stubby and thin, from his pocket, then took a pocket knife from his pocket and shriveled down the lead end to a sharp point. Then he bent down to the monkey's level and said, 'Pietro?', like that, questioning, like asking an older brother to solve a calculus problem. And at the same time, he held out the sharpened pencil for the hairy fingers to grasp. The monkey looked, then grasped familiarly.

Ned felt Wanda's hand hard on his arm.

When the monkey's man began to wind his box, the hairy half-man rose on two legs and pivoted around, to the tones of 'Lord He Wuz Doin Her Wrong' – then sprung into the air while his master wound on, toward the startled dog which had been released by the other man.

Ned looked on in horror, still not able to comprehend the portentous form of the dear Mama Harper.

The monkey was in midair. His hand held the sharpened pencil over his head. He held it like a dagger as he flew. And when he landed, the way Ned knew he would, with himself facing the butt part of the dog, astride the dog, with his tail lashing securely around the dog's neck, he used the harmless pencil with the plunging certainty of death.

The dog yiped with the first downward stroke, which had pierced its anus. It began to go around in a circle, trying to throw the unthrowable monkey from its back. Its cries were screams of unmortal terror, and Ned felt himself cringe inside with the sound of them.

The dog's scream caught a sustained note. It began to run around in mad circles. But the monkey was chopping away, and finally had chopped down to the root of the animal with the bloody pencil. He chopped, and chopped, and chopped.

The dog's screams ended; it fell to its side with snapping sounds, feet kicking, trying to kick the pain out. It frothed at the mouth and tried to catch the moving-away monkey; its eyes became glazed, like a drunk's. Its owner watched it die as the monkey still chopped away, and it seemed as though the monkey chatter was the chatter of blood as he made it fly all about him.

Some of it got on Ned and Wanda.

The crowd opened up to let them through, but the last they saw was the monkey standing victorious over the dog, bloodily unmarked, and looking down in the dead dog's face as though he were saying. 'It was all a game. Why don't you get up now?' He threw the pencil to the laughing crowd.

yes, he was doin her wrong . . .

'Cops!' someone said behind them. The crowd began to scatter.

Something made Wanda and Ned run now. They didn't have to tell each other that they should run: the coming morning sun told them, the new fresh breeze arising, the outside voices applauding death. Yet even as they ran, they knew, were clued inside, that this would never come about, what they were trying to do.

'It's two o'clock, Ned,' Wanda said, passing a store clock.

'We'll make it,' he told her, but doubt grew stronger that they wouldn't.

The night careened against him, because of Weed. The station-house loomed ahead. He thought Wanda said, 'This is it,' but she didn't – it was him saying it and not knowing it. He gripped the three bills tighter.

The inside of the place was moorish eccentricity. A lot of people stood around the space in front of the cages, waiting for the Limited to Detroit. Ned parted from Wanda – but didn't want to – in order to get the tickets.

The ticketman grinned at him, as though he knew who Ned was, and Ned recoiled, almost backed away. Then he knew it was Weed again – but still, in a way, it didn't seem to be at all.

He gave Wanda one of the tickets while they stood waiting

near the gate. Away, howling in the new morning spray, the steel chariot bellowed its nearness and told all of them to get ready for the new arrivals, the old bon voyages.

Ned began to tremble, and Wanda felt him trembling. He felt himself almost crumple as the train wheezed in to the outside track.

Then Ned, with his world unscrewed by Pot and the fear of the unknown, turned to see the faces of two accusers, waiting, like he, for the train. He saw Doris, but she had seen him first, and now turned to look at the woman beside him.

Doris wasn't what Ned would have expected her to be, seeing him like that with another woman. Hers was a What-is-she? look at Wanda, or better, Why-is-she?

Ned tried to shield Wanda from her gaze, but Doris only looked vacuous, and resigned, and sure – and victorious, like the little monkey. She looked toward Ned as though he had never existed.

She took the boy by the hand and led the little demon in Ned's every feature, up to them, till she was in front of them, till Ned could not turn Wanda and himself away any further, except by running, and she said, 'Say goodbye to your father, David.'

'Goodbye,' David said, and stuck out his tongue when no one was looking.

Ned was speechless, but Doris didn't press him. She went on past with the boy when the train came in.

Ned turned to follow, but couldn't. It was as though his feet were planted in the cement, as though they had a premonition of what was coming, on and after the train, and they would let him go not another step.

He could not meet Wanda's beautiful eyes, he could not make himself cognizant of her flesh. He was like a dehydrated prospector, finding a mother lode in search for water, and cursing what he had found.

'Ned . . .' Wanda said, but it was more a Ned of I Realize, I Know, rather than a pleading Ned, with hell to follow if he heard her. He felt her hand drop from his arm.

'Sure . . . sure, Ned.'

He turned to see the funny-looking face of Cullen, the

cop Ruckson and Wanda had told him about – and in the background of the station, by the door, he saw Ruckson, himself, and knew the little man had followed him this far – followed him right to the gates of capture, he loved Ned Land that much.

'You're under arrest on suspicion,' Cullen told him with trembling lips, clamping handcuffs on and letting the uniformed cop with him grab Ned and frisk him. Of course they found the can of weed.

When Ned looked again, Ruckson was gone. Wanda had begun to fade away to the edges of the crowd, looking at him with a quiet gaze, beautiful and tall and his woman: for as long as he lived, he knew she would be his woman.

'Let's go,' Cullen said.

As he went by, Ned was smiling at her. Not happy – smiling – but happy, too, in the way he felt about the way it had happened. He made the policeman stop, and he gave her the albums. He saw her blue, whore-painted eyes, and in that instant he bent to kiss the soft whore mouth. He knew what she would do with the albums; his eyes told her.

Then Cullen took Ned out, looking back at her once, apologetic fright within his eyes, and frightened love.

Wanda went slowly out of the station with the records.

They were waiting on him when he came in, but he did not see them immediately. He saw her. And the way she was lying there on the floor.

He didn't understand, and they, the police, did not understand him and the way he slowly bent toward the body, as though seeing it in existence this way for the first time.

'Coral?' he said.

One of the uniformed policemen moved toward him, but Bill Mullins held him back, and all their faces were illuminated over him, waiting, as he stooped by the body.

'Coral, baby?' he questioned, then made his hand go to her quiet breast and settle its bigness there. For the first time, she did not repulse him or argue at his affection, and he felt a deep warmness inside that reflected the gentle smile on his big mouth. He had begun to cry, but did not realize it.

'Coral, I'm sorry what I done . . . about the record shop man. You believe that, please. I don't know,' he said, grimacing a little, 'I just kept thinkin *he* was bad, when it wasn't him at all, 'cause I couldn't know whether he was good or bad, not knowin him. I saw all this, Coral . . .'

She was silent and listened while he spoke, in a way that he had wished to God for so many times.

'Like you said, Coral honey, it was me, the way I was thinkin – that's what made you, wasn't it?'

He paused in speaking for a long time, but she still did not answer, and he could find no hint of anger on her quiet face.

'It's bein locked up, what does it to a man,' he said. 'I tried to explain it to you a lot of times, but I couldn't get started or get the right words together. I guess we all locked up, one way or another. Even the record shop man's locked up now, so I guess he'd understand, too, what I'm tryin to explain to you.'

A tear fell into her face, but she still did not move, and he began to realize she was dead.

He looked around and saw them waiting.

'All right, Burris,' Mullins said quietly.

His conception was so strangely unsettled that he stood almost eagerly.

'All right, Burris,' Mullins said again, as though it were understanding that caused him to agree that everything was truly all right.

They led him out in the hall, where the neighbor from below who had called them stood staring opened-mouthed into his wet face, an unbelieving hand clutching at the throat of her old housecoat.

'We'll need to see you later today,' Mullins told her, but she did not seem to hear as they went down the stairs.

Outside, the enormity of her death suddenly struck him and he could not stop crying.

And the new morning shone as though it were the Creator's most remarkable achievement.

A dew had come to the outside air. The new morning felt clean and fresh to her, but the dew was really tears in her eyes.

Across the street she saw a tall yellow man looking over, his head bent down, watching the police car taking her man away, looking like Cullen might have looked if he were a tall yellow man looking over, his head bent down.

It was as though the music of Ned Land kept going around inside her head. She walked with a free step in the outside air.

The sweet, slow music of a dead Brown trumpet came to her as she approached the shop, loud from the loudspeaker. Across the street, in front of the house with the red candle, a hearse pulled off.

She saw the man called Ruckson waiting within the shop.

And with a gash of gesture, with a hand upon her heart to feel that it was still beating, with a new tear like the new morning, a course of weird new current running in her blood, she put her hand on the door and opened it to the inside: in fact, she laughed as she came through, a tinkling thing that Ned would have loved – and she faced Ruckson with an unafraidness she had never known before any man in thirty-four years.

'He turned the shop over to me last night,' Ruckson said, eyes tight. 'I didn't want it, and I told him what he was doin to me – how he was blowin my plans about San Francisco.' He looked at her, without the sympathy she expected. 'But he blowed a lot of plans, I guess – his included.'

She turned to go.

'Don't you worry, kid,' he consoled her. 'Ned'll only do a year – two at most. He ain't got no record; they'll go easy on him. But don't you worry: when he comes back, he'll get everything that belongs to him.'

'Sure,' Wanda said, still crying, going out, leaving the door wide, 'he'll get everything.'

The music blared goodbye to her. But it was only goodbye for a little while. She still had the ticket Ned Land had given her, and his love. They both had tickets on a common trip, would one day meet on their way there.

She walked surely toward the train station in the fine new morning.

Gazing after her, the little man shook his grim head and wished for God to look down on Ned.

Then, cursing his and Ned Land's luck, Ruckson went and kicked the damned door shut.